FIRESTORM
OF
Dragons

Edited by

Michele Acker & Kirk Dougal

Save a Tree Program

At Dragon Moon Press, our carbon footprint is higher than average and we are doing something about it. For every tree Dragon Moon uses in printing our books, we are planting new trees to reduce our carbon footprint so that the next generation can breathe clean air, keeping our planet and it's inhabitants healthy.

FIRESTORM
OF
Dragons

Dragon
Moon

www.dragonmoonpress.com
www.firestormofdragons.com

Firestorm of Dragons

ISBN 10 1-896944-80-9 Print Edition
ISBN 13 978-1-896944-80-7

ISBN 10 1-896944-82-5 Electronic Edition
ISBN 13 978-1-896944-82-1
CIP Data on file with the National Library of Canada

Dragon Moon Press is an Imprint of Hades Publications Inc.
P.O. Box 1714, Calgary, Alberta, T2P 2L7, Canada

Dragon Moon Press and Hades Publications, Inc. acknowledges
the ongoing support of the Canada Council for the Arts and the
Alberta Foundation for the Arts for our publishing programme.

Printed and bound in Canada
www.dragonmoonpress.com
www.firestormofdragons.com

"Come not between the dragon, and his wrath."

William Shakespeare, *King Lear*

CONTENTS

"Never laugh at live dragons."

J.R.R. Tolkein, *The Hobbit*

DRAGONSCALING!

JOHN TEEHAN

So, you want to go dragonscaling!

Of all the ultra-extreme sports: beanstalk climbing, griffin baiting, and in-line rugby, dragonscaling is by far the most fraught with peril. You wise readers should examine your intent to take up this pastime right up to the moment you've inserted that very first piton into the dragon's hide. Beyond that point, of course, it's far too late to change your mind.

Dragonscaling summons that deep-seated need within the human soul to put oneself into recklessly dangerous predicaments for pure entertainment. Perforce, the sport requires the delicate strength of a figure skater on thin ice, the pulse-pounding endurance of a long distance runner, the nerve of a cliff-diver, and about three hundred pounds of pure, uncut chutzpah. Defeat will mean saving your loved ones the cost of a funeral casket, but survival will have you walking away with a feeling of accomplishment, victory, and not an insubstantial amount of money.

So climb aboard! Just remember to mind those ropes! This is going to get tricky, so read everything presented here and anything else you can get your hands on. You're in for a hell of a ride.

A Short History of Dragons in North America

Sometime between 2010 and 2015, the exact year being subject to debate and legal obfuscation, genetically engineered dragons intended for amusement parks escaped from a crèche located in Medford, Massachusetts.[1] The dragons, once in the wild, began mating at a prodigious rate and then spread throughout northern New England and southeastern Canada. At first the escaped dragons, smaller than the common wild dragons of today, were considered merely a nuisance. However, given their unstable genetic development at the time of escape - and the fact that a dragon will eat anything that both moves and is smaller than itself—the nuisance turned to near-catastrophe as this new breed of wild dragon grew to Brobdingnagian proportions, quickly surpassing the West Texas Jabberwock as North America's largest land animal.

The impact of wild dragons on the landscape soon became evident. Up and down New England, moose and deer grew scarce. Direwoves and coyotes that had been forced to move to less draconian neighborhoods began feeding on domesticated pets and livestock, thus denigrating rural economies as summer

---

1 The insurance report is purposefully unclear on the exact dates, although it reveals that there was more than one incident of escape. It may be of interest to note that this Medford lab rests on the site of the former home of Etienne Leopold Trouvelot, whose carelessness in the late nineteenth century resulted in a continent-wide infestation of gypsy moths, which remained a problem well into this century.

tourism plunged and locals abandoned their homes. The United States Department of Fish and Wildlife, together with the Maine Office of Tourism and several Provincial Ministries of Tourism in Canada, joined to campaign for a year-round open season on wild dragons in a desperate bid to restore the previous ecological balance.

As a result, hunters, exterminators, and other hardy souls ventured north eager to add a dragon's head to their trophy collections. Much to their chagrin however, dragons proved exceedingly difficult to kill. Dragonhide turned out to be extremely thick and impervious to most conventional firearms. Attempts to slay dragons by employing surplus military missiles and napalm proved more destructive to the general landscape than the dragons had been themselves, and the original zeal to erect a stuffed dragon in one's backyard dampened.

Within ten years, wild dragons took up residence in every North American state, province and territory north of thirty-three degrees latitude. At that point, the breeding limit of wild dragons collided with the carrying capacity of the available land, with the result that the number of hatchlings per nesting season soon decreased[2] and leveled off to the point where urban areas were relatively dragon-free.

In the short history of dragonslaying, one particular hunter managed to succeed where many had failed, and single-handedly put a considerable dent in the early North American dragon population. That man was former New York senator, retired Yankee shortstop, and big-game hunter Edward W. Feldt.

Feldt had considered the problem of dragonslaying while vacationing at a hunting lodge outside of Fairbanks, Alaska. He learned about Inuit hunters who wrapped raw meat around small canisters of nitroglycerin as a method of hunting sabre-toothed cats, and realized that this method, when applied to dragons, would not only be effective, but also stood a good chance of preserving the outer hide for taxidermy. Feldt

2 For a better picture of the variations on the original dragon phenotype, consult The Audubon Society's *A Guide to North American Dragons*. Unless otherwise specified, this article focuses on the common adult *draconis americanus* which, from snout to tail, measures up to three hundred metres and weighs about twelve hundred metric tonnes.

ordered a dozen oliphunts from a genetics laboratory in Nome and spent three days force-feeding them plastic explosives and detonators before herding them north into Brooks Range where a two hundred and fifteen-metre dragon had recently been spotted. He penned the herd in a valley, concealed himself among some tundra brush, and waited. On the second day, an adult blue dragon came crashing through the tree line and consumed two of the packed pachyderms. Feldt set off the explosives by remote and observed the results.

First came a series of muffled popping sounds as Feldt watched the dragon's stomach expand abruptly, stretching like a balloon, then collapse. A few seconds later, smoke poured from the dragon's mouth, nostrils, earplates, and hindquarters. It staggered a few yards and collapsed-stone dead.

Within six months, Senator Feldt had reached the Department of Fish and Wildlife's hunting limit on dragons and was awarded a special dispensation to bag a hundred more. For each dragon slain, he earned a considerable bounty and made further profit by selling carcasses to museums, occultists, and specialty food concerns. By the following year, hundreds of hunters took up baiting dragons with explosive laboratory-brewed animals such as oliphunts, moas, quagga, dodos, Irish elk, and-for larger dragons-mastodons. It was a perfect method marred only by occasional mishaps attributable to human error when a few booby-trapped animals prematurely detonated, raining body parts down upon hunters and indignant local townships.[3]

After a year of traveling the northern regions, the thrill of hunting dragons had waned for Feldt. Over the next few years, he stalked man-eating unicorns in Africa, defended Ulan Bator from a migratory invasion of yeti, spoke to record-breaking audiences on a worldwide lecture tour, and discovered the remains of Prester John's legendary kingdom high in the Andes. It was in those mountains where a tragic misstep

3 The use of revived-extinct species or custom-designed animals based upon mythological creatures as explosive bait has raised much debate and criticism from animal-rights groups across the globe. When Congress passed legislation in 2052 protecting artificial species, the use of booby-trapped bait had already become obsolete.

resulted in a colorfully-winged, fifty-metre snake eating him. Thus ended a legendary career.

On Dragonscales and Dragonscaling

In 2045, a remarkable chance discovery changed the world overnight. A Minnesota graduate school student named Sally Leung arrived in her lab one morning to discover that she had failed to remove a sample of dragonscales from an acid wash the previous evening. During the night the scales broke down to a fine silt-like substance which radiated a faint blue glow. Leung investigated further and began cataloging a host of unexpected properties which make dragonscales so sought after today. Leung and subsequent scientists discovered tantalizing differences between the gene structure of the original dragons that escaped the original Medford lab and contemporary wild dragons. These apparent mutations affected not only the size of the dragons, but the biochemical composition of their scales.

As many know, the remains of acid-treated scales possessed characteristics that promoted cures to a host of human afflictions including the common cold, psoriasis, kidney stones, menstrual cramps, foot odor, chapped lips, pink-eye and male-pattern baldness. It was a pharmacological dream-come-true. Furthermore, distillation of by-products from the acid treatment produced a high-yield nutritional tonic capable of sustaining one for seven days on nothing else but that and sugar cubes.

It also made an excellent mixer.

Despite the great benefits dragonscales held for mankind, they afforded little in the way of physical protection for the dragons themselves when compared to their thick hides. The glittering, rainbow-hued scales provided no camouflage coloring whatsoever and scientists were at a loss to explain any natural benefit or function the scales provided for dragons. In the final analysis, however, the value dragonscales offered mankind turned out to be the best defense the dragons could have hoped for. Blowing up dragons just for their scales proved shortsighted as dragonhide, upon the animal's death, secreted a toxin that nullified the scales' more useful attributes. Only naturally shed scales maintained the integrity of the valuable compounds.

In light of these new developments, the Department of Fish and Wildlife removed the bounty on dragons, and dragonslaying ceased as a sport. As the scales became more valuable per kilogram than gold, people flocked to dragon-populated areas to search for dropped scales. (Some also took this as an opportunity to go mushrooming when in season.) Many of these prospecting holiday-makers, ignorant of the territorial tendencies of dragons, were never seen again. The United States government stepped in and licensed geographical regions to corporations that agreed to meet rigid safety requirements. Private citizens cried foul and claimed that corporations were given an unfair, possibly illegal, advantage. Nevertheless, the US government and others, under United Nations decree, continued the practice and collected substantial taxes on every bushel of dragonscales gathered.

Then in 2047 the sport of dragonscaling arrived on the scene.

Elvis Jackson, a professional rock-climber, was scaling the southern side of Angel's Window when a two hundred-meter dragon passed beneath him and snagged his lead rope between its bony backplates. The dragon pulled Jackson from the rock face and dragged him along the north rim of the Grand Canyon. After a short fifty mile jog the dragon, who hadn't noticed Jackson tangled in ropes behind him, settled down for a nap.

16

After loosening himself, Jackson gathered his wits and studied the situation. He noticed an irregular patch of scales hanging loosely from the dragon's hide. Curious, he reached out to grasp one of the scales and it dropped off easily into his hand. More importantly, doing so didn't seem to disturb the dragon's slumber. Encouraged (and perhaps addled by his recent ordeal), Jackson scaled along both sides of the dragon until he filled his duffle bag with scales far fresher than any found shed on the ground. Halfway down the starboard flank, the dragon awoke without warning. Jackson quickly cut himself free, slid down the dragon's rump, and ducked into a small cave opening just as it came fully awake. Despite having sprained an ankle in the fall, Jackson felt his way through the darkness while the dragon roared outside. He resurfaced two miles away and limped back to civilization with a bag full of the freshest, most valuable dragonscales ever collected to that date.

The Arizona authorities fined Jackson and confiscated his scales, but a new extreme sport had been born. Jackson himself never risked a repeat of his adventure, but others who heard his tale embraced it as the ultimate challenge and imitators answered the call. Realizing that there would be no practical way to prevent these daring adventurers from doing what they wanted, the government, ever-accommodating, decided it would be simpler to license and tax them instead. While the corporations maintained their monopoly on free-shed dragonscales, only licensed dragonscalers were allowed to collect scales from the dragons themselves.

The North American Dragonscaling Association (NADA) was established in 2049 to train, test, and license dragonscalers as well as assess the value of the collected scales and collect fees. In 2050, NADA also took on the task of monitoring the dragon population to ensure that the corporations were not tempted to capture and contain live dragons for illicit scaling. This fear was unfounded, of course, as there is no force or corporation on Earth that can contain a live dragon for very long-particularly when mating season comes along.

Dragonscaling Organizations and Resources

As a beginner, your first step is to locate a dragonscaling organization within your community. Be sure that the organization is accredited by the North American Dragonscaling Association and has at least one Master Scaler in its membership.

If no organization exists in your area, you can visit several on-line resources such as www.dragonscaling.org and www. dragonscaling-usa.com. In addition, you can participate in two related Usenet groups: alt.sports.dragonscaling and alt.suicide.exotic.dragonscaling. (Both groups post FAQs monthly.) Despite the fact that the Internet allows you to get in touch with dragonscalers from across the globe, there are no accredited dragonscaling organizations that operate solely in cyberspace. As always, any information found on-line should be treated with caution.[4]

Armchair dragonscalers will want to subscribe to *The Dragonscalers Journal* and its sister publication, *Scaly Tales*, both of which appear on newsstands in alternating months from NADA Press and are available for subscription.

Preparations for Dragonscaling

Proper equipment is a must. All equipment should be NADA-approved and purchased from a licensed retailer; second-rate gear should be avoided at all cost. There is no room for error in dragonscaling. A loose piton, a frayed rope, or a poorly constructed carabiner can result in disastrous mishap followed by an abruptly fatal end to your adventure.

Beginners should select thirty-five centimeter carbon-steel pitons and a sturdy hammer with a rubber grip. Choose rope that is certified for five hundred kilograms and is carbon poly shielded. Climbing boots and gloves should all have no-skid pads where appropriate and be fitted with climbing claws. If your dragonscaling adventure occurs close to mating season, avoid colognes, perfumes, and scented soaps and shampoos. Most licensed outfitters carry a no-scent bodysuit and deodorant which will also help mask your presence.

While you do have a choice, it would be wiser to use

18

---

4 While on-line recipes for dragonbane sound neat, there is no evidence that it is effective. Beware of mixing myth and reality.

climbing claws that can retract into your boots or gloves so you don't get stuck to the dragon when you need to make a quick escape. You'll find the majority of safety concerns involving dragonscaling have more to do with getting away from the dragon safely than with climbing the dragon itself. Wear a hands-free radio in order to keep your ground crew apprised of your progress and to receive warnings of weather conditions that may affect your climb or escape. In recent years, some dragonscalers have begun to adopt backpacks with spring-action aluminum gliders for those cases when they want to leave the dragon's back as quickly as possible. Purists feel this is cheating and refer to these devices as 'chicken wings.'

Harvested scales can be kept in a wide variety of commercially available mesh bushel bags which can be dropped from even the largest of dragons without bursting. While scale-poaching is almost unheard of, prudence suggests purchasing bags with unique frequency code emitters so your ground team can locate and collect your scales after the dragon has left the area.

Another piece of equipment that has become popular and controversial of late is the Scale-Tugger™ made by Dragontech Ltd. The present controversy comes from veteran climbers who feel that dragonscales should be collected by hand and not with a tool that rakes and gathers whole square metres at a time; but to date, there are no official standards on the methodology of dragonscaling so long as the scales are collected straight from a live dragon's hide. The sport has relied upon a tradition of sportsmanship which changes with each new generation of climbers. At the last North American Dragonscaling Conference, the supervisory board voted against enforcing revised sets of rules and regulations, but as new technologies enter the playing field, standards will eventually need to be set in place in order to preserve the legitimacy of the sport.

Equipment considerations aside, only those individuals in peak condition should attempt to take up dragonscaling. Once you've got your gear, even before you shop around, consult with your physician, priest, insurer, lawyer and astrologer (just to be thorough). Then take a long hard look at your life and ask yourself if life has truly become so dull that you seek to pepper it with a few terrifying jaunts into dragon territory. If the answer is the affirmative, you may then prepare to actually go climb a dragon.

Selecting a Suitable Dragon

Never select an awake, alert dragon. Not unless dragonscaling for you is just a complicated form of suicide. Always go for one deep in slumber. Fortunately, dragons are generally heavy sleepers and during most times of the year they will snooze peacefully through earthquakes, hurricanes, and local elections.

Unlike their domestically engineered brethren, wild dragons are territorial creatures and gather together (a group of dragons is called a gatling) only during mating season. Avoid scheduling your adventure between the sixth and eighth full moons of the year.

Otherwise, the sort of dragon you select should be determined by your level of experience, skill and the amount of excitement you seek. Larger dragons have more scales and are slower to wake, but difficult to begin one's assault on. Smaller dragons are more nimble and dangerous, but easier to begin climbing. There is no noticeable difference in temperament when comparing male and female dragons, nor in comparing colors. Should you be eaten, you'll find that all dragons look the same from inside.[5]

So where do dragons live?

Generally wherever they please; but-given their size-

5 The author wishes to say a word concerning the rumors of fire-breathing dragons: Balderdash! They exist only in legend. Despite reports from numerous witnesses, the geneticists involved in the creation of the original dragon species insist there was nothing in the design that could reproduce effects associated with the fire-breathing myths of old. No methane burps. Nothing.

Qualified investigators have examined some of these claims and have uncovered nothing that a careless ground team member and an unextinguished cigarette couldn't explain. There is no such thing as a fire-breathing dragon.

locating dragons poses no huge challenge. They roam remote areas and feed off herds of custom-designed meat-animals provided by the region's corporate sponsor. Dragons are most often found patrolling wooded and semi-wooded areas such as the American northwest, New England, and British Columbia. While they will live in areas of extreme heat such as the American southwest or in frigid regions such as the Nunavut tundra, dragons tend to prefer more mild climates. On rare occasions, a dragon will take up residence on a small island, but only if the interceding water can be easily forded and there are plenty of animals and dragonscaling teams nearby to sustain its considerable appetite.

NADA maintains an on-going database of dragon activity and registers all expeditions. Accessibility and proximity to rescue stations are factors in some regions being more popular than others. To keep certain dragons from becoming over-harvested, NADA recommends that you reserve your dragonscaling expedition a year in advance.

Scaling the Dragon

You're trained, equipped, somewhat insured, and utterly determined-so let's go! You've chosen a medium-sized dragon that is presently napping in the middle of a small valley and its back glitters with multicolored scales. The ground support team, located a kilometer behind you, wishes you luck via your headset. You've approached the rear of the dragon from downwind and now you're ready to hammer in your first piton. Have you really thought this through? So be it.

Beneath the scales, the hide of a dragon lays approximately twenty centimeters thick. There are not many nerve endings near the surface of the dragonhide so it's relatively safe to begin by hammering pitons into any part of the dragon that looks like a good starting point. The best initial grip is along the broad base of the tail and, with pitons and rigs, work your

21

way up to the back ridge-plates. From there, follow the spine up to the wing-joints where the choicest scales await. Be sure to wear gloves when pulling yourself along the sharp barbs which jut out along the spine. Adjust ropes at regular intervals so you have something to grab on to should you need to.

You need not concern yourself with being too delicate while affixing your pitons or using climbing claws. What you do have to be alert for, however, are nightingale scales. Named after the legendary floorboards in Japanese castles that 'sang' when stepped on (thus alerting guards to the presence of salesmen and assassins), stepping or leaning on a nightingale scale jolts the dragon to a sudden and very annoyed state of wakefulness. Likewise, should you insert a piton beside one of these deeply-rooted scales or attempt to pull one free, your adventure ends in short order. The dragon will come alive, turn and, unless you've managed to maintain a good hold, snatch you with its jaws and devour you on the spot.

Talk about an exhilarating sport!

Enthusiasts of dragonscaling lore have yet to create reliable guidelines in how to recognize and avoid these disconcerting traps—not for lack of trying. Nightingale scale placement, color, luster, and thickness all vary from dragon to dragon as well as from season to season. At the moment, there are no usable statistics predicting how many such scales exist on any individual dragon, nor where they would be concentrated-so climber beware.

While the chances of scaling a dragon's back without tripping a nightingale scale are better than winning the national lottery, the odds are still pretty appalling. Generally, one doesn't scale a dragon, harvest the choicer scales, and then simply depart. One scales the dragon and harvests scales until the dragon inevitably awakens. Many dragonscalers feel that the greatest challenge is to see how long they can remain on the dragon before this happens and ground teams often hold side bets on how long you'll last. You can tell how confident your team is by the odds they give you.

Currently, the longest time record for dragonscaling was achieved by Michael Diamond of Cincinnati, Ohio who began his climb at six o'clock on a Monday morning and collected 24 bushels of dragonscales over a period of three days before a passing griffin plucked him off the sleeping dragon's back and ate him.[6]

Escaping the Dragon

Once the dragon has woken up, the dragonscaling portion of your adventure is over and the escape phase of your adventure begins. The typical dragon takes ten to fifteen seconds to become fully alert. That doesn't give you much of a head start-especially if you have been harvesting your scales along the wings. While the dragon is still reaching for full wakefulness, its head may reach around in reflex and snap at the area where the nightingale scale was triggered. Watch out.

Smart dragonscalers will have prepared ropes along the port and starboard sides of the dragon in order to rappel down at the first sign of activity. Don't be standing when the wings begin to stir; many climbers get caught unawares and are swept off to their doom before they can grab hold of their lines.

You should also have your escape route mapped out well in advance. An abruptly woken dragon will pursue you relentlessly through valleys, swamps, forests, campgrounds, hills and mountains. Thankfully, they are not as fast as one might suppose and they rarely reach speeds over a hundred and twenty kilometers per hour. All-terrain vehicles are useful to a point, but they will run out of fuel. The dragon, on the other hand, will continue the chase for as long as you remain in its territory (and then some). Endurance is key.

Some dragonscalers choose airborne escapes via gliders,

23

6 Michael Diamond was the youngest in a family of three brothers and two sisters, all of whom had taken up dragonscaling. With the exception of Michael and his eldest sister, Honoria, all of the other Diamond siblings hit nightingale scales three minutes into their climb and did not survive the experience. Honoria Diamond-Jones, who retired from dragonscaling after her younger brother's misadventure, went on to write the best-seller, *Scaling Down*, and is now an anti-dragonscaling lobbyist in Washington, DC.

skimmers, helicopters, small jet planes, or hot-air balloons. Dragonwings, after all, were designed for aesthetics, not for utility; so while some dragons may be able to climb mountains and even cliffs, they are not skilled flyers. At best, a few smaller specimens may be able to glide short distances when given a substantial updraft and a running start; but if you've given a dragon either of these advantages, you've given it far too much.

Dragonscalers who collect scales for sport, rather than for profit, don't care much for air escapes but prefer the challenge of overland evasion. A minor faction of old-school dragonscalers believe that the ultimate sporting gesture is to escape on foot or, at best, a mountain bike. Understandably, the percentage of dragonscalers who feel this way becomes smaller with each passing year as their escape-related fatalities rise.

Postmortem

So assuming you've done your homework, planned each step three times over (at least!), and have escaped intact, the only thing left to do is to head back to the clubhouse. There you can get your scales appraised and logged, tell your tales of adventure, and plan your next outing.

Dragonscaling is as exhilarating a pastime as it is profitable and dangerous; but only serious scalers need apply. If you don't feel sufficiently warned of the inherent dangers of spiking into, climbing, scaling, and escaping a dragon, then the mournful fact remains that you may, indeed, have what it takes to be a dragonscaler.

Good luck! And may your pitons never split.

DRAGONKEEPER

CHRIS AZURE

The Chinese characters were smeared on the rocks in mud-red paint. Sean Morrison regarded them curiously as he sat by the gentle stream winding its way down the hillside to the Sha Tin valley below. Yesterday there had been nothing on the rocks, and today, some sort of message. Someone had once used this place as a shelter, evidenced by the bundles of clothes and scattered food utensils that lay strewn under the little bridge spanning the stream, but none of that had been disturbed as long as he'd been visiting. Certainly not in the past day or so.

His school's lunchtime bell rang in the distance. Maybe he should have taken those Chinese lessons after all. He knew one of the characters said "dragon," a word that cropped up everywhere in Hong Kong, but that was about all his limited Chinese reading abilities allowed him.

Footsteps approached on the trail above. He looked up. Amanda Choi stood at the top of the rocky incline in her school uniform, clutching a small plastic bag. She'd cut her hair to chin-length which brought out the natural round shape of her face, but her big eyes had narrowed into a glare. Somehow she managed to constantly look annoyed whenever she was with him.

"You have to stop skipping school," she said, shuffling down the incline to join him. "You're going to get kicked out if you're not careful!" She clutched his shoulder to steady herself.

"They'd never do that," he grinned.

"They might if you don't show up by the end of the week," she added, refusing to share his amusement. "And if you don't come back soon, I might have to tell them where you're hiding."

"Okay, okay," he sighed. "I'll be back on Thursday. Friday for sure."

"You better," she said. "Anyway, I brought you this." She handed him the plastic bag. Inside were a small polystyrene lunch box and a plastic spoon.

"Lunch? What makes you think I'm hungry?"

She shrugged. "Who else is going to cook for you?"

"You cooked this?"

"I bought it at school. You owe me ten bucks." An inkling of a smile crossed her lips.

Sean opened the lunch box and began scooping up the fried rice. "You should come here every lunchtime," he said between mouthfuls.

"Why do you come here anyway?" she asked, sitting down on the rock next to him.

26

"It makes a nice change from sneaking back home as soon as my parents are out for the day. Anyway, it's nice to just sit back and listen to the stream sometimes. Take in the wonders of nature."

She raised her eyebrows. "But don't you get bored?"

"I get bored more easily in school... but look. See this writing over here on the rocks? It only showed up today. Can you read it for me?"

Amanda sighed as she stood and walked over to the writing. She squinted her eyes in puzzlement. "It says something about sleeping dragons and the children of dragons. It's written in a very strange, old style."

"Who would write something like that?"

"A crazy poet, I suppose. Or someone as bored as you."

He laughed. "Yeah, too bad I don't write Chinese. I could add my own little verses. Maybe I'll do some in English."

"I'd rath..."

Before she could finish, their conversation was interrupted by a raspy old voice screaming at them in Cantonese. A clean-shaven old Chinese man with scruffy hair and clothes, looking like some sort of well-kept homeless man, stomped down the rocky slope towards them. He carried a leather bag in one hand and waved a bamboo stick in the air with the other.

"What's he saying?" Sean asked.

"I'm sure you can guess. Come on, this must be his shelter." They scrambled up the slope and back to the trail leading to the school, the old man screaming after them. Sean could still hear him from the trail, but the sounds soon turned from raspy shrieks to something sounding like horrendous attempts at either Chinese opera or karaoke.

"What the hell is he doing?" Sean asked, pausing momentarily.

"He's singing, or trying to at least. See, I wasn't far off. He's a crazy performance artist." Suddenly the ground trembled. Trees shook, discarding a few leaves. Birds took to the air. Amanda grabbed a tree trunk. Sean grabbed Amanda. Even as they steadied themselves, the ground trembled again, but this tremor was deeper and softer, like the purr of an enormous lion within the hill itself.

"That old man did something," Sean said, turning back towards the stream.

"Don't be absurd," she replied. "It must have been a tremor... I felt something like this once after an earthquake in China somewhere."

"I dunno... let's go see," he replied, grabbing her arm and pulling. She stumbled along behind him. "I think there's more to this than mere insanity." They crept through the woods towards the rocky incline. From the cover of the trees, they watched.

The leather bag lay open by the old man's feet. It held an

impressive selection of papers, some glass jars, a few paints, and an oversized, mud-encrusted egg.

"What is that?" Sean whispered. He received no response. The old man stuck several white paper notes onto the rocks, and danced. The cacophony sprang from his throat once again. The ground shook a third time, as though even it couldn't stand his singing, and this time Sean and Amanda held each other for support. The old man continued. "Can you understand him?" Sean asked. Amanda shook her head, but watched silently.

"Don't wake up, stay rested in the bones of the world," she said. "Now it is time to bring forth new life from your heavenly dreams."

"What?"

"That's what he's saying. More or less. It sounds more poetic in Cantonese. I still think he's crazy."

"But those tremors... and that egg. It could be a dragon, like the rock said! This is just the sort of crazy I'd like to learn more about!"

The old man picked up the papers again and flung them into the stream. Then he scooped up some water in a jar and packed it into his bag. He grabbed his bag and returned to the trail.

"We have to see what he does next!" Sean said, inching towards the trail again. The school bell went off in the distance.

"Sorry, Sean," she said. "I'd better get back to school."

"Aww, you can be late just this once, can't you?"

"I don't think that would be a good idea."

"Okay, how about this? Come with me today, and I'll be in school the rest of the week. Starting tomorrow."

"You promise?"

"I promise. Now let's go before we lose track of this crazy old man!"

The old man led them across the Sha Tin hills. It wasn't long before they were sweating and panting their way up the trail, hiking through the approaching cloud of humidity that would soon have Hong Kong enshrouded in its blanket. The old man had no trouble keeping up the pace, but Sean and Amanda struggled to keep close enough to not lose him around the next bend or dip in the path.

As they reached Needle Hill, one of the dominant peaks on the side of the valley, the old man stepped off the trail into a small clearing in the trees, and poured the jar of water onto the ground. Sean cringed as the man did his unwanted karaoke performance once more, and braced himself for the expected rumble. It was faint, but he was sure he felt something. Then the old man left.

"See, he did cause the tremors!" Sean said as they dashed down to the valley floor after him. They reached ground level and wove their way through a series of narrow streets and bike paths toward the train station. The old man disappeared through the turnstiles. Amanda immediately cast Sean a stern look, a look that distinctly said *"Don't even think about it,"* but he just took her hand and led her through the turnstiles and down to the Kowloon-bound platform. The station wasn't particularly busy at this time of day, but they did their best to mingle with the other passengers and keep out of the old man's way as they followed him onto the train, boarding the same car two doors down. Fortunately, he was either not paying attention or had terrible eyesight.

The old man alighted at Mong Kok station. They followed him through the streets, bustling even at this time of day, until they reached Tung Choi street, the northern part of which was lined entirely with pet shops. Most of these shops sold only fish and aquariums, as best suited Hong Kong's housing situation, but some sold dogs, cats, rabbits and more exotic pets. The man disappeared into a reptile shop.

"A lizard's egg! That's all it was!" Amanda cried out.

"Not even crocodile eggs are that big." Sean began walking towards the shop.

"Wait!"

"We've come all this way already."

Amanda relented and followed him inside. The shop was dimly lit and filled with rows of tiny terrariums, barren apart from a few rocks and shrubs. Tiny lizards and snakes hid in what little shelter they had, or stood completely motionless on the open rocks. A number of larger reptiles, such as pythons and iguanas, added a little variation to the mix. The old man was nowhere to be seen, but another man, a gawky twenty-something with black-rimmed glasses, supervised the shop. A thick curtain at the back of the shop guarded any hidden secrets from snooping sixteen-year-olds.

"Can I help you?" the gawky man asked in reasonable English, but with a heavy Hong Kong accent.

"Just looking," said Sean. He glanced at Amanda and nodded very slightly towards the man. Sean peered into the tanks, inching towards the ones at the back, near the curtain. Amanda walked up to the shop assistant and started chatting in Cantonese. The assistant led her around the store, apparently eager to discuss his products with her. Amanda appeared just as eager to listen.

Sean slipped behind the curtain. A narrow corridor led back to several doorways. The first opened to a tiny kitchen. The second proved rather more interesting. It was lined on three sides with bookshelves holding ancient books, atlases and all sorts of messily-stacked papers. The back wall, however, held shelves of terrariums, just like those in the storefront. Unlike the ones on display, however, these were brimming with decoration. Each tank housed a tiny landscaped garden with pebbles and a miniature hill. Blue and green mood lighting shined through whatever bonsai trees and shrubs had been added. More importantly, most of the cases held small reptilian creatures of various colors. Dragons!

30

The miniature beasts vaguely resembled the dragons of Chinese myth. Their bumpy, camel-like heads and serpentine bodies wound their way around the trees and rocks. Tiny legs barely reached the ground, but ended in sets of nasty-looking claws. Sean saw no actual horns or beards, like in typical depictions of dragons, but maybe they'd grow them when they were older. These dragons were about the size of cats. They must just be babies. They looked far more real than he'd imagined, but still otherworldly in their near-luminous reds and purples and blues. The dragons slinked to the glass as he approached, and watched him with wide-eyed curiosity. Each of them wore a little red paper collar with gold Chinese writing.

"Amanda!" he squealed. Some of the dragons cowered in their cages. Others raised their heads in defiance. He heard running, followed by shouting. Amanda appeared in the doorway. He slammed it shut and turned the lock as soon as she was through.

"What... oh my god!" she screamed, dashing towards the tanks, frightening even more of the dragons into their corners in her haste. "They're beautiful!" Two voices, one raspy, screamed from the other side of the door, and a fist banged furiously.

"They're all labeled," Amanda said. All of the tanks, including those that housed only landscapes, had a Chinese label.

"What do they say?"

"Each of them has the name of a hill, and a date," she said. "Look, *Ma On Shan, January 18th. Fei Ngo Shan, March 2nd.* Here's one with today's date," she said, pointing to a tank that had some landscaping but no dragon. *"Lion Rock."*

"That must have been the egg in his bag," Sean said. "What about this other empty one?"

"Needle Hill, May 6th."

"That's where he poured the water. You think..." He grinned. Alarm crossed Amanda's face. "Well, we could just fit one of these little babies in our pocket and run away with it instead," he suggested.

But before he could do anything, the door clicked open and the two men stomped through. The shop assistant grabbed Sean by the neck, pinching it sharply. He tried to shake him off, but the man had a firm grip.

31

"Leave this place. Don't come here again!" the young man said as he threw Sean out onto the street. Amanda, following untouched, rushed to him.

"Are you okay?" she asked, pulling him up.

"Absolutely," he replied, rubbing his neck and ignoring the crowd of onlookers. "We know exactly where to pick ourselves up a dragon in three weeks!"

Sean kept his promise to Amanda, even going to school for the next few weeks, but the anticipation was driving him crazy. He spent most of his classes just pretending to pay attention as he thought about the prospect of digging up a dragon's egg.

"We'll have to go up there a day or two early," he said to Amanda one lunchtime. "To make sure we beat the old man to it."

"Are you really gonna do this?"

"Sure, and so are you!" He squeezed her hand, feeling the blood rush to his head.

On the fifth of May, armed with a small spade, they made the hike up to Needle Hill after school, taking care as they approached to make sure the old man wasn't around. There was no evidence of either him or dragon activity, but they remembered roughly where he'd poured the water. Sean began digging immediately.

"Careful," Amanda said.

"I'm being careful," he replied as his spade tore through a bunch of tree roots.

"Give me that," she said, snatching the spade from him. She dug carefully and slowly. Sean sat down on a nearby rock.

"What's in that water of his that makes a dragon appear underground anyway?" he asked.

"We don't even know if this is going to work."

"I'm pretty convinced. Do you think there are fully-grown dragons swimming around in the stream?"

"That stream was tiny. Something a little more magical than that, I would think. If a dragon even turns out to be here."

Finally, the spade hit something solid. A hard white surface appeared beneath the soil, and the two of them began scraping it away. When the egg was free, she pulled it to the surface. It was smooth and grayish white, about the size of a rugby ball. Sean gave it a knock.

"Don't do that!" she snapped, pulling it away from him.

"Sorry. But now we've got our own dragon! This just leaves one question. My place or yours?"

"Yours, of course. My parents won't even let you come over.

32

I can't imagine what they'd think about a baby dragon."

"Mine it is then," he said. And he kissed her.

The egg sat motionless on the desk in Sean's bedroom. He'd forbidden the maid from entering his room and had taken up the shocking new habit of actually cleaning it himself in honor of Amanda's regular visits. His parents, when they came home late at night, knocked on his door a few times, but he kept it locked and pretended to be asleep. They never pushed too hard for a response.

Every morning Sean would stare at the egg for an hour before bundling it in towels and shoving it in his schoolbag. He'd peer at it constantly during classes, watching for any small sign of movement.

Every lunchtime, he and Amanda retreated to an isolated part of the school and brought it out. Occasionally it shook a little, but it never went beyond that. Amanda was a different story. Now they spent almost all their time between classes wrapped around each other, even in full view of the rest of the students. Going to school had never been easier! And, back in Sean's apartment, when they weren't eyeing the egg, it was pretty much the same story.

One lunchtime they went for a short walk up to the stream. The old man's papers and painted writing were gone, but there was a note attached to one of the rocks.

"He wants his egg back," Amanda said as she read it.

Sean grinned. "Of course he wants it back. He must get thousands of dollars for something like this. What else does he say?"

"That dragon is dangerous. If you keep it, the mountains will be angered and will rumble. Your dragon will cause unspeakable terror. It must be returned immediately. Return the egg to my shop or face certain destruction."

"Forget thousands... he must be getting millions for it if he's that determined!"

"What if he means it?"

"He doesn't. He's obviously just bitter. Why should he be the

33

only one allowed to have a dragon? Him and the millionaires, that is. Anyway, we're dragons too."

Amanda smiled. "You think we can raise a dragon better than anyone else because we were born in the year of the dragon?"

"Sure! They're practically family!" They both laughed. He threw the note into the stream and watched it float away.

One Saturday morning, Sean woke to find the egg trembling. He called Amanda immediately and she rushed over.

"It must be frightened," she said as they watched the egg shuffle towards the edge of the desk. Sean rolled it back to safety.

"Maybe it's just bored from being stuck inside an egg for weeks."

"Or hungry? That's a point, what do these things eat anyway?"

"Oh." He just stared at her for a moment, hoping she'd somehow come up with an answer for him. "What did that old man have in his case?"

"No food. Unless they eat paper or paint."

"Well, we do have some stuff in the kitchen. We'll just have to see what it likes, I suppose. Whenever it breaks out of that shell."

Throughout the morning, the trembling became more vigorous until finally the shell cracked. A hole formed, and a tiny bright red snout poked itself through, its big nostrils sniffing the air. Sean and Amanda watched in fascination as the tiny creature dropped itself onto the desk, dripping egg slime all over the polished surface.

Sean reached out and touched the dragon. It immediately leapt away, floating slowly down to the ground, and disappeared into a dark corner behind the computer.

"Would you stop doing that?" Amanda complained. "Go get that food you were talking about. Maybe we can lure him back out."

"How do you know it's a he?"

"Either way, I'm sure it probably eats. Now go!"

He dashed out and grabbed whatever he could find - sausages, a loaf of bread, chocolates, dry-roasted peanuts - and rushed back into the bedroom again.

"Frozen sausages?" she asked.

"Well, if you'd like me to go back and fry them up..."

"Whatever. Let's see if he likes any of this other stuff."

They waved the chocolate behind the computer, but received no reaction from the tiny thing. Nor did the dragon respond to the peanuts Sean scattered across the floor, much to Amanda's dismay. The loaf of bread, curiously, appeared to be the winning ticket. No sooner had he removed a few slices from the packet when the dragon dashed out, toppling the computer tower, and snatched the bread in its tiny camel mouth.

"They're bread-eaters?" Amanda asked.

Sean grinned. The dragon didn't stop at just a few slices. It launched itself into the bread bag and gobbled the lot, even taking some of the plastic with it. Then, still inside the ripped bag, it curled up and went to sleep.

"There's no way I'm going to school next week," he declared.

Unfortunately, it was exam time, and Amanda pressed the issue, dragon or no dragon. She bought a pet carrier so he could leave the dragon safely at home, but he just couldn't concentrate on his exams when he knew what was waiting for him. Hopefully he'd scrape by as he usually did, but this was definitely not going to be his best performance ever.

Every day after exams, Sean and Amanda both rushed back to his place and took turns feeding and playing with the beast. The dragon was growing, already almost as big as the ones they'd seen in the shop. It started off as a rather timid creature, constantly dashing behind the computer tower or under Sean's bed whenever it was released from its cage, but gradually it became more confident and scurried out to interact with its surroundings. Sometimes it would gaze into the computer screen or mount the desk to get a good look at itself in the mirror, an image it clearly recognized as its own. Soon, the dragon was much livelier and more playful, eagerly whirling itself around their arms and using their bodies as climbing frames. It didn't fly, but when it leapt, it soared through the air

35

in slow motion as though in its own personal time bubble.

But the dragon continued to grow larger, until it outsized even a cat. Playfulness turned into destruction, and no amount of bread could convince it not to smash up Sean's room. It thrashed around the room restlessly. It knocked huge dents in the wall, cracked the mirror, and worst of all, smashed his computer to oblivion. He managed to grab and immobilize it during these outbursts, but it was stronger than it looked and any attempt to restrain it turned into a lengthy wrestling match. It wasn't long before he needed Amanda's help just to get it back into its case.

"This is impossible," she said. "Soon it's going to be as big as us."

"I've been thinking about that," he replied. "Those dragons in the shop... most of them were several months old already."

"And?"

"And they were all still smaller than our dragon. I think I know what those collars were for. All we need is to get one of them for our own dragon and no more problem."

"Good luck getting one," she said.

One day as the two of them tussled with the dragon; it let out a high-pitched squeal. In response, the entire building shook. Books toppled over and action figures fell to the ground. Unlike the tremors from the previous month, this one didn't stop. The room just kept shaking, as though Hong Kong had decided to relocate itself to a fault line.

"This is too much!" Amanda screamed, stumbling towards him. "The old man was right! The mountains can hear him!"

The dragon screamed and writhed, knocking Sean off his feet. Amanda brought the case over and they struggled to shove it in and lock it. The case continued to jostle as though given a life of its own, but at least it was more manageable.

"We have to take it back!" Amanda declared, grabbing the case by the handle and staggering out of the room.

"Wait!" he said, chasing after her.

She didn't stop, but zipped down the emergency stairwell

to ground level and out towards the road, Sean close behind. As soon as they set foot on the ground, the trembling grew stronger. People rushed outside, clearly afraid their homes were going to topple to the ground. The hills behind the complex seemed to physically stir. He swore one of them was glaring at him. They fought their way through a small crowd onto a minibus that would take them down the hillside, the driver looking as stunned as everyone else as they sped down the trembling road.

Once they reached the valley floor, the tremors died down until they faded away.

"You can't take it back!" Sean protested as the minibus made its way to the train station.

"Are you crazy? Do you want another earthquake?"

"Look, it'll be fine," he said in defiance of all evidence. "We just have to learn how to look after it. How to stop it becoming agitated, and more importantly, how to stop it agitating the hills. Who knows, maybe all we need is the collar. The old man knows. And as long as we don't give the dragon up to him, maybe he can be convinced to tell us."

"I don't think that's going to work."

"Maybe not, but at least we can try. Just give me one chance. If they refuse, we'll give it back. I promise. Come on, how often do chances like this come along?"

She sighed. He knew he'd have his way.

They waited in a little cafe by the station for about half an hour, feeding slices of bread into the pet carrier under the table until the dragon finally settled down to sleep. They still had to go through a tunnel beneath the hills to get to Kowloon and wanted to avoid another earthquake if at all possible. The café's television was broadcasting news in Cantonese about the earthquake.

"Was it serious?" he asked.

"No," she said. "They're confused about the epicenter. There seemed to be several, but it wasn't as serious as it felt. No major damage."

"Excellent!" he grinned, but quickly straightened his face when she glared at him.

They reached the reptile shop without incident. Sean wanted to leave the dragon at Amanda's, giving them a better bargaining chip against the old man, but she was having none of it. After consistent pestering, however, she had relinquished control of the pet carrier.

They stepped into the shop nervously. The shop assistant raised his eyebrows in alarm as soon as they entered. "Do you have any idea what you've done? There could have been serious damage!"

Sean raised his own eyebrows. "You heard about that already?" Then realized a radio was on beneath the counter. "Well, you know there was no actual damage then."

"You were lucky. A few more moments and hundreds of lives would be on your hands."

"Don't blow things out of proportion."

The old man appeared from behind the curtain, and immediately started screaming in his raspy way. He screamed at the young man, screamed at Amanda, and screamed at Sean. He noticed the pet carrier in Sean's hand, and screamed even louder.

The young man nodded towards the old man. "He wants you to hand over the dragon."

"Obviously, but I'm not going to do that."

"Sean," Amanda whispered behind him. "Let's give it back."

"Listen to her," the young man said. "If you don't, the consequences will be extreme. You may cause the destruction of Hong Kong. Your dragon is growing too quickly."

"It's okay," he replied. "Just give me one of those collars, and tell me how to keep the dragon from being agitated. Does it have something to do with excessive amounts of bread?"

"You cannot be allowed to keep it!"

"And how much are you selling it for anyway? This dragon came from nature, it's not yours!"

"It is ours!" he growled, the old man still rasping away in the background.

"Greedy bastards!" Sean said and marched towards the curtain, pet carrier still in hand.

He shoved the old man to one side and dashed into the dragon room. The old man was soon after him again, his desperate cries filling the room as Sean opened the nearest tank. The blue dragon cowered slightly, but made no sudden movements as he reached for it. He grabbed the collar. The old man ran towards him and shoved him aside with surprising strength, just as the collar came loose. Sean spun to the floor and looked up to see the tiny dragon growing rapidly, months of suppressed growth transforming the beast into a mountainous heap of a thing. As it grew, its own tank and the surrounding tanks shattered. As the dragon kept growing, one tank after the next shattered, sending a shower of shards across the room. One shard pierced Sean's cheek. He screamed in pain. The old man cried out too. A swarm of tiny dragons darted from their broken cages to safety in the bookshelves, hiding behind the largest books they could find. The old man chanted desperately and quickly. The collarless dragon toppled from its shelf and fell. Its tail struck the ceiling as it arched through the air. Plaster and concrete rained to the floor as the dragon thundered down on the old man. He rasped his final rasp as the dragon crushed him.

Amanda appeared in the doorway and gasped as she caught sight of the huge thing. "Sean!" she shouted.

"Stay out of here," he yelled back, but she dashed towards him anyway.

The shop assistant appeared in the doorway and grabbed a large book and several white papers from one of the shelves.

39

"You idiot!" he said. "I'm not ready to deal with this."

The dragon stepped towards the man, raised onto its hind legs and tail as though about to pound him into the floor. The assistant shouted out a series of words as he read from the book. He flung the papers towards the dragon, one by one. The dragon's growth slowed and then stopped. As the final piece of paper hit, the dragon began to solidify, its scales turning stony and its limbs stiffening. The rocky dragon statue crashed to the ground. Amanda shrieked.

Several of the tiny dragons had been crushed, though others clung to the bookshelves. Their own red dragon was safe, cowering in the pet carrier in the corner of the room. But the shop assistant himself was no more, the only evidence of him the old book that had fallen away as he was crushed. As for the old man, he was under there somewhere too.

"Sean..." Amanda said in a quiet voice as the motion stopped. "Are you alright?"

"I'm fine," he said, pain from the shard in his cheek stabbing him as he spoke. "The old man saved me. I don't think he meant to." Amanda sunk down next to him, and they stared at the hill in the middle of the room. "The hills. They were its parents. The hills are all dragons."

He woke to a gentle but persistent prodding on his shoulder. He was curled up in the corner of the room near the door, a purple dragon snuggling next to him. Amanda's face loomed over him. It was red, the remains of dried tears dotting her cheeks.

"What... what's going on?" he asked.

The small hill still rose up in the center of the room, its peak almost scraping the ceiling. A few dragons scuttled across the rocks. He noticed a large red banner, a larger version of the red collars, circling the hill's base. He pulled himself up. His neck was stiff, and might have bothered him had it not been for the sharp prodding in his cheek. A small bandage was taped to his wound where the glass had been.

"How long have I been asleep?"

"A few hours. How are you feeling?"

"I'm okay. Well, not really." A knot tightened in the pit of his stomach as he thought of the two men. "I'm sorry. I was stupid."

"Yes," she said.

"Has... has anyone seen the damage?"

"Not yet. I locked up the shop. I've been doing some reading."

"Reading?"

"This is important, Sean. You have to listen. The old man and his assistant weren't selling dragons."

"Hmm?"

"Just listen." She picked up the book the assistant had been reading from and began to translate. *"The ancient dragons have slumbered for ten thousand years. Their sleeping bodies form the backbone of our world - our hills, our mountains. But as humanity encroaches upon them ever more, they become restless. It is our duty as dragonkeepers to see that they remain in slumber and bring no danger to humankind. But even in slumber, dragons enter heat. Even in slumber, dragons want progeny. Our further duty is therefore to breed the dragons. These small dragons should be kept for one year, then returned to nature and sent back into slumber as tiny hills on the backbone of the world."*

"What about that one," he asked, pointing to the room's rocky centerpiece.

"I've taken care of it. It has no connection to the bones of the world, and will shortly wither and die. It's all written here. Sean, this is all about you now. The old man's duty was to have passed to his assistant. Now it's going to have to pass to you."

"Me? But..."

She narrowed her eyes. "We're going to take all the surviving dragons and leave this place. We can keep them on my building's roof until we find a better place. Then you're going to walk the hill trails of Hong Kong, appeasing the slumbering dragons and doing everything these books say."

"I can't read Chinese."

She glared at him. "Then I'll translate while you write it all down. Those two men died because of you. I won't let you run from this responsibility, Sean. You wanted to take care of a dragon. Now you can take care of them all."

41

Sean smeared the Chinese characters onto the rocks with mud-red paint. The brush strokes looked a bit sloppy, but then so had the old man's. *Slumbering ancient, do not awaken. Release your energy, bring new life to dragonkind.* Not quite as poetic or incomprehensible as the old man's version, but it had much the same effect. He just needed to leave the characters here to sink in, and return tomorrow for the rest of the ritual.

The school's lunchtime bell went off in the distance. No longer his school. Now it was just Amanda's school. He sat on the rocks and waited.

"Hi." Amanda appeared on the trail above, wearing a smart red shirt and black trousers. She held a small plastic bag and smiled at him. Her hair reached her shoulders now.

"Hi." He smiled back as she stepped down the incline towards him. "How was your first day back?"

"Not bad." She handed him the lunch box. "I'm glad I don't have to wear a uniform this year, but I wish it was still summer. I'm already missing dragonkeeping with you."

"Well, there's always evenings and weekends."

"I still have to study."

"Just weekends then. I'm sure we can work it out."

"And you'll be okay doing this on your own during the week?"

"Absolutely. I think I've finally found something I enjoy."

She smiled. "I know I shouldn't be happy about everything that's happened, but this has really changed you. You finally have a sense of responsibility."

"I think my parents would have something to say about that. They're not too happy about me quitting school. But I'll worry about them later. There are more important things here."

"The dragons really give you something to care about, hmm?"

"I'd say it was more than just dragons." And without another word, they kissed.

LESSONS

KIRK DOUGAL

Laughter and voices rose in the air and rang back from the walls, mixing with the sounds of running feet, echoes multiplying until it seemed ten times the number of children played.

"Quiet!" Mother yelled, her eyes closed tight against a burgeoning headache. "Stop it and let me have some peace." A glance outside revealed the rain still pounding on the ground, splashes of mud leaping up in response to the drops. "If you all sit down and promise to be quiet, I'll tell you a story."

"Hurray!"

"Yes, Mommy, a story."

"We'll be good, Mommy."

In a few short moments, Mother looked down at her three children lying on the floor, unblinking eyes returning her stare with only the sounds of their heavy breathing filling the air. She felt the knots in her neck relax as the blessed silence washed over her. Her enjoyment of the moment was cut short, however, by the sound of her eldest child clearing his throat.

"Ah, yes," Mother said, settling herself more comfortably, "a story. There once was a young woman who lived with her parents in a city on the edge of a large forest. One day..."

"Hello, Father," Sally said, looking up at the sound of the kitchen door opening before returning her attention to the dough she kneaded. "You're home early from the shop." She looked up again when she heard her father sigh. "What's wrong?"

He sat down at the table, the chair groaning beneath his weight as he plopped onto the seat. "Nothing. Is your mother home?"

"I'm right here," Sally's mother said as she walked into the kitchen from further in the house. Her smile faded when she saw the look on her husband's face. "What has happened, dear?"

"I received a message today." His fingers tapped a disjointed beat on the tabletop. "It was from my mother."

"Is anything wrong with Grandma?" Sally asked.

Her parents exchanged glances before her mother answered.

"No, dear. She wants to sew your Blessing Day dress herself."

Sally was thrilled at the idea of her grandmother making the dress announcing her entrance into womanhood. The old lady lived in a house deep in the neighboring forest, away from the bustle of city life, but her skill with a needle remained legendary. She was sure the dress would be beautiful.

44

"Oh how wonderful," Sally exclaimed. "When will we leave?"

"You will leave first thing in the morning," her father answered. "But you will go alone. Your mother and I were not invited."

The next morning, the sun had barely shown its full body above the city buildings before Sally walked out the back door of the house, a cloak pulled tight around her body in the chill. A voice cried out and she waited until her mother walked through the doorway.

"I wish you were going with me," Sally said. "Maybe you and Grandma could work on my dress together."

"No, dear. I know you're looking forward to a dress only she could make for you." Her mother sighed before worry clouded her eyes. "Now listen to me, Sally. Don't talk to anyone on the way and don't leave anything behind on the trail. Above all else, stay on the main path. Don't try any shortcuts. Do you understand?"

"Yes, Mother."

Sally made her way into the woods, skipping and laughing, even singing to entertain herself as she traveled. The morning flew by and soon the sun climbed high enough to pour its light onto the path she walked. The temperature rose as well and Sally removed the cloak that felt so good in the crisp morning. As she slung the garment over her arm, a rumble shook her stomach.

"Now's as good as any to eat lunch," she thought. "The next time I see somewhere to sit, I'll stop."

Sally watched for a downed tree or stump to use as a chair but she walked for a long time with no luck. Paths occasionally broke off from the main road, some almost as large and well kept while others were little more than game trails, tempting her to try a different way to her grandmother's house. Yet, she remembered her mother's orders and stayed on the path. After a while, however, she came across a route nearly as clear and broad as the road on which she walked. Better yet, she could see the trunk of a fallen tree only a hundred or so steps down its way.

"Surely that is the nearest place to eat and get off my feet for a while," she thought. "Mother wouldn't expect me to walk all the way to Grandma's without a rest."

Sally walked down the side trail and soon reached the fallen tree. It had been a mammoth old oak, its trunk wider than one of her strides, but it must have been hit by lightening since it had rotted from the inside-out until it died and fell. She spread her cloak on its gnarled bark, settled down with a sigh, and quickly attacked the sandwich her mother had packed.

45

The meal was a memory of crumbs on her dress when she leaned back and let her legs hang limp. The air in the woods smelled fresh, no stink from the tannery or smoke from a smithy to foul her nose. She sucked it in great breaths, like a squirrel hoarding away nuts against the winter snows. It was when Sally stopped that she noticed how quiet the woods had become. Only the buzzing of flies broke the silence.

"Hello," she said, her voice a small squeak. "Anybody there?"

"I'm sorry. So few people travel down my path and I did not want to frighten you off."

Sally could not find the speaker in the shade of the nearby trees but it sounded as if he was over to the right.

"If you didn't want to scare me, you shouldn't have been sneaking around. Why won't you show yourself?" A whiff of smoke tickled Sally's throat and threatened to make her cough.

"As I told you, I get so few visitors and my appearance usually startles people."

The smell of smoke grew stronger and the voice was now behind her.

"Well, I promise not to scream," Sally said. "Please show yourself so I know who I'm talking to."

"As you wish." The voice came from her left.

Part of a nearby trunk appeared to peel away from the rest and walked into the light. The voice belonged to a young dragon, barely taller than the girl while standing on his hind legs. Sunshine rippled across his scales in a kaleidoscope of greens, browns, and golds, accentuating the blinding white of his claws. Before he turned to face where Sally sat, she received a glimpse of two hand-sized wings on his back, quivering in a nearly translucent arc.

"So what brings you down my path, young human?" The smell of rotting eggs floated on the dragon's breath when he spoke and mixed with strong remnants of smoke.

46   Sally could barely draw a breath—partly from the stench causing her to gag and partly from the fear gripping her heart.

"I'm going to visit my Grandma who lives down the main road." She swallowed and swore the gulp echoed in the silence. "I'd better be on my way or I won't make it there before dark."

The dragon opened his mouth and laughed. It sounded like a rough blade sliding over a whetstone, making the hair on Sally's neck stand. She only noticed the dragon's teeth.

"Well then, you're in luck. The road you've been on winds around and follows the base of these hills, taking you well out of your way before reaching your grandmother's house. This path, however, goes straight over with only a little climb to pay for the shorter distance and it comes out nearly at her back door. What do you say to my walking with you?" He waved one stubby foreleg with a flourish, a talon pointing the way. The warnings of Sally's mother rang in her thoughts.

"No thank you, kind master," she said, sliding off the trunk to stand on shaking legs. "I will take the road I was told to use." After as deep a curtsy as she dared with her jellied-knees, Sally walked back to the road, sparing only a quick glance back when she turned. The dragon still stood in the path where she had left him.

Her feet beat a steady rhythm on the road, her gaze darting from shadow to shadow in a terror-filled dance, sometimes lingering on a spot until she passed and other times flitting around too fast to follow. She did not notice the gathering clouds between the treetops above her nor hear the echoes of distant thunder, only noting the change of weather when the first drops of rain splashed on her face.

Only then did Sally realize she had left her cloak on the trunk beside the dragon.

Meanwhile, the dragon wasted no time once the girl walked out of sight. He scooped up her cloak and ran down the path in the opposite direction. Up and down the trail undulated yet it held to a straight line, finally climbing the largest hill in a gentle ascent.

The dragon ran in an odd fashion, on his powerful hind legs for several strides before leaning forward to use his undersized forelegs to regain his balance and then back to just two. Only a few years removed from the egg, his undeveloped wings tried unsuccessfully to beat the air and add lift to his movements. Regardless, the wyrm covered the ground with breathtaking speed.

His sprint was fed by Sally's cloak trailing from the sides of his mouth, flapping in the passing wind like twin banners announcing the approach of a lord. Her scent rose from the fabric and swam into his nose, flooding his senses and causing his mouth to water. The dragon had intended on sneaking close enough to surprise the girl from behind and eating her for lunch but he had not lied when he said not many people traveled down his path. A deer he could kill without cunning and conversation; Sally offered a titillating game of cat-and-mouse.

The dragon broached the big hill, his speed increasing on the downward slope. The rain was drumming steadily when his trail merged with the main road again, a little cottage standing a short distance from the meeting. He threw Sally's cloak around his shoulders and pulled the cowl up until only the tip of his snout showed.

His feet had barely moved off the steps and onto the front porch before the door flew open to reveal a gray-haired woman.

"Sally dear, I've been worried sick. You shouldn't have dawdled in these woods, especially with the weather. Come inside, girl, before something worse than a cold gets a hold of you."

The dragon stepped inside before throwing back the hood, firelight dancing across his fangs and scales.

"You have no idea, old woman," he growled before swiping once with his tail, snapping her neck and killing her instantly.

The dragon licked his lips but decided he did not have time to eat the woman before Sally arrived. Yet, there was no reason he could not have a little snack. He dragged the body into the nearby bushes, draining her blood into a pitcher he retrieved from the house before slicing off long strips of flesh with his talons. These he blew on with his breath, roasting the meat while the skin curled up and crackled. He had no more than sat down at the table to refresh himself, however, when stout shoes clamored on the porch. The dragon threw Sally's cloak in the corner and jumped into bed as a knock sounded at the door.

"Who is it?"

"It's Sally, Grandma. Can I come in?"

"Of course, girl. Let yourself in."

Sally opened the door and stepped into the cottage. Rainwater dripped from her clothes and pooled around shoes caked with mud. Her hair lay plastered against her head while her arms clasped around her body, trying to keep in some heat.

"Where are you, Grandma?"

"I'm in bed you silly girl," the dragon said from the darkened back of the cottage, out of the reach of light from the lantern on the table. "This foul weather has brought on a cold."

"I'm sorry to hear that. Can I get you anything?" Sally took a step toward the bed.

"No, stay there!" The dragon wanted the game to continue for a while longer but he realized he had spoken too forcefully. "No, girl. I'm fine. Take off your shoes before you track mud all over my house."

Sally sat in the chair beside the table and stripped off her shoes and stockings. A coughing fit wracked her body as she straightened.

"Grandma," she asked once it stopped. "Is this red wine?"

"Yes, girl. It's a strong vintage with a salty taste but it will help that cough. Have a glass and then eat some of the meat strips on the plate beside the pitcher."

Sally poured herself a cup of her grandmother's blood and gulped down several swallows before stopping with a gag.

"I've never liked wine much, Grandma, but that tastes horrible. Are you sure it hasn't gone bad?"

"No, it is very fresh. Perhaps I should let it age some more. What do you think of the meat?"

Sally felt a little queasy after the wine so she only nibbled at first on the meat. It was not long, however, before she gobbled down the rest of the strip of her grandmother's flesh.

"This is very good. It's a little tough but it has good flavor. What kind of meat is it?"

The dragon held back a smile, fearing his white fangs would be visible in the gloom.

"Oh, just some old bird that was nesting around here." The smell of the old woman's blood reached his nose and spittle began to gather at the corners of his mouth. The game needed to be brought to a quick conclusion. "Why don't you take off that wet dress before you're sick like me."

Sally stood up and undid the long row of buttons down the front of her dress. She slipped out of the garment and draped it over the back of the chair to dry before stepping toward the bed.

"Well that won't do, girl. Your underclothes are just as wet as your dress. You'd better take them off, too."

Sally felt a chill travel down her body and she wondered if there was a draft blowing through the cottage. She drew the shift over her head and stepped out of her small clothes. A feeling of exposure swept over her and she wrapped her arms over her bare breasts.

The dragon licked his lips at the sight of the girl. Her skin glistened in the light of the lantern, drops of moisture gleaming jewels on her skin. He could not have cared less about her nakedness except the glimpse of her round breasts and healthy body promised a succulent meal.

"Come lay in bed with me, girl, and we will stay warm together." The dragon's voice was breathy with anxiousness.

Sally nodded her head in agreement and walked to the bed but vulnerability made her feet stumble. She felt like she was walking out of the light of day into a dark and forbidding cave, the lair of some beast lying in wait. Only a step from the bed, she paused to draw a deep breath and brought a hint of smoke to her nose.

"Grandma, do you have a fire burning? I smell smoke."

"No, child. Now come here and join me so we can discuss your future." His breath rasped with the control it took to wait rather than leaping from the bed. A red tongue slithered from his mouth and licked at his snout, the fork forcing his lips back to reveal fangs.

Sally's foot rose to take another step but there it stopped. Stench hung in the space between her and the bed, a rotting stink mingled with smoke that made bile rise in her throat - the same feeling she had when she met the dragon. The barest hint of glowing white confirmed her worst fear. She screamed and ran for the door.

The dragon was caught off-guard, already scooting closer to the wall to give the girl room to slide under the covers. He leaped up to chase her but his talons tangled in the bedsheets and he tumbled to the floor with a howl, scorching the floor in his anger.

Sally reached the door and threw it open, bare feet slapping first on the wooden floor of the porch and then splashing in the mud of the road. Another scream leaped from her throat but in her mind it was a final cry of despair. She dreaded the feeling of talons ripping into her back, the smell of putrid breath overwhelming her senses even as she continued to run down the road.

Wrapped up in waiting for her death, Sally nearly ran headlong into the horse trotting toward her. She screamed again but cut it short, a gasp ending with a cough when she saw the man in the horse's saddle. His armor found some way to shine even with rain pouring over it in rivulets and the sun hiding behind black clouds. She had no time to catch her breath to beg for help before his gaze rose from her naked body and glared at the road behind her.

Spurs raked down the horse's side while the man's curse echoed over the sound of his sword clearing its scabbard. Sally leaped to the side, her feet slipping in the mud, and fell to the ground in a puddle. She rolled over just in time to see the knight's sword cut through the dragon's neck, the head flying off with a spout of black blood.

Mother sat up straighter and studied the faces of her children. They sat motionless at her feet, still enthralled by her story.

"So tell me, what lesson can we learn from this tale?" she asked.

"Don't go through the forest by yourself."

"Don't talk to strangers."

"Always listen to your mother."

Mother shook her head back and forth, the scales on her long neck glistening golden red. She reached behind her and dragged a body from the back of the cave.

"Fine lessons all, but not the one I'm looking for," she said. Mother ripped a leg off the dead knight, using her talons to pull the armor off and let it clank hollowly on the stone floor. Flame shot from her mouth and the smell of roasting meat filled the air, causing her children's tongues to lick greedily at their snouts.

"No, my beloved brood, the lesson is simple." The dragon mother tossed the leg to her children and watched them ravage it before she continued.

"Never play with your food."

51

THE DRUID'S DRAGON

BOB NAILOR

"I can smell you, mortal, so heed my warning." The dragon's deep voice resonated through the air.

The great beast stood up and stretched his massive wings into the starry night sky. The moon cast silvery shadows on the surroundings, reflecting off the dragon's scales and glinting in his green eyes.

The man knew not which caused him to shake more—the dragon's words or his own fear—but he held his ground.

"My name is Doodahn," the dragon bellowed, then turned and lowered his mighty head to face the man. "Mere mortals die when I receive the calling. I fear I know not when the calling will happen, but for now, you are safe."

The huge dragon looked about, scrutinizing the surrounding

trees that created this glen in the woods. In the distance the beast saw the stone monoliths of the circular altar.

The man, holding a medium sized urn, had stumbled from the dense growth of trees and happened upon the sleeping dragon. If he hadn't tripped over the greenish brown tail, Doodahn would've remained sleeping and the man would've been on his way, neither of them realizing the other existed.

"A dragon in fear?" the man asked hesitantly, expecting a blast of sulphurous fire to cleanse him from the planet. "What calling?"

The dragon eyed the man suspiciously, leaned down and sniffed at the urn, then raised his head to full height.

"Very well, mortal," Doodhan said. "Do you know of the time-weave?"

The puny man shook his head and clutched the urn closer to his body. The wax seal was unbroken.

"You've never heard the word before?" the dragon asked.

"Never, great Doodahn," the man replied and lowered his head. "Would you honor me with that knowledge, please?"

"A mortal who knows his place," the dragon said. "Very good." Doodahn swelled with gratification and pride. "Have you ever heard of blood-bond?"

"That sounds disgusting," the man said. "Never."

"And what of Druids," Doodahn said and again lowered his head to face the humbled man, his green eyes piercing the soul of the man.

The diminutive man hung his head and stared at the ground for a few moments, then again looked at the dragon. "Druids?" the man echoed. "They were once a mighty religious sect." 53

The dragon reared his head into the air. "So, you know of Druids?" His voice rumbled the surrounding area; the huge head plummeted toward the earth to again face the man. "Once?" he said loudly. "What does once mean?" He lowered his voice. "Are you a Druid?"

"Once," the man uttered.

Doodahn rose to full height.

"The word," the man shouted. "Once. It means..." He nervously shifted his weight. "It is a very obscure word to define, mighty Doodahn. Let me put it into another sentence, perhaps you will understand its meaning. Once you were asleep, but now you are awake."

"Fine," the dragon replied. "I understand the word once. So, again I ask, are you a Druid?"

"I've studied many religions," the man mumbled and waved a hand into the air with a flourish. "Christianity, but I'm not a Christian; Judaism, but I'm not a Jew. I've studied the Druids. They existed centuries ago and are said to have been very powerful. From what I can tell, they disappeared and no longer exist, or at least they no longer exist in that capacity. Even today there is much we don't know or understand of who the Druids are or what they did and didn't do. In fact, Doodahn, in today's society, dragons don't exist either."

"I knew the Druids," Doodahn said. "A treacherous lot. They are who I fear."

The dragon again lifted his head into the air and scrutinized the area. Doodahn then cocked his head to one side and returned to the man on the ground.

"You said I don't exist," the dragon said. "If that be true, then who and what am I?"

"You are Doodahn," the man said laughing. "A great dragon that doesn't exist. At least, not in today's society. What can you tell me of the Druids for my studies?"

"They tricked me," Doodahn said. "I had been fighting with a knight and was severely injured. I sought refuge in a wooded area. My wounds were seeping. A Druid found me and promised to heal my cuts. He said I would sleep and when I awoke I would be healed."

"That doesn't sound unfair to me," the man said.

"That is the only truth he told me," Doodahn replied. "He cleansed my wounds, but the blood he kept, placing it into jars, similar to the very one you hold. Have you any knowledge of the amount of blood he took?"

"None, Doodahn," the man answered.

"They need to use only one drop. That's right, a single drop of my blood, to perform the time-weave and blood-bond. My wounds were gashes. Blood was oozing onto the ground. That

54

Druid gathered enough blood to last for many, many years, even centuries."

"You're lucky to be alive," the man said placing the jar to the side of a large boulder. He scrambled on top of the stone and sat down.

"Lucky?" Doodahn bellowed and unfurled his wings. "I'm lucky? Imagine being at the beck and call of a mortal's slightest whim. They perform a blood-bond that locks my soul with another, usually the victim's. At that moment, I no longer have control. Their ceremony is the only thing that matters, especially the final consummation of the act."

The dragon folded his wings back against his body and arched his neck.

"Tell me, mortal," Doodahn said, "since we are talking so much, what is your name?"

"My name is Arthur," the man said, "but most of my friends call me Artie. I would be honored to count you among my friends."

"Artie," Doodahn said. "A strange sound, but it has interesting tonal qualities. I shall call you Artie."

"Doodahn, you mentioned a ceremony. Could you explain it, or at least elaborate on any details?"

"The time-weave and the blood-bond are a part of the Druidic mastery of the universe," the dragon said while curling his tail about himself and lying down. "How can I explain it?"

The man watched the dragon gaze into the distance, into a place that the mortal couldn't see.

"Do you know why the cock crows at sunrise?" Doodahn said.

Artie shook his head, wondering why the great dragon had asked the question.

"They know time," Doodahn said. "Their internal clock beats to it. It courses in the blood within their veins. Time is part of their being." The dragon blinked absently and slowly. "My blood is like that of the rooster. I understand and am one with time."

Doodahn looked at Artie and he could see that the man didn't understand.

"Artie, my dear mortal friend," the dragon said, "you age. Why? Because time passes. That is how you understand the concept."

Artie shook his head affirmatively and knew that he was getting older just sitting on this hard stone while they spoke.

"But that is a fallacy," Doodahn said. "Time isn't passing. Time is coursing. Your blood is coursing through your body. It is wearing out, tearing down time. When you've used up the time within your blood, you die."

The man rubbed his forehead; it throbbed from the explanation which he didn't understand.

"Are you telling me that time doesn't exist except inside my body?" Artie asked. "Time is my blood?"

"I'm saying that time exists in each and every living thing," Doodahn said. "Druids knew this and used it against me."

"Against you? How?"

"It is said that time will weather that great boulder you sit upon down to many grains of sand. Is that not true?"

"Yes," Artie replied. "In the passage of time that would happen."

"If I chip or crush that boulder, has time passed?"

"No," the man replied.

"So, do you understand now?" Doodahn asked. "Time is an existence inside living creatures. Inanimate objects, such as your magnificent boulder seat, endure but do not tell time."

"I'm not sure I understand," Artie said.

"You see the boulder today," Doodahn said. "Tomorrow when you come back, if I had crushed it, would you know how much time had passed? If I hadn't crushed it and you came back to this boulder two hundred years later and only found a small stone, would it have told you anything?"

"I think I understand," Artie said. "What of the Druids?"

"They had learned the secrets to gather the forces of time and funnel it," the dragon responded just as quickly. "It became known as a time-weave. They built sacred altars, huge monolithic stone structures with the correct magnetic properties to accentuate their time-weave."

Artie became excited. "I am familiar with these structures, but how did that involve you? How did they force you? What was your play in all this?"

"During their ceremony they would mix a drop of my blood. Remember I mentioned the jar with my blood in it?"

"Yes," Artie replied. "Continue."

"A drop of my blood and a drop from the sacrificial victim. With their chanting, mathematical formulas, and ability to blend and control time, they were able to create a blood-bond between the donors of the blood; a blood-bond between the victim and me."

"But," Artie said. "I've studied Druidism and never found any definitive truth to human sacrifices or blood rituals, let alone something this involved."

"I curse the day that Druid crossed my path and healed me," Doodahn said. "It has been my bane for centuries."

"But you live, Doodahn," Artie said. "You're alive."

"That is a truth. I live, but always in fear of the calling; their calling." Doodahn sighed heavily.

Artie stood up and stretched. The stone that he had been sitting upon had taken its toll and he needed to move. He looked at it and realized that he couldn't tell if it had aged or not, it looked the same to him.

"Doodahn," Artie said, turning his attention once again to the dragon. "You've mentioned the victim. Can you explain why you used that particular term?"

"Just as I'm a victim," the dragon said, "so is the human that is blood-bonded to me. During the ceremony the blood is heated in a copper bowl. As the blood heats in the bowl, so does the blood in my body. Dragons cannot endure this heat too long or they lose control of their senses."

Artie nodded his head in a gesture that he understood and he leaned back against the boulder.

"When the time-weave is invoked," Doodahn continued, "I must attend the ceremony. For every moment that I don't attend the calling, my blood's time is diminished at an increased rate. That, Artie, is the penalty for disobedience."

"So," Artie said, "just ignore the calling and age. How old can a dragon get?"

"Unfortunately I can't ignore it, Artie," the dragon replied. "Remember the blood-bond? I can't stop the rage in my blood. Together, the bond and the weave are more than I can endure. There must be a cleansing."

"My sympathy, dear Doodahn. When was the last time you were called?"

"It's been years," the dragon said. "Many years. If you have spoken the truth and Druids no longer exist, then perhaps I'm free of this savage servitude to their religion."

"But Doodahn," Artie said, "what happened to the mortal victim? You're still here."

"My blood boiled and raced through my body," Doodahn said. "I would burst upon the ceremony and hover above the monoliths, unable to leave, watching in fascination and attempting to control my reasoning. The copper bowl kept heating. Finally, I would lose my senses and blast the bowl and the human in a ball of fire. When I finished, there would be nothing left except the stone altar."

Artie was immediately reminded of the altar stone he had examined earlier in the day. It was stained in blood and smudged with fire's ash. It hadn't made sense at the time. Now it did.

"Doodahn," Artie said, "if it was the blood in the copper bowl, why did you destroy the human?"

"I was cleansing time," the dragon replied. "Our blood had been mingled and I needed to purge the mortal's from mine. Cleansing. The bowl was a symbolic link to the real link between the mortal and me. Our bloods had been mixed, but dragon blood must remain pure."

"It seems a senseless death," the man said. "I've never seen that part of Druidism."

"Artie," Doodahn hissed, "Druids never kill senselessly. The sacrifice was necessary. While I destroyed with fire, time was being released from the mortal. The Druids, harmonizing the vibrations of the stones, would use the freed time to see into the future."

"Fortune telling?" Artie gasped.

"No," Doodahn said. "Fortune telling is chicanery. They read the future, the vibrations of time, to see where time would lead them. The Druids were involved in understanding the matrix of time."

"It would seem that I've completely misunderstood what

Druids were," Artie said, and once again stood up. "Druids and time." He reached down and carefully picked up the jar. His heart raced in this new knowledge; knowledge that he had never been able to glean in his studies of this latest religion.

"Druids enjoyed nature, for nature is time," the dragon said while watching the man. "Are you leaving, Artie?"

"I fear I must, mighty Doodahn," Artie replied, now fully understanding how to use the strange thick liquid in the jar he had found. The wax seal had been somewhat difficult to pry away, revealing the green bile under the lid. It had a foul smell and Artie, thankful that the wax remained intact, had quickly re-sealed it.

"Perhaps our paths will cross again, Artie," Doodahn said.

"They will cross," Artie replied. "We will see each other very soon. I'll call to you, my friend."

The man smiled and hastily retreated toward the woods, holding very securely his new-found jar of valued dragon blood.

"I need to cleanse your blood from mine," Doodahn whispered. "Forgive me my new friend, Artie, but the jar scratched you when you opened it. Even the smallest trace must be erased."

The full moon shone upon the opening and the monoliths in the distance glistened in the light.

Doodahn sat up, spread his mighty wings, arched his neck, and then blasted the would-be Druid. Doodahn could see in the burst of time vibrations that there would be no more Druidic callings for him now that the last jar of his blood had been found and destroyed.

Dragon Eye, P.I.

Karina L. Fabian

"You can't be a gumshoe! You're a dragon!"

I get that a lot. Not the "gumshoe" part—where'd she dig up that dime-store novel word, *The Faerie Book of Mundane Slang?*—but the part about my not being able to be a private investigator. Speciesist, if you ask me, but no one ever did.

She had walked into my office in the warehouse district, the echoing click-click-click of her fancy boots on the concrete floor fortunately waking me up from my nap before she got to my desk. Where was that mutt I got? Ol' Hot Dog was supposed to guard the place.

Oh, yeah. Ate him. Been a tough month.

For a minute, we just looked at each other. I knew what she saw: a quarter-ton, North African Faerie Wyvern, six-foot-two at the shoulders when I'm sitting down, with a five-foot tail. The lighting in the warehouse didn't do my red-and-black hide justice and I had collected a few scars over the centuries—all very recent to my reckoning. Still, my sunburst-yellow eyes glowed with a feral light, my cheek crests flared dramatically, I was largely muscled, and I had upper and lower canines the size and sharpness of a Bowie. If I had reared up and unfurled my wings, I'm sure I'd have been the most terrifying thing she'd ever seen. In fact, if it hadn't been for that run-in with St. George, I'd still be the most terrifying thing anyone had ever seen, without making any kind of display. God bless St. George, the muscle-bound pain in the tail.

She, of course, was as human as my saintly nemesis, and expensively dressed while trying to blend in with the locals: artistically rather than realistically torn jeans, patent leather jacket that tried to pretend it was vinyl, a vintage Dead-Head t-shirt that would bring in enough money to keep even me fed for a month. Her hair had the braids and curls and wisps in all the right places, yet somehow managed to look like a professional job. That look that says she's used to people serving her and having her conveniences conjured up by magic rather than technology. I'd seen the type before. They come to the Mundane side of the Gap slumming, and if they're lucky, they go home to Faerieland with a story and maybe an STD. If they're not...I wondered where her bodyguards were hiding, and how fast they'd be in here if I reared up and made her scream.

I didn't bother. I needed money, not thrills. Instead, I lifted one taloned foot. "No shoes, but I have stepped in my share of gum. Humans are terrible litterbugs."

"Aren't you small for a dragon?"

"I'm big enough to do the job. You have one for me?"

"Why aren't you off terrorizing the countryside, devouring virgins and stealing treasure?"

Tact, she had not. I treated her to my half-snarl—I couldn't afford to lose a client, no matter how rude—and said, "Did you come here to insult me, or were you just hoping to find a down-on-his luck human male to throw yourself at?"

"I'm not that kind of lady!"

"And I'm not that kind of dragon. Now that we've established that, do you have a job for me, Princess?"

She gasped and pulled herself back. "How did you know I was a princess?" she whispered.

Actually, I called all female virgins "Princess." Millennia of habit.

"Sherlock Holmes may have liked to give away his trade secrets, but I don't. Now, what can I do for you, Princess?"

"Call me Valerna. What else can you do?"

Well, she recovered fast. "Sure, 'Valerna.' Like my ad in the Yellow Pages says: Lost treasures recovered. Virginity verified. Hired muscle. Wisdom of the ages; experience of millennia. Reasonable prices, flights extra. Just causes only."

"My cause is just. I'm sure of it." But she looked a lot less sure of herself than she had since she'd sauntered her way into my lair—sorry, office. "I need you to find something that was lost or stolen. A family heirloom." She pulled out a photo, one of those kinds used by museums or insurance agencies. On black velvet rested a necklace of heavy stones of a warm, golden hue that utterly clashed with Valerna's pale complexion. I turned my head and squinted. I thought I could make out small objects inside each stone.

"Amber?" I asked as I pocketed the photo. She looked like she was going to object to that, but thought better of it.

"Yes, some of it magically forged. They were last seen somewhere in the palace garden two days ago—it was a state party, my... formal coming out."

I nodded knowingly, though the puzzle was just coming together. Princess Galinda Tavendor's Coming of Age Party was big news, here and across the Gap in Faerie. A Faerie princess wouldn't come to the slums of the Mundane world seeking my help unless she didn't want Daddy to know something. "And how would the state jewels of Tavendor end up off the neck of its heiress?"

She blushed, but seemed to relax as she thought back to what was obviously a pleasant memory. "Galendor, of the House Eternal Winds of the High Elves. He was trifling with me, and I knew it, but it was oh-such fun, and I didn't let things get too out of hand... "

"You don't need to tell me." I tapped my nose. "Sure it wasn't Galendor that... ?"

"Of course not! Elves are beings of honor, and Galendor more so." She sighed in a sickening way, and then abruptly turned practical. "Besides, the garden was my idea. No one was supposed to be there and it's oh-so isolated and perfect for a merry chase, and once I realized the necklace was missing, we retraced our steps looking for it. And I'm quite sure he didn't hide it on his person—I mean, his outfit was too tight, you know how Elves dress." She was blushing again, but rallied. "I thought perhaps a jay or crow took it to its nest."

I decided not to comment. *Crows. At night. Sure.* "Can you get me something it's touched?"

"Well, I handled it the most that night… "

"And I'm sure you've washed. Your dress?"

"Low cut. And laundered."

"Well, find me something if you can. It'll make the searching easier, especially from the air. Otherwise, all I can do is sniff out amber. If it's in a nest, that may be enough, but if not… Now, as to my price."

We quickly settled on a sizable herd and grazing lands. I even helped her concoct a story about it being a charity job for the poor. I knew plenty of poor who'd help me manage the herd. They'd run the "farm," get some breeding going. Faerie cows are a delicacy in the Mundane world; a smart family could do well for themselves. Me, I'd be happy with the culls.

A regular food supply and another good deed against my debt. Things were looking up.

She soon left and, now that I was listening, I heard several footsteps outside as her bodyguards joined her, some at discreet distances. They knew their business. Good for them. I tried to turn my thoughts to my business, but my stomach got in the way. It'd been a long time since desperation made me turn ol' Hot Dog into a… well, you can guess the pun.

I spent the next couple of hours wandering the nearby slums, ridding them of vermin. Rats taste vile, but enough of them will fill you up and it's another good deed, right? By the time

I was sated for the next couple of days, the sun was halfway to the horizon. Still enough time to check out "Valerna's" idea. My sniffer was good to find amber for hundreds of yards, but I didn't think they'd appreciate a dragon flying over their territory for grins, so I headed to my favorite restaurant to barter my services for a cover story and a little something to take the rat taste out of my mouth.

Half an hour later, I was through the Gap and airborne over Palace Tavendor, a large banner announcing "Grandma Natura's All-You-Can-Eat Friday Buffet!" trailing behind me, the sweet taste of mutton scraps in sauce still on my tongue. I made a few fly-bys of the garden, and then moved in ever-widening circles over the surrounding parks and neighborhoods, scanning the trees and seeking the warm scent of amber. The city guard took potshots at me, but their aim was lousy. What hurt worse were the kids pointing and laughing. I hate billboarding.

As the sun went down, I abandoned my search and headed back. It was raining on the Mundane side of the Gap. Figures.

"Grandma" untied the soggy banner from my tail and insisted on paying me a bonus, so I took my hard-earned cash down the block to the Colt's Hoof to slate my thirst and see if Costa was making his usual appearance.

I got the standard glares and hairy eyeballs when I walked through the door, but I was used to them, and the Hoof serves all kinds, so I settled myself at the end of the bar where there was no stool, confident I'd be ignored.

"Sh—ay, aren't you kind of small for a dragon?"

Well, so much for that. I gave him my 'Do you really want to mess with me?' stare. Usually that stopped them, but this elf had obviously had a tankard or twelve too many and was looking at me with a tight, half-mad grin like Hot Dog used to get when he was about to vomit something he never should have eaten in the first place. I hoped this guy didn't have similar plans. "I'm big enough to do the job," I growled.

Instead of being intimidated, he tossed a friendly arm up to my shoulder. "Oh, c'mon, don' be… urp… like that. Never sheen a dragonon-on before. Lemme buy you a, a drink. Yeah. Hey, bartendeler—a bloody Mary!" And he fell to the ground, laughing at his own joke. And I had thought the embarrassing part of the day was over. There were days when I so wish I could still breathe fire. Just a spark would have ignited this guy.

Just then, Jerry Costa walked up. "Hey, Vern. Ordered take out again?" He glanced at my drunken antagonist.

Balmy suddenly stopped laughing, so I took the opportunity to turn my head slow and dramatic-like—easy to do when your neck is two feet long—and gave him The Grin. Suddenly Balmy was sober and out the door as if I had set him on fire.

Now it was Costa's turn to laugh, though it was more of an appreciative chuckle. We've played that particular shtick before. He pulled a stool next to me. "Buy you a drink?"

"My treat today." I ordered a beer for him and a Virgin Mary for me. Might as well get the joke right. Besides, when I wanted to get drunk, I headed to the Texaco for a few gallons of ethanol. Lonely but cheap, and I was a mean drunk. Be meaner if I had my fire. Damsels and Knights, I missed my fire.

Costa interrupted my brooding. "What brings you here—and with money? On a case?"

The rest of the bar had gone back to their drinks and their business, so I handed him the photo. "Heard it might be making the rounds." I didn't say any more and Costa knew better than to ask. The fewer questions he asked me, the fewer lies I needed to tell, and I didn't need any more black marks.

Costa was a first-class fence until his missus made him go straight. Now he owned a chain of pawnshops and a fancy jewelry store. Cliché, I know, but it kept him in the know with anyone who's buying or selling stolen goods.

"Fat chance of that," he replied. "That's the Mystic Necklace of Tavendor. Each one of those jewels holds a religious relic from a major world religion—yours, and ours now. Only an idiot wouldn't notice the power signature. Even on the Mundane side, we check now."

"Even Mundanes can learn."

Mundane was the catchword for creatures from the non-magical side of the Gap that links our two universes. And if you think Mundane is insulting, just try calling a barbarian swordsman from my universe a Faerie. Now, I may have had

65

the wisdom of the ages (at least what my good deeds have earned back for me), but even I didn't understand the physics. What I did know was that a nuclear experiment here somehow interacted with a High Magic experiment in my former world and boom! We're connected. It was a rough time for both sides: a lot of technology, especially iron, is harmful to the Faerie, and more than few magical items have crossed into the hands of inexperienced Mundanes with disastrous results. A lot of strong trade and environmental laws had settled things down, though there were still movements to close the Gap. Most of us have adjusted. Some, like me, have even benefited.

Still, there were those who had to try to break or at least bend the rules. Bet Princess's Coming Out Party had lots of Mundane industrialists attending.

Costa seemed to be thinking along the same lines. "Didn't I see a picture in the paper of Princess Galinda wearing these at some party? You'd think they'd take better care of them."

"Flaunting their religious beliefs—or lack thereof," I explained to my friend. "The Tavendors are notoriously atheistic. I doubt the royal household has a single person who ascribes to any religion. Which, when you think of it, makes them the perfect caretakers, since so much of the power depends on belief or the twisting of belief."

We finally got our drinks. "St. George!" Costa raised his glass and took a huge gulp.

"St. George!" I replied.

"His curse is our blessing."

It's an old ritual between us, and one of the reasons I liked life on the Mundane side. See, Faerie dragons can't be killed. Ever. Pierce us, we heal. Burn us, we rise from the ashes. Slice us to bits, whatever's most alive will grow back. Not always easy, not always fast, usually painfully, but we cannot be killed. Didn't stop folks from trying, though, which was why so few of us were out and about to 'terrorize the land, devour virgins, and steal treasure,' as Princess Galinda so delicately put it.

St. George, though, was smart, and it didn't take him long to figure things out, so he tried a different approach. He cornered me in Ethiopia—the Faerie Ethiopia, that is. What a great gig. They really respected dragons there. Just show up at the gates and they'd toss out the livestock. Better than take-out Chinese. Anyway, St. George bound me with the Power of God and his own personal will. He took everything from me—my size, my flight, my power, my fire—and gave me only one way to return to my former glory. I've got to earn back my former powers through constant faith and good deeds. And you can imagine how hard that was in the land of Faerie. Throughout history, dragons were The Enemy. Who was going to believe one had changed? Few wanted my help; the ignorant wanted to kill me, or to try, anyway. Used to be an annoyance; after George, it was downright hazardous to my health. It took fifty years just to find a priest willing to listen to my confession. Eight hundred years of trying, and I'd gotten back a third of my height, less than that of strength, some of my wisdom, and let's not talk about my puny healing abilities. At least I could smell properly again. Handy skill.

Mundanes, though, were more than willing to accept my help. I might not get paid well, but my store of good deeds was on the rise, and being a P.I. was interesting work. The Gap was like an answer to a prayer—and believe me, I'd prayed.

Costa was staring at his glass thoughtfully. "Wonder if the Popes know about it?"

"The Popes?"

"Yeah, it was on the news today. Both Popes are coming for the 25th anniversary of the opening of the Gap." Despite himself, Costa grinned at the old joke. The clothing designers must have been crying with joy the day the scientists coined that phrase.

"So?"

He tapped the center jewel of the necklace in the photo. "That's St. Peter's knuckle in there—your St. Peter. Wonder if someone's planning to pass it to one of the Popes in hopes of getting an Indulgence?"

Indulgence. A remission for temporal punishment of sins which have already been forgiven. It was an Indulgence that got me my flight back. Suddenly a whole new set of possibilities was opening before me. I finished my drink. "Let me know if you hear anything,"

67

I said as I grabbed the photo. Costa looked a question at me, and then shrugged. He knows how I get when I'm on a case.

"Come to our house for dinner after church, Sunday," he said as I tossed some coins—a combination of Faerie and Mundane—on the counter.

"What? So I can play pony for the kids and fashion model for Rita?"

Jerry's got five kids, all under 11, so I got swarmed when I visited, and Rita'd taken it as a personal challenge to clothe me. I didn't mind, though. The kids were great and I loved the attention. And it's nice to have clothes. Not that I need pants —Faerie dragons are androgynous and housebroken, which I've had to explain to more than a few Mundane proprietors and cops—but vests with pockets definitely come in handy in my business. Besides, she'd gotten really good over the years. The one I had on right now was easy to put on, even without thumbs and with the challenge of my wings, and it had lots of hidden pockets for the usual tools of the P.I. trade. And Rita said the color brought out the gold in my eyes.

"She'll make you chili verde," he sing-songed back. He knew I couldn't resist her chili. She made it extra special for me; it's as close to breathing fire as I've come in eight centuries. I gave him a real grin before I left.

As soon as I was back on the street, my smile faded. The rain had stopped and I made my way through the damp streets on automatic, my mind on our conversation in the bar. The Faerie Pope would know it was stolen goods. Would the Mundane Pope have any use for a Faerie relic? Holiness is holiness, and our St. Peter was just as important as the Mundane's. Would he grant me an Indulgence—and would a Mundane Indulgence have the same effect? Or could the necklace itself restore my abilities? St. Peter probably had more power in his knuckle than St. George had in his whole holy muscle-bound body. But if I took the necklace for myself, I'd be just as bad as whoever stole it in the first place. Just like good deeds worked to restore my powers, bad behavior set me back.

I'd just gotten to the front door of the warehouse when an elf materialized out of the shadows and jabbered at me in High Elvish.

"Oh Great Wyvern, Fellow Citizen of the Golden Land, Land of Magic and Beauty, Where the Eternal Winds blow gentle on the softly blooming meadows of Caraparavelenciana, where once you flew with grandeur and strength, heed me and aid me. For throughout time, we of the Ancient Folk and your people, the masters of the skies..."

"Listen," I cut in. "It's been a long time since I've had a good, long conversation in a native tongue of our land, but I'm cold and I'm on a case. So could you just spit it out in Mundane?"

Even in the dim light, I saw him switch mental gears. Poor guy. Who knew how long he'd been working on that speech? He'd even looked up my old hunting grounds. That's class. Faerie Elves, just like Mundane legends, are extremely long-lived, and their speech reflects it. They have to plan half an hour ahead to ask where the bathroom is.

"Princess Galinda has been kidnapped," he said. "I knew she was working with you to find the necklace and I think I know who took it and her. I need your help."

Wow. He spoke Mundane real good. "Galendor, I presume? You've got some explaining to do." That's usually enough to get the desperate good guys talking, I've found, and Elf Charming was no exception.

"I'm afraid it's all my fault. My dark cousins..."

"Funny. You don't look Unseelie."

He did look pained. "Dark in spirit, dragon. They challenged me to engage in love games with the Princess Galinda. To... see how much of her gilding I could convince her to remove." He paused to sigh theatrically. *Now, where had I heard that before?* "She was as fair as the espali flower which blooms only in the most clement of springs... Sorry. I thought it was a game. I wasn't prepared for her to enchant me so."

Ah, interspecies love. So cliché. "The necklace?" I prompted as I pushed past him to unlock my door.

"When we couldn't find it, I knew I had been tricked. When I could not convince my cousins to return it, I hastened to confess to her, only to find her missing. Can you help me find her?"

"Just be glad the necklace is the only thing she lost that night. Come on, let's get my harness. Flights are extra, but we

69

can discuss my fee after we find her." I may have just found my way around my moral dilemma. Kings used to offer half their kingdoms to the lucky sod who saved their daughter—believe me, I know—so maybe King Daddy would be willing to part with just one family heirloom...

I admit it, my mind was on treasure when it should have been on work, so when Galendor's 'dark cousins' jumped us, I was caught completely off guard. Still, I managed to beat off the first half-dozen. Then one of them got under my guard with a lucky swing and everything went dark.

When I first woke up, I thought they'd knocked my vision all funny, but once the fuzziness cleared, I realized that the room was just as I was seeing it. *Too bad*. We were in a long abandoned, decaying church, the crumbling statues of saints defaced and desecrated. Candles everywhere made the shadows move eerily and reflected off the faces of black-robed elves. Galendor was chained to the walls, his sword gone and his clothes dramatically torn. I was bound to the floor with manacles on all four legs and a collar around my neck. A crude band bound my wings against my back. I was inside a chalk circle, in the center of which was etched a pentagram, one amber stone set into each point. I squinted and saw that the one with St. Peter's knuckle was on the point nearest me.

In the center of the pentagram was who else but the Princess. They'd dressed her in flowing scraps of sadrae, a material as smooth as silk yet mostly sheer with a slight iridescent quality that caught and reflected the candlelight. Very expensive, royal dowry stuff. I'd had a couple of bolts in my hoard, back in my pre-St. George days. The princesses used to ask their knights to try to swipe it on their way out. Which, of course, was why I kept it. Ah, good times, good times. Still, from the way Princess Galinda was laying, gagged and terrified, with robed and cowled elves chanting and making preparations around her, I didn't think she was thinking honeymoon.

One thing about the Faerie. They never miss a cliché.

"Well, this is cozy," I said to no one in particular. The right guy would come to gloat soon enough.

In the meantime, I tried to reach under the vest, as if to scratch. No luck, thanks to the chains. I used my tail instead. They hadn't bothered to chain it; it wasn't the threat it used to be back when I had my full size. *Evil Overlord Mistake Number One.* Number Two was leaving me my vest. Beside me, there was a groan, a shout of "Galinda!" and the sound of chains being pulled ineffectually. Yep. Galendor had started to come around. I let Elf Charming struggle; it was good cover for my own activities. You try picking your own pocket with your tail.

Still, I got what I needed and was discreetly working on my collar when none other than the headman himself came over. I could tell he was top elf because he was the only one in red. "So you awaken—and just in time, too," he leered. I looked at him and waited.

"You'll never get away with this, Adrenoglandanpau'ertrep pin!" Galendor shouted.

Right on time. Like I said, Faerie and cliché.

"Oh, do be quiet, Galendoropynphordaladys," Adren sneered. "I have already gotten away with it. In just a few minutes, the moon will reach its zenith, I will kill your beloved human, and my plan will be in motion."

"Full moon's tomorrow night," I volunteered smugly. I started scratching at my back legs with my tail.

"Fool dragon, I know that! You think my plans can be achieved with the power from one pathetic little virgin girl? She is but one piece in my little game. I will sacrifice her to gain control of you. Once I have control of your mind, dragon, I will use you for my next step—to kidnap the Mundane Pope!"

"Let me get this straight—you're sacrificing a pawn to get a knight to gain a bishop? Why aren't you after a king?" I'd finished my back legs and had moved up to my front, and was making an effort to stand real still without seeming to on purpose.

Fortunately, the Chessmaster was too wrapped up in his

71

Evil Overlord Gloating to notice. Mistake Number Three. "No wonder you can't afford better than that dump of a warehouse," he sneered. That hurt. "The Pope is the most powerful virgin of the Mundane world. While the authorities of two universes are seeking out the evil dragon, I shall sacrifice him and gain enough power to accomplish my true goal—to close the Gap, unite those Faerie stranded in the Mundane world, and take my true place as Supreme Ruler of this Earth!"

It was so hard not to laugh. Fortunately, Galendor didn't miss his cue. "You fiend!" he cried, and Adren turned to volley a few clichés with him, villain to hero.

One more leg…

"And," whispered someone just within my peripheral vision, "If you survive, My Master has promised you to me. A little payback for that scene in the bar."

I didn't need to turn my head to know it was my intoxicated elf friend—I could smell him. I rolled my eyes.

"I wouldn't have eaten you. I don't like my food pickled."

He made to reply—with the staff he was holding—when his Master interrupted. "Balmasloshenwastredintauxikus, enough! You had your chance with him earlier this evening and failed me! Now, take your place. The ceremony begins!"

Adren stood behind the altar, with it between him and us, so we could watch in horror, I'm sure. The elves stepped quickly into position within the circle and renewed their chanting. Loudly. Galinda struggled and screamed through her gag. Galendor shouted a heartfelt "NOOOO!" and just to be helpful and—well, you know—the wind started to howl outdoors.

With all the noise, no one heard the click of the manacles hitting the ground or the tinkle of my locksmith tool as I dropped it. Even luckier for me, everyone was intent on Galinda. I guess all her thrashing did something for them. Must be the sadrae.

Adren raised his knife. As Galinda's screams came faster and higher pitched, he paused for effect. The blade gleamed in the candlelight. Typical.

I wasn't as fast as I used to be, but I was pretty quick for my size. I left Galendor chained where he was—he was safer outside the circle—and darted in, head first. I butted aside the nearest elf, glad to see it was Balmy, snatched up St. Peter's knuckle with my teeth, and kept right on going to the altar. I threw myself over Galinda, taking the knife in the wing and back. It was a tainted blade and, appropriately, hurt like hell, but I bit back my screams and put my trust in the relic in my mouth and the God of all worlds, faerie and mundane.

Within the circle, chaos swirled. I was sure I heard otherworldly roaring and bizarre screeches, and I felt something tear at me, actually sheering scales off my hide, but it could have been the wind or maybe the elves. I wasn't opening my eyes to find out.

Then suddenly, silence.

Funny how silence can seem as deafening as noise.

"Gert ovv meeh."

Oops. I'd almost squashed the person I was supposed to be saving. I lifted myself gingerly off her, undid the straps that held her to the altar and gave her the relic stone, which she hastily wiped on her gown. She got up easily, pretty much unscathed despite everything she'd gone through. Couldn't say the same for her abductors. In fact, you couldn't say anything about her abductors. They were gone. All of them. Just empty robes scattered neatly along the edge of the circle. Galendor was still chained to the wall, looking like someone who'd seen all the horrors of the Apocalypse and lived. Maybe he had, come to think of it. Otherwise, he seemed fine, except that there were three of him and they kept blurring in and out of focus...

73

That was a month ago. I don't remember much of it, except that there was a lot of praying, ointment, a wizard, and a veterinarian or three. It all worked out, though. My scales have pretty much grown back. Whatever it was that I had loosed with my half-baked plan had ripped them off, along with a couple of layers of underskin, but I was healing faster than I had in eight hundred years. Not only did Galinda pay her bill in full, but she took care of my medical expenses and tossed in a nice cash bonus. Nothing but beef and mutton for me from now on. Galendor has given me the High Oath of Service, a kind of elvish mega-IOU that I can cash in on later. He and Galinda are getting married at Spring Solstice. I get to be best dragon. Best of all, King Daddy was only too pleased to grant me my boon, not that I needed it. You'd be amazed how much clout there is in saving the world. Costa had a new setting made for it, though, so now St. Peter's knuckle is neighbors with mine. Wonder what ol' George would think of that?

I'm back in my lair—office—and back on the job. I'm still in the warehouse district, though I invested in some better lighting for my place. The work is interesting, and besides, I'm needed here. I'm still the same size; like I've said, I'm big enough to get the job done. There are a few changes, though.

Rif and Raf, the Sheltie and Rottweiler I rescued from the pound both start yapping as I let blow a 6-foot cloud of flame over their heads. I just toss them some scraps and laugh.

It feels good to be packing heat again.

POISON BIRD

SARAH R. SULESKI

Birdie Kass had always lived next door to me. She was my best friend. We were inseparable for a time; Birdie and Will, Will and Birdie. Say it real fast and it's almost like one word. One name. One person.

I made other casual friends throughout my childhood, but Birdie was the only one who was there nearly every step of the way. One of my earliest memories is of us playing together as toddlers in the sandbox in back of my house; Birdie's hair was the color of damp sand and her little head was bent over a tower she carefully patted smooth with her gritty hands. I like thinking of her that way.

She was an only child and both her parents were devoted to their jobs, always working late at the office or off on business trips it seemed. Mr. and Mrs. Kass used to hire an old woman to live in their house and raise Birdie for them, but she died when Birdie was eight, and after that they figured Birdie was old enough to take care of herself and the house. They bought her anything she asked and let her put any sort of animal in the house that she wanted to.

Over time she amassed many animal friends: a couple of dogs, a few cats, a gerbil, fish, garden snakes, mice, a potbelly pig, raccoons, caterpillars. You name it. But her favorites were her birds. She bought several cages and put all sorts of feathery creatures in them. Cockatoos, canaries, lovebirds, doves, parakeets, pigeons.... She also managed to tame some wild birds. They were still flighty and wild around me, but devoted to her. After a while her cages sat empty and her attic was filled with birds. The windows hung open and they came and went as they pleased. But they always came home, to Birdie.

She did not make as many human friends. In fact, the older she got, the less and less she associated with other kids. Because I lived right next door I was the only one who continued to hang around with her and only I knew what she did with her free time.

She liked to play with fire. Experimenting, she called it. We would buy illegal fireworks together and set them off down by the river, but Birdie had to go for something even better. She balled up some tin foil and ruined her microwave with it, blowing out some of the wiring in her house. No problem. She called the electrical company herself and paid for it using money from selling a stereo and TV—which I hadn't known that she owned. I began to wonder what Birdie did at night, when I was sleeping, or when I was at school and she was truant. I didn't skip school with her because she didn't ask me to.

I wondered if I should say something to someone about it. But I didn't, because you just don't snitch on your friends like that. I simply tried to be with her more often, to protect her from herself. All she needed was someone, I reasoned, to give her attention. Birdie's parents were never around, and Ms. Porter, the old housekeeper, had spent her last days sleeping in front of the TV. Everyone left Birdie to herself.

I decided to be her 'protector,' even if she didn't know it. If she did, she wouldn't like it because Birdie didn't like boundaries, or guardians to enforce them. All I wanted to do was make sure that I was there to stop her, if she decided to set herself on fire or something crazy like that. That was the idea.

Instead, I ended up becoming a partner in her crimes, watching out for her while she shoplifted or helping her lug something heavy out of a house. How we didn't get caught was a mystery to me, but we always got away scot-free. We set a lot of things on fire down by the river and buried the charred remains in a small cave nearby. My conscience bothered me, but Birdie was confident. She seemed to appreciate my 'help', so I told myself it was for the best. I could say no, I reasoned, if she got any *really* crazy ideas.

Collecting pets was her 'public' hobby, the one the other kids knew about. Only I knew about the fire and the constant stealing, and the other things she just talked about doing. She wanted to fly, she often told me. Not in a plane or a hang-glider or anything like that. *She* wanted to fly, like the flock of birds in her attic.

By the time she was fourteen she had been in the animal phase for a couple years and her pet collection was as complete as it would ever get because she was about to begin a new phase. Me.

Meanwhile, I had a crush on a girl named Susie. She had long, wavy blond hair and big blue eyes, and a figure that made everyone think she was at least eighteen. Half the guys were crazy about her and the other half were just crazy. I plotted and planned how I could make Susie notice me and like me back. I was just a freshman in high school and she was a sophomore, over a year older than myself, but I wasn't about to let that deter me. So what if I wasn't anyone special. I wasn't tall, or muscular, or handsome, or athletic, or even smart. I couldn't even call myself a nerd or a geek; my grades weren't good enough for that. Too much time spent "protecting" Birdie to spend time on homework or a hobby. Birdie was my hobby and I didn't think Susie would be interested in that.

Birdie always made clever plans, no matter how insane her ideas were, so I went to her for some advice. It was late in the school year and I was running out of time to woo Susie. It was a very warm spring day and Birdie was sitting on the picnic bench in her back yard, feeding a squirrel peanuts from the palm of her hand.

The squirrel might eat from Birdie's hand, but at my coming it scampered away up the maple tree and sat on the branch above the bench, where it could stare at me and the peanuts with mixed emotions. I told Birdie about my problem —how just about every other guy had more of a chance with Susie than I did, unless I did something really special to get her attention.

"What have you tried?" Birdie asked with an analytical expression, brushing back wisps of sandy brown hair from her eyes. She did that when she was forming a plan, as if she must first clear herself of all distractions.

"I've said hi to her..."

"And..."

"And on Valentine's Day I bought her a really nice card..."

"What did she say about it?"

I shrugged, reluctant to admit, "I didn't sign it."

"So what else have you done?"

"Nothing, really." I shrugged again.

She rolled her eyes—dark chocolate brown eyes framed in long lashes. Funny, I'd never really thought about them as pretty, though many times I'd found myself staring at her as the reflection of flames danced in them on dark evenings down by the river.

"Willie," she said (everyone else called me Will), "you haven't actually done anything. You know how many people, boys and girls, say 'hi' to her during a day? And an unsigned card? There's no way she's gonna link that to you."

"I know, I know, I'm stupid. But I can't think of anything," I complained, putting on my most pathetic "help me!" face.

"Well, you'll have to find a time when she's alone, then go up to her—"

"She's always got her girlfriends hanging around and boys following after her."

"She can't all day long. Just watch closely. And when the time comes, what you do is—"

"What?" I asked eagerly, telling by her voice that she had a really great plan coming.

"I'll tell you if you don't interrupt me," she said. "What you do is go up and kiss her."

My enthusiasm abated just a little. "Uh....You think she'd like that? Shouldn't I at least say, 'Hi, I'm Will,' or something?"

Birdie shrugged. "If you have time. But if you expect her to actually think about you, you have to do something shocking. Something none of those other guys have tried. Come on, haven't you ever read one of those romance novels they sell at the grocery store? Nothing drives a woman wilder than some mysterious guy coming up and kissing her into submission."

I was still skeptical. "Would you like that?" I asked, but knew it was a stupid question as soon as I did so. Birdie loved the shocking and indecorous.

"Even if I was a little startled, I'd think about it a lot afterwards, you know?" Birdie explained. "Susie will do the same thing. You'll be on her mind, making her heart flutter when she thinks of your touch. Oh yeah, this is the thing to do, trust me."

I thought about it for a moment. None of the guys at school paid attention to Birdie, though she wasn't ugly and she had as much feminine accoutrements as Susie. But she didn't have quite the same aura Susie did. I never really thought of Birdie as a girl, for some reason, and apparently I wasn't the only one. On the other hand, Birdie had been reading grocery store paperbacks, and so she knew more than I did about romance and stuff, I guessed.

"They go for it?" I double checked.

"Totally," she nodded.

"What kind of a kiss, though? I mean, I never kissed a girl before and I don't really know how, what if I bang me teeth against hers or something?" I sounded like an idiot and I knew it, but there was only Birdie and her animals around and this matter worried me.

"Well, if that bothers you maybe you should practice first."

"Huh?"

"Practice. You don't want to be sweating like a pig from

nerves, so you have to get confident about your kissing abilities," Birdie elaborated patiently.

An uncomfortable silence settled down around us. Or at least I was uncomfortable. Birdie looked pretty placid to me. "You...want me to kiss...you?" I choked.

"What's the big deal? You need practice bad and who else is going to help you out? It's just me, anyway," she rolled her eyes again, as if my reluctance was completely ridiculous.

"But..."

"It'll be a totally platonic kiss, Willie, you'll just be trying out the basic maneuver, so later you can concentrate on the passion that'll knock Susie off her feet," Birdie assured me.

There was something about the term, "basic maneuver" that really turned me off and I had about as much desire to kiss Birdie as I did the squirrel in the tree. "I can't," I declined. "It wouldn't be right. I mean, that'd be like..."

"I get it," she said, "I'm *sooo* disgusting to you, that even a platonic, scientific practice kiss is impossible. Okay, but don't blame me if you do something really stupid to Susie and screw it all up."

"That's not what I meant," I objected. "It's just the whole idea of practicing like it's a sport or something. And...scientific? That's like...dissecting frogs or something. I can't, I mean, you've got to be in a mood to kiss, it's not something you learn."

"All the erotic pleasure comes after you've mastered the basics," Birdie proclaimed sagely. "Normally you can be patient enough to learn with the person who turns you on, but in your case you've got one kiss to impress her. It has to be memorable, it has to be perfect, there's no time to ease into the smooch, got it?"

"Uh, I didn't even say that I was going to go through with this," I backed off. "I still think she might slug me, or something."

"Okay," she chirped lightly, shrugging as if it were no skin off her back. "Then you'll have to figure something else out on your own, 'cause that was my suggestion."

I just stared at her for a moment, thinking hard, and then I said, "Shit," when my mind drew a blank. I was so bad at romance, it was just pathetic.

She smiled and the look reminded me of when she watched flames consume some new theft. I wanted to get up and run away, far from her ideas and plans, out of sight of her brown eyes and smiling lips, which I was contemplating kissing - the most bizarre thought I'd had in our relationship to date.

"Hey, you don't have to kiss me," she said with a hint of mocking laughter in her voice. "I'm just giving you advice. You could go ask someone else to teach you how, you know. Like Susie. Maybe 'Hi, I'm William, would you teach me how to kiss?' is just the line to turn her on."

That made me angry. She was sitting there laughing at me! Making fun of me for coming to her for help! And what did she know anyway? All she'd done was read some trashy books. She didn't know one damn thing about real life and she had the nerve to laugh at me. I glared at her for a moment and then decided that I would be the one to "teach" that smug bitch what it was like to be kissed.

I grabbed her and smashed my mouth against hers. She was a lot softer than I'd thought she'd be and she yielded to my kiss willingly, letting me be in control. Actually, she didn't taste half-bad either. She was a lot easier to kiss once she'd shut up about basic maneuvers and platonic science.

I let her go and watched for the reaction. Girls were supposed to sigh dreamily and melt once you'd kissed them, or at least that's what one of my friends claimed. Birdie sat back and wiped the corner of her mouth with the back of her hand. "Hmmm..." she said. "You want to get her attention, yeah, but I'm thinking 'attack mode' might be a little too much."

"Huh?" I stared at her dumbly for a second. Then I remembered. Oh right, Susie. No, I wasn't planning on kissing her like that; I wanted Susie to like me. I didn't want Birdie to like me, I wanted her to submit to me, to melt into jelly in my arms and sigh, not wipe her mouth off and nonchalantly categorize my kiss as "attack mode."

"There are all sorts of different kisses between a tentative peck and a mashing," Birdie said, sounding like she was beginning a lecture.

"God, Birdie," I cut her off. "What kind of a cold fish are you?"

Birdie narrowed her eyes to slits, and said in a clipped manner, "How many different kinds are there, William?"

Uh oh. I knew that look and that tone. I backed away a little and said, "Uh..."

"Besides, I thought this was about Susie, not me. I'm just trying to help."

I wasn't going to try kissing her again, now. She'd be more likely to set my hair on fire with a match than melt into jelly. I stood up and took a step back. "Yeah, well, that did help. Thanks. I'll tell you how it went."

"Do."

I turned around and stumbled back through the bushes into my own yard. I'd do homework, I thought. Yes, lots of homework tonight, because there sure wasn't going to be a burning party at the river that I was involved in.

Sometimes I lie awake at night and wonder why I'm such an idiot. Anyone else would never have fallen for the trap Birdie had set for me. But I did. I can't even say I did it blindly, because that would be an excuse. I knew that what I was doing was certifiably moronic, but I did it anyway. Why? Why did I ever do anything that Birdie told me to do?

As you can imagine, Susie wasn't swept off her feet. In fact, I didn't even get to kiss her, since I moved too slowly and she saw what I was doing in time to hit me with her science book. "What the hell are you doing, dweeb?" she squealed, backing away.

I didn't have an answer, of course, because I had no idea. What the hell was I doing? My heart wasn't even in it anymore, not since I'd kissed Birdie. And now I hadn't even managed to get Susie alone, and so her friends started to laugh. I'd never been so red in my life and I ran from them like I was escaping the Gates of Hell.

I went searching for Birdie. I couldn't find her. Apparently she was playing hooky again. Birdie came and Birdie went, always whenever Birdie wanted to. I stood alone in a deserted hallway, knowing I was late for class, but thinking about her.

All the guys thought she was unattractive and the girls thought they were above her, the few times they thought of her at all. But Birdie had the world on a string. When no one notices you, you can slip through life on your own terms, I thought. She could go anywhere and do anything, because no one cared enough to stop her. Besides me.

I skipped class for the rest of the day and ran home to find Birdie. She was there, in her house, in her attic with her birds.

"You knew that was going to happen," I said, standing in the doorway, panting from my run down the sidewalks and up the two flights of stairs.

She was sitting in an old wicker chair, surrounded by an assortment of feathered friends, perched on her head and shoulders and lap. None of them had shitted on her, like birds would usually do. They respected her too much for that; they knew you didn't crap on Birdie, it just didn't happen. When I came storming in, they screeched and jumped up in a flurry of feathers, beating their wings in an effort to get out the window quickly.

Birdie stood up and said in an even voice, "Of course. Those girls are all the same, Willie. But you had to find out for yourself. They don't accept you unless you play by their rules. Susie—she would never love you like I do."

"Their rules? What about your rules? And you think it's loving to humiliate me in front of everyone?" I steamed.

"Tough love," she smiled. "Like I said, you had to see for yourself. You do see, don't you?"

"Oh, I see, all right. Everyone's got rules they want everybody else to play by and you're no different, so don't act so self-righteous," I declared.

She shook her head, and a feather came lose and floated to the floor. "I hate rules," she said. "That's why I let you be humiliated, I didn't just tell you to forget about Susie. You wouldn't have listened, because that'd just be a silly rule: 'Forget Susie'. You have to want to. So do whatever you want to, right now. You look mad, Willie. You want to hit me? Do you want to?"

"Yeah, right. I'm not in the habit of beating up girls."

"But that's my point. You and your habits. Why don't you do something different? Break the damn rules."

"Yeah, but if I break those rules, I'll just be following your rules, which kinda defeats your point, doesn't it?" I felt a moment of pride, pleased with myself for catching her inconsistency.

"Are you trying to be clever?" Her eyes sparked with annoyance. "Because you're just ignoring my point with your little nitpicking."

"What is your point? What do you want from me, Birdie?"

She shook her head again and turned away, walking over to the window. There was a cushioned bench in front of it and she sat down, twisting around so that her back was to me and her elbows rested on the sill. I'd seen her like that before, staring out the window. God only knows what she thought about, because it overlooked the woods and not the street, so the view never changed.

"Stop trying to be like one of them," she said after a moment, the words almost lost on the breeze. Her tone of voice had changed; she sounded softer, sadder, as if the whole ordeal pained her.

I went over and sat next to her, knowing that I was doing what she wanted me to do, as always. But I was starting to feel as if I were the one who should be apologizing for even noticing Susie to begin with. "I like them," I protested half-heartedly, "especially Susie."

Birdie turned to face me. "They don't like you. Or me. Are you going to fall all over yourself trying to please them?"

I shook my head. "You're right. About one thing anyway," I relented. "Why do I need to think about anyone else, when I've got you?"

Her lips curved slowly into a smile and with a blink the harshness left her eyes. It was replaced with a fond expression, as if I were one of her cute little critters. She traced her fingers along the side of my face and replied, "Yeah. You've always been my only real friend, Willie."

I sighed and leaned forward, resting my head on her shoulder, nestling my face in the hollow of her throat at the base of her neck. She smelled vaguely of bird feathers, but also some sort of flower scented perfume. I closed my eyes and felt better as her chest moved in the soft swell of breathing underneath me. It was easy to think of nothing else, that way.

Birdie kissed my head and ran her fingers lightly through my hair, saying, "It'll be alright, just you and me."

"Don't talk, Birdie," I replied, lifting my face a little to kiss the underside of her chin. It felt good just to breathe in her scent and be highly aware of her soft body close to me.

She fell silent and just stroked my head like a mother comforting a child and that was all right with me. I'd been smacked around and called names by Susie, but Birdie knew how to relax me, when she wasn't telling me stuff I didn't want to hear. I didn't want her to start educating me about basic maneuvers I could practice on her. No, I wanted to be in control, now.

I raised my head and looked at her. Her eyes were shut, but she opened them to look at me. "You wanna fly?" I asked and kissed her before she could say a word.

Birdie was not disappointing. I'd never thought of her as a girl like the others and she wasn't. She was better. And she wasn't naive, no, not Birdie. She was a virgin up until then, don't get me wrong, but somehow Birdie just knew everything about anything. She knew exactly what she was doing, all along.

She knew how badly I wanted to control her and she knew how to use it to control me. I thought I was getting my way and so after that I kept coming back to her. Home to Birdie, just like her pets. We all flocked to her. I felt powerful and in charge when I made love to Birdie, like a real man. All the while I was losing myself to her more and more. It didn't begin with the intimacy. She'd been in control before then. But she knew just what it took to overthrow my defenses completely.

85

I still told myself that I could stop whenever I wanted to, draw the line wherever it had to be drawn. Birdie liked to experiment with everything, test all the borders she could, and so it wasn't long before she decided we needed ways to spice up those plain old orgasms. And I gladly played along with whatever game she devised, no matter how bizarre or, at times, dangerous. I thought

I was one lucky puppy; my after school activities beat the hell out of the other kids'. To think, they did homework.

My mother once asked me, when I was sixteen, if there was anything I wanted to admit about my relationship with Birdie. I told her there wasn't and she was pleased. She said she was just checking, to see that I didn't do anything I'd regret later. She believed me, just like that. I couldn't help but feel an uneasy conviction that Birdie's control had something to do with it; my mother was not that gullible. Usually.

No one noticed Birdie but me; no one had ever caught her stealing or discovered her fires. If I hadn't been there to distract her, she'd probably have become a terrifying arsonist, impossible to trace. I wouldn't put it past her to burn down a building. But they'd never catch her. No one noticed her.

When I was eighteen and had graduated from high school, I decided, out of naivety, denial, blindness, or sheer stupidity — whatever you want to call it—that we would get married. Why not? I was so wrapped up in her that such commitment held no fear for me. And why would she object? We had spent the last four years devoted to each other. Devoted to each other, how silly that sounds, now. She was never devoted to me.

Birdie had dropped out of high school fairly early. Her parents didn't do anything about it. Maybe they didn't even know. Mr. and Mrs. Kass were like ghostly figures hovering on the border of Birdie's life. When not off on a trip, they came home late at night and left again in the early morning, passing away into their business world without ever paying attention to their daughter. It was how Birdie wanted things to be.

I went to her, proud of my new diploma, with visions of how I'd build our life together in my head. I thought that she loved me; I thought that I loved her. It was a lie I believed so firmly that I'd blinded myself to anything that contradicted it.

She'd gotten rid of most of her pets, one way or the other, but she still had all her birds. They were around her always, but they fled as I came near, though you'd think they'd have gotten used to me by now. She was sitting in the back yard, with one of her books.

"Birdie."

She looked up, a cool expression in her eyes. They weren't like chocolate today, more like petrified wood. I didn't think of it 'til later. I continued on blithely with my mission.

"Ever since I graduated, I've been thinking about the future," I said. "I've got some colleges lined up. I guess I'll go into journalism, I was pretty good in English class, better than the other subjects anyway."

She didn't reply, just stared at me aloofly, waiting for me to continue, but looking like she didn't really care if I did, or not.

"I guessed you weren't going to college; that's alright, and all. You don't need to. But I'd like you to come with me, of course," I declared.

"What?"

"I want us to get married."

Her face changed. If it were at all possible, her eyes grew colder, but with a burning cold that seared me with her gaze. A look of disgust twisted itself onto her mouth as her eyes narrowed into slits, and she said, in a clipped voice, "Are you that stupid, or did you just think I was lying all this time?"

"I...no...but...what are you talking about?" I stammered.

She got up from the bench, slamming her book shut with a snap. "You think I'm going to settle down with you, have children, and become a nice little housewife to come home to after a stimulating day at work?"

"But..."

"Haven't you ever listened to a thing I've said to you, Willie?" she demanded, anger in her voice that I hadn't heard before. Not clipped, desperate.

I scrambled for something to say, 'of course,' or 'yes,' but she was right. I'd never listened; I didn't like it when she talked.

"I'm sorry. What's wrong, Birdie? What have you been saying?" I asked, trying to conciliate her.

She made an incredulous noise and ran her hand through her hair, pulling at the roots a little. "Damn you!" she suddenly exploded and threw her book at me. Its hard pointed corner struck my shoulder and it fell to the ground.

"Hey," I squeaked, my voice cracking a little like it still did when I was scared. I didn't know what I'd done to deserve this

87

curse and assault. I stood up and moved toward her, but she held out her hand in a warning gesture.

"Don't touch me, that's all you ever do. I told you a thousand times what was on my mind, but you were too busy sucking on my breasts to listen, you bas—"

"Tell me now!" I pleaded, feeling myself slipping into panic. "What's the matter, what do you want from me, what?"

"What's the matter? What's the matter?" she screamed back at me. "Everything's the matter, Willie. Me, you, the whole world. I'm the matter! Look at me for once, just look with your eyes, what do you see?"

I tried. I really tried. But all I saw was Birdie: thin tanned face, brown eyes, sandy hair hanging down past her shoulders, full chest hugged by a white tee shirt. Birdie. "I see...the most beautiful girl I know," I said helplessly.

She just stood there, waiting for something more. Demanding something more.

"I see...um, anger. Lots of anger," I continued, swallowing nervously.

She turned away, shaking her head. In that moment, she gave up on me, but I still didn't see it. "Well, the answer's 'no'," she said. "I can't stay here, with you or anyone else. I'm going."

"Going where? And we won't stay here, we'll go to someplace far away, a college in a different state, even," I persisted.

"That would still be here, Willie," she replied. "I'm leaving and you can't come with me, I guess."

She started walking back toward the house and as I realized that she really meant to leave me, forever, my confusion gave way to rage. "No!" I barked. "You are not doing this to me! If you think I'm going to let you get away, you're wrong, dead wrong! I'd die before I let you have someone else! I'd...I'll...kill you, bitch! You get that?"

She stiffened when I called her a bitch, but she didn't break stride and so I yelled, "You're my life, Birdie, my life! You walk away from me and it's all over!"

I ran after her and grabbed her, spinning her around to look at me. My hands burned where I gripped her arms, but I ignored the sensation. I shook her. "You can't turn me off that easy, don't you get it?"

"Let me go!" she screeched, her face contorted into hatred as she dug the heels of her palms into my chest and tried to twist free.

"No!" I pulled her closer, falling back on the only way I'd ever been able to control her, so I'd thought. When I kissed her, my lips stung like they were touching fire and her hands felt like cattle brands burning straight through to my lungs. I inhaled sharply, in shock, and a flare of sulphurous gas shot through my body. Hot, choking, very hot. I can't breathe! God! I'm on fire! For a terrifying instant I thought that I would spontaneously combust. Then she kneed me hard in the groin and I fell to the ground with a whimper. Even her bony, sharp damnable knee was hot and burning.

"I said not to touch me," she declared, a strange coolness returning to her voice. I lay curled up on the ground, gasping, and watched her go in through the back door without a backward glance for me. Stinging bile rose up into my throat and I retched all my lunch and I swear part of my stomach onto the ground, before rolling away and flopping onto my twisting midsection.

It was a moment or two later when I heard birds screeching and crashing against the attic window frame. I rolled from my stomach onto my back and stared up at the sky. I saw her birds fly out the attic window, cawing in terror. I closed my eyes and breathed hard. The blue of the cloudless spring sky was burnt into my vision and I could still see it against the black of my eyelids. I had never been in so much pain before and I could imagine my bones turning into ash. When I opened my eyes and took a peek at my hands, I saw them red as if I'd stuck them into open flames. My blood felt hot and stinging, like I'd swallowed poison. Maybe I had.

I drifted out of consciousness, never passing out completely, but swimming through a feverish haze of half-reality. I saw fire in my mind. I saw Birdie sculpting castles of flame in the sandbox, holding onto me with the amber fire-mirrors of her eyes. I tried to get free but I couldn't; she was everything, the only thing, and I was consumed. I fought my eyes open to look at the sky again, or at least I thought I did; I couldn't know what was real and what were my own burning hallucinations. I saw another of Birdie's birds flying away, but it seemed large and strange to me, like a great eagle with bright, fiery-colored plumage. To my fevered mind it seemed the bird propelled itself high into the sky and then drifted for a moment on a current of air, red wings outstretched.

Fire suddenly spewed from its beak, curling away into the air like the bright explosion from an aerosol can and a lighter; a little trick I remember Birdie had shown me when we were just children. I knew then that I must be losing my mind, maybe it was melting like the rest of me, and I could think of nothing but fire.

I squeezed my eyes shut, clutching at the overlong grass blades as if to assure myself there was still something real under me. "Oh..." I groaned, reluctant to get up from my grassy bed. It felt cool against my burning body. The ground was nice, firm, and safe.

I opened my eyes again to see if the illusion of the dragon-bird remained, but it did not. The sky was empty. I sat up enough to prop myself up on my elbows and then I felt the loss.

She was gone. I knew it. It was like when a loud noise is suddenly cut off and your ears ring with the absence of it, the profound quietness of the noise being no longer there. Birdie was my noise and suddenly she had gone quiet.

My head felt clearer. Maybe clearer than it had in years. The world around me snapped into sharp focus and I thought, really thought for the first time, about what had just happened between me and Birdie. I staggered to my feet and ran into the house, even though I knew she wasn't there. Once inside I wondered why I had run. I couldn't run to where Birdie had gone.

I wandered all over the place, staring sullenly at spots that held memories of her. I felt like a fool as I dwelled on the last four years, especially. Why hadn't I listened? I only began to understand a very little now, an understanding mired by confusion and uncertainty, but Birdie was no longer there to explain to me what I had missed up 'til the very last.

I went up to the attic and found myself kneeling on the cushioned bench, staring out the window at the tree tops. And the sky.

She'd always wanted to fly.

A Reptile at the Reunion

Sandra M. Ulbrich

I was mopping up puppy piss in the waiting room when a client brought in his bearded dragon. For a moment, I was tempted to dump my dirty water in its carrier. How could these people love such scaly nuisances? I could understand cats and dogs, but dragons? I don't know what made me more homesick: the human with foreign ways or the smaller version of the animal that had led to my exile here.

"Bitsy's not passing her eggs," the man told the receptionist. "They have to be aspirated."

Once, I could have solved the problem without damaging either dragon or eggs. But a dragon bite had drained my magic.

The man sat down and took his dragon out of the carrier. He glanced at my nametag. "Hi, Sybil." He smiled. "Would you like to hold my dragon?"

I gripped my mop tightly so he couldn't foist the animal on me. "Sorry, I'm busy."

"Don't be scared; she's friendly."

"I'm sure she is." I glanced down at my left arm, making sure my smock covered the scar on my wrist. "But I've had bad luck with dragons in the past."

Bad luck was putting it mildly. The dragon I'd run afoul of hadn't been a two-foot-long bearded dragon kept as a pet, but a real one, man-sized and fire-emitting. Still, I should have been able to banish the pest, especially with my best friend Ninya immobilizing it. Except her spell had backfired and the dragon bit me. Every time I held a bleeding animal, I remembered watching my own blood spurt onto green leaves, wasted like the magic that drained from me with the dragon's bite. A second stroke of bad luck had diverted me to this world while I was seeking a magicologist who could help me. I trundled my mop and bucket into a storage closet and retreated into the back. Better to check a dozen fecal samples than assist the vet with the bearded dragon.

An hour later, I wasn't sure checking samples was better than dealing with dragons. The smell didn't bother me as much as the paperwork and the boredom. By the time we closed for the night, all I wanted to do was go home, warm up some leftovers, and surf the Internet—the closest thing to magic on this planet. So I was astonished to open my car door and see a cream-colored envelope resting on the seat.

"What the—how did this get here?"

It rose up as I spoke, confirming its unearthly origins.

93

"Something wrong, Sybil?" the vet asked, pausing as he walked toward his own car.

"Oh, no. Just—something I didn't expect to find." Something that might finally bring me home.

He shrugged and kept on going. I wanted to open the envelope right away, but I didn't want to draw any further attention to myself. So I drove off, however, I couldn't wait until I got home before reading it. As I waited to make a left-hand turn, I examined the envelope. *To Miss Sybil Heathermoor*, it said, *From the Alumni Office at the University of Magic—Magvergence.* The handwriting looked familiar, but I couldn't remember whose it was. I tore the envelope open with a fingernail and a sheet offered itself for my reading pleasure.

Dear Magvergence Graduate, it began in ornate writing with gold ink—different from the writing on the envelope. *Chancellor Ninya Thorndale takes great pride in inviting you to your ten-year class reunion...*

Chancellor Ninya? I laughed so hard I had trouble making my turn. *Is this a joke? The reunion part is believable, but not her title. She's not strong enough to be chancellor; she couldn't even bring me back to Magvergence.*

I batted the invitation to the seat. A second sheet fell out; silver ink on it glittered at me in the same loopy sprawl I'd seen on the envelope. Maybe this invitation wasn't from Ninya after all. As construction slowed traffic to sulkiness, I read the second message.

Unlike the invitation, the note was short. "Sybil, I had no idea where you were until I found your location in Ninya's files. What are you doing on a mundane world like Earth? Please come to the reunion. I need to talk to you—and I miss you. Kit."

Kit. I traced his handwriting with my fingertip. Hadn't Ninya explained the situation to him? If he'd been involved from the start, I wouldn't be stranded here. Perhaps I should have visited him before leaving Magvergence; next to Ninya, he was the best friend I'd had at the university. I'd secretly wished he'd courted me, but he was a shapeshifter from another world and only Magvergence, specially created as a plane for magicians from many worlds to meet and trade skills, could have brought us together. Was he still there, or had he returned home for a shapeshifting bride?

The maintenance man still hadn't replaced the light bulb in the hallway of my apartment building. Nothing ever got done promptly in this non-magical world; I couldn't wait to escape. As soon as I shut the door behind me, I held the reply card next to my mouth. "Yes, I'll come," I said. "But you'll have to arrange transport for me."

My words appeared on the card in the same blue-and-black ink I'd used at the University. Kit had a fine memory for details. He'd also provided an envelope with sufficient return magic, so I stuffed and sealed it. It disappeared, taking my self-confidence with it. Was it really a good idea returning to Magvergence and facing all of my other friends who still had magic? I'd have to explain what had happened to mine over and over. What if it was too late to recover it? I sighed. At least the reunion beat facing the dragon again.

The day of the reunion, I paced in my bedroom, skirt swishing around my ankles as I waited for Kit to activate his transport spell. For the third time in five minutes, I tugged my teal sleeve down to hide my scar. My battered leather satchel was already packed with personal items and common Earth things, like chocolate and spices, that would make nice gifts for Kit and Ninya. I'd also bought gold jewelry for barter on Magvergence. Everything else could stay in this plane. Outwardly I was ready; inside, I was torn between anxiety and anticipation.

At the appointed time, Kit's spell manifested as a man-sized oval of light in the center of the room. I grabbed my satchel, took a deep breath, and stepped through. For three steps it was like walking through a black tunnel; then light returned, so bright I had to shut my eyes.

"Sybil! I'm glad you came," a familiar voice said. "You look... you look wonderful."

"So, do you forgive me for leaving so suddenly?" I asked. I hesitated before opening my eyes, unsure of what I'd see.

Kit sat on the same old stump I'd studied on when the weather was warm. In human form, his cheeks were as round as eggs and he'd started to bald, like most of our male professors, but his eyes were still the same friendly shade of blue. He wore a navy blue robe with gold symbols for Transformation embroidered on it. We stared at each other like we were test questions we couldn't answer.

"How's your cat—what was his name, Sphinx?" I asked.

"No more problems with his fur?"

"No; he hasn't run afoul of Ninya's spells lately." A frown puckered his eyebrows.

"It was an accident—"

"Maybe, but I never liked the way she tested experimental spells on animals, especially when they didn't work."

"She's not that bad; she helped me adjust to Magvergence when I was homesick. And I didn't come back to start another argument." Feeling greatly daring, I touched his left hand. No ring, but that didn't tell me anything; his world didn't practice the Earth custom of wedding bands. "It's good to see you again, Kit. I missed you."

His smile warmed me as he put his hand over mine. "I missed you too."

We held hands for a moment. "I'm glad you stayed on Magvergence," I said. My hand tingled from his touch. "Who else from our class is here?"

"Well, Ninya, for one." He picked up my satchel. "She's the chancellor."

"She is? I still can't believe it. How did she manage that?"

"I'll tell you as we walk."

Kit had transported me via one of the outdoor Jumping Circles, a carefully maintained circle of willow trees budding with pale green. Afternoon sunlight slanted through the branches. I took in a deep breath, enjoying the unpolluted fragrance of spring as he led me down the path following the river toward the university. He was silent as a couple of students ran past us, books and papers peeping out of their satchels.

"Ninya's power increased after you left," he said once we were alone again. "Remember that time in Transformation class when she turned a horse into a fly?"

"And the fly turned back into a horse five minutes later." I grinned, remembering how the panicked horse had bolted through the building, leaving a manure trail.

"Right, but she did it again. This time the horse stayed a fly."

"Well, that might not be increased power so much as increased skill."

"I thought that too at first," Kit said, "but I didn't notice any change in her technique. That's why I started to think maybe she'd found a way to increase her power, so I've been monitoring her spells. Sometimes they're still erratic, but sometimes, such as during the Successor Trials after Chancellor Moorman died, they're nearly twice her normal power."

It made no sense, unless... no. Despite a sudden sour taste in my mouth, I shook my head vigorously. "I have no idea how she managed that."

"You don't? I thought she might have told you something. You were her closest friend."

"I haven't heard from her since I left Magvergence." I snapped my mouth shut before more bitterness could escape. Maybe, even with her extra power, she hadn't been able to trace which plane I'd landed on. She'd be happy to see me again, I was sure.

Kit raised an eyebrow but said nothing.

After a couple of minutes filled with only bird calls, I asked, "What happened to the dragon?"

"The dragon?" He looked at me as strangely as if I'd explained to him how cars ran without magic. "What dragon?"

"The one that bit me. Did Ninya finish the job and banish it?"

He smoothed out his robe with long strokes. "The only one I know about occupies an abandoned pear orchard about ten miles south of the university."

That was where Ninya and I had gone. Why would someone abandon a fine orchard because of one dragon? I wondered if I should go back there and face it. Maybe throwing stones at it from a safe distance would make me feel better.

Before I could decide, Kit asked, "What were you doing on Earth? Isn't it hard to use magic there?"

"I wouldn't know." I kicked over a small pile of stones. "I don't have magic anymore, Kit. That was why you had to transport me here."

"No magic... oh, Sybil." He looked ready to cry. "I can't believe it. Are you sure? Perhaps there's interference on Earth. Why don't you try a spell now? It ought to work here."

I knew it wouldn't; after the dragon bite, I'd tried working magic before seeking a magicologist. But he was so determinedly optimistic I had to try. *Maybe I ran away too soon. Maybe my magic returned after my body had more time to heal.*

We'd stopped by a bank of violets, so I plucked one and spoke a simple spell to make it double in size. For a moment I felt a faint response, as if my magic emanated from somewhere else. Then it died, leaving me with a still-tiny flower.

Kit looked more downcast than I felt about the failure; I'd gotten used to it. He stared at the flower before saying, "Let's go to the banquet hall, then."

I felt as invisible as a ghost at noon as we stepped onto university grounds. Ivy smothered all nine towers, distinguishable by the banners above each entrance. Students sauntered among them; light danced in their impressionable faces as they hailed their friends. None of them would call my name. None of my classmates would either, once they learned of my handicap.

I halted by Fourth Tower. "Kit, wait. When does the reunion start?"

He glanced up at the sun. "We still have a few hours."

"Then let's go somewhere else first." I took a deep breath for courage. "I want to go to that orchard you mentioned. There's something I need to see there."

He looked at me, shrugged, and led the way to the Jumping Room inside the tower. Nine circles of various sizes were outlined in different metals on the floor. We stepped into a small bronze one, our backs grazing as we made sure we were completely inside the circle. His back was clammy, but that's not what made me shiver. What if the dragon attacked me again? Kit rushed through the jump spell as if he knew I wanted to change my mind.

The miasma assaulted me first, a mixture of rotting fruit, methane, and a trace of rust. *Dragon. Once you smell one, there's no forgetting it.* It had to be close by. I scanned the twisted branches of the trees, ready to run if I spotted the dragon.

"So why is this orchard abandoned?" I asked.

Kit drew smoke letters that blurred when I tried to read them. After we were shrouded from possible eavesdroppers, he said, "All I know is that the farmer left after Ninya became chancellor."

"And you think she had something to do with it?" A familiar world and familiar face made me use old habits; I absently gestured the smoke away before remembering the spell wouldn't work—except it did, and it made two bubbles of air, one surrounding me and one hovering above a tree branch.

"It... it worked." I stared at my hands, too stunned to be happy. Kit smiled for me. "I knew you couldn't have lost your magic, Sybil! But did you mean to make two bubbles, or was that an accident?"

I had no idea how to answer him. As I studied the second bubble, it grew larger, glinting green. It took me a few seconds to realize why.

"Oh, hell." I stepped backward, nearly slipping on a soft pear. "The dragon."

The dragon landed several yards away from me. It folded its wings, letting the scaled skin brush the grass, then raised its streamlined head and stared at me as if it remembered me. Magic echoed between us like a long-forgotten word shouted in a still room.

"Something about the dragon feels like you," Kit said as he stared at it.

"The dammed beast drained my magic when it bit me." I showed him the faint scar. "I thought my magic was gone for good, but it had it all along. Maybe I would have realized that if I'd stayed in Magvergence, but Ninya said she'd send me to a magicologist on another plane, and I wound up on Earth instead. Another of her wretched accidents..."

The words trailed off as I reexamined my memories. When Ninya had healed my arm, had her eyes shone with concern —or glinted with malice? Why had she ushered me out of Magvergence before I could consult one of the professors here? Had the holding spell's failure been the accident she swore it was—or had she planned it all along?

"It was no accident. None of it was." My mouth tasted as dull as rust. "She robbed me of my magic so she'd be more powerful than me. And here I thought she was my best friend..."

Anger seeped like acid into my stomach, then erupted, burning my face and pooling in my palms. Even the hair on my forearms felt repulsed by it. My jaws ached like overstretched rubber bands as I clamped them shut.

"I'm going to kill her," I pronounced sentence.

"Sybil…"

"Don't try to talk me out of it, Kit; she deserves it. She deserves worse; what would be worse than death…?"

"Sybil…"

"Maybe I could exile her to Chicago and let her find out what it's like to live without magic. I'd love to see her play in traffic." I kicked an unripe pear at the dragon, but it didn't connect.

"Sybil, forget the traffic games. This is more serious than you think." His face looked pasty. "She's got to be using your magic herself. That would explain how she became chancellor. She'll lose her position when everyone finds out she earned it unfairly."

Her cheating seemed trivial after the way she'd betrayed me. "Well, we can accuse her of that too when I denounce her. Let's go." The natural Jumping Circle formed by some of the trees had been distorted by shrubs, so I hiked my skirt, ready to march back to the university and storm Ninya's office. I'd learned a lot of rude comments and gestures in Chicago, and I planned to demonstrate them all to her.

Kit grabbed my arm, throwing me off balance as I kicked another pear. "Be sensible for a moment, Sybil. You can't just go up to her and expect her to hand your magic back. She could transform you—look out!"

He shoved me to the ground and threw himself on top of me as the dragon flew over, releasing fruit-scented flame from its most dangerous end. A few licks landed next to my satchel, but they died immediately. I hoped Kit had had his robe enchanted against fire recently. Thanks to him, I'd experienced nothing worse than bruises and scrapes, though I'd have to clean my dress before the banquet tonight.

Kit threw a holding spell on the dragon; his spell interfered with my ability to sense my magic, but given the circumstances, I didn't object.

"Are you all right?" he asked.

"I'm fine, though I'd be better if you got off of me."

"Oh. Sorry."

He pulled me up, but he didn't release me. "Sybil," he whispered, staring at me. His pupils were vertical slits, and he seemed taller and stronger than he had a moment ago. I'd met many kinds of men back on Earth; some of them had even asked me for dates. None had attracted me as much as Kit did now, even when I wasn't sure how to approach him. I stroked the stubble on his chin before reaching up to kiss his lips. It was a gentle kiss, but he seized on it as if it was his first one. His beard—no, fur—tickled my cheeks.

His face had a feline cast once we broke apart. "Sorry about the partial shift; it happens to my people when we..." he stopped, sounding embarrassed.

"Oh." *No wonder he'd never courted me.*

"No one back home makes me want to lose control like that. If only things were different...." He stroked his fur until it disappeared into his skin, then shook himself, becoming professorly again. "So... before we confront Ninya, you have to reclaim your magic, or at least prevent her from using it."

"Good idea," I said as I tried to think about magic and dragons, not Kit. "But how do I get it back? Convince the dragon to bite me again? I'd rather not, thanks."

"Do you know if Ninya used any magic to transfer your magic to the dragon?"

"I wasn't paying attention; I was busy getting my arm eaten."

He ignored my Earth-learned humor. "Well, since you don't know, the best thing to do would be to check the dragon for enchantments. I hope I can break any spells Ninya laid. She's had plenty of time to reinforce them...."

He strode to the dragon and grasped its wings. I flinched, but his holding spell was more effective than the one Ninya had cast for me. He closed his eyes. "Protection," he muttered. "Binding... oh, bless it, she's cast Linking on it!"

"Linking?" Bad news; that meant she could use the dragon's senses no matter where she was. "Is it active now?"

"It was," a voice like honey from poisonous flowers said behind me. "Now, I don't need it anymore."

I wasn't sure it would work, but I automatically warded myself as I turned to Ninya, my best friend turned worst enemy.

101

After so many years, I finally saw her true face. No magic could disguise how thin and mean her lips were, or the way her face naturally assumed an I'm-better-than-you-are-and-don't-you-forget-it expression. I'd seen her wear it lots of times, mostly directed at younger students in hand-me-down robes. She'd never directed it at me before and I was surprised how unhappy I felt falling from her grace. I wanted to apologize for something, anything, so we could be friends again. *You fool; she's the one who should apologize*, my better sense told me. *She tricked your magic from you, and you still want to be her friend? She's not worth it. Blast her now before she does something!* But how could I with my magic trapped inside the dragon?

Kit advanced on all fours, his robe taking on black-and-orange tiger stripes. "UnChancellor Ninya," he said with a snarl. "So you did cheat after all. Everyone wondered when a second-rate magician like you won the position."

"Second-rate? Second-rate?" The veins in her neck looked like cords. "Try calling me that when you're a second-rate statue!"

As she gestured, I could feel her draining my magic from my dragon, making me light-headed. I tugged back, but the holding spell blocked me. But I did reclaim some of my power before Kit was lost in marble. It wasn't enough. His legs became columns supporting his fleshy body. He hadn't finished his own transformation, and the mixture of stone tiger legs supporting a human torso made Ninya's spell even more appalling.

"Don't worry about me, Sybil!" Kit called. "Just get your magic back!"

As a natural shapeshifter, he could break the spell on his own. He had the easier task; I still didn't know what to do. But I had to do something.

"Why, Ninya, why me?" I asked, inching toward the dragon. "You would have done all right if you'd just practiced more. Is being chancellor worth more than my friendship?"

"No one teases me or nags me to practice now that I'm chancellor." She smoothed her dishwater-dull hair like she was her own lover. "And they can't compare me to you anymore." The temperature of her voice dropped below freezing. "My parents always asked me, 'Why can't you be more like your friend Sybil? She doesn't need three hours of practice to master a simple spell.' Don't they know how hard it is to remember all the details and summon magic at the same time? You never understood that either – you never had problems tapping into your magic reserves." She sobbed. "Well, if I didn't have your talent naturally, I thought maybe I could get it some other way —take one more step and Kit is gravel."

I halted. *So much for pity.* But I'd learned on Earth there were plenty of ways to accomplish the same goal. Maybe I could convince the dragon to come closer. But first I'd have to break Kit's holding spell on it from the inside out. Better yet, maybe I could trick Ninya into breaking it for me.

"I still can't believe you're strong enough to be chancellor," I said. "You couldn't transform Kit completely if you practiced until our next reunion."

"Silly Sibie, you wouldn't say that if you'd seen my Successor Trials. Or have you turned against your other friend too? I suppose it is untidy leaving him like that...."

Frowning, she worked her way through a master-level breaking spell to undo Kit's holding spell. My magic felt stronger, as warm as if she'd lifted the lid off a pot of boiling water. We reached for my magic simultaneously, neither gaining an edge. The dragon twitched its tail as if trying to decide who was the better target.

"Flame her, you miserable beast!" Ninya shook a branch at it. "Flame her before she kills you!"

Would I have to kill it to get my magic back? I had more sympathy for it now than I did for Ninya. The dragon wasn't evil; it was both Ninya's pawn and victim. It was even prettier than her. The client back at the clinic would have loved this dragon. Maybe I needed to love and forgive it too.

"Come to me." I knelt and extended my hands to it. "Come to me, and I'll give you warmth and trees and rocks and fresh fruit."

Perhaps hosting my magic made it more sensitive to my words. It tilted its head and blinked one green eye at me. Then it crawled toward me. I hoped it didn't want to bite me again.

"What are you doing?" Ninya shouted. "Flame her, don't bite her! That could ruin everything!"

103

She must have panicked, for she sent out an amoeba-like blob of unformed magic, just as she used to do during practice sessions. Raw magic could kill my dragon with random effects. I lunged for it to shield it, touching its snout as the magic enveloped us both.

Pain like being ripped open, stuffed with old and new elements, and hastily stitched back together... a sense of falling ... freedom beating against my back... chilly air leaching heat from my scales... fermented pears churning in my stomach....

My stomach? I didn't eat any pears! Ancient instincts overrode thought as I adjusted to my new perspective.

"Sybil!" a man screamed. "What did you do to her, Ninya?"

"What did she do to my dragon – and my magic?"

Her magic? I snapped my teeth in annoyance as my scales tingled. Every time this woman visited, she weakened me. Not any more, not ever again. My methane sac rumbled in anticipation.

We must catch her off guard, another, wiser part of me said. *Here's how.*

I willed my flame to seek my enemy, no matter where she was. I pictured how she might stop my flame and told it how to pass through her shields. Still facing her, I raised my tail and farted a lovely stream of methane. My glands ignited it as it left me. A blue fireball curved over me and swung straight at her.

"Sybil, no!" She raised her barriers as she threw her hands in front of her face. "We used to be friends!"

More magic taught my tongue how to move against my teeth in strange but familiar ways. "You never were my friend," I said.

My fireball melted through her barrier. A high-pitched scream hung in the air for a few seconds and echoed in my skull. The smell of burnt flesh contaminated the redolence of luscious fruit. But I was hungry, so I nosed a bruised pear. Time to replenish my gas supply.

"Sybil, Sybil." The man's voice sounded rough as shed scales. "Sybil, I know you must be confused and frightened, but everything's going to be all right."

I knew that voice; I remembered it as a friendly one. "Sybil." The man edged closer, one hand outstretched. "You're not just a dragon; you're also human. If you remember, you can change back." He stroked my head. I flinched, but it didn't hurt. In fact, his warm, naked skin felt nice. He touched me again, as bold as if he'd done it lots of times....

And I remembered when he'd touched me, held me, before. "Kit!" I said. My dragon-self receded as my human-self took control. My training as a vet tech helped me recall the differences between this body and my human one, and I transformed back. Pain gripped me again as my senses dulled and my claws softened into fingers.

"Kit," I said again as his face came into focus. "I'm glad you're all right..." I threw my arms around him and blotted my eyes against his shoulder. I wasn't sure who I cried for: him, me, or even Ninya. Maybe I cried for lost innocence; never again could I look back at the good times I'd had with Ninya. Everything was tarnished.

"I was worried about you too." Kit stroked my head until I ran out of tears. "Can you still feel the dragon inside?"

The pears smelled appetizing. "Yes."

"Then you're a shapeshifter now, even if you're stuck with only one animal form." He grinned and pulled me closer. "Don't worry; once you learn to control the change and keep your human self from being lost in the animal, it can be fun. Perhaps it could be something more...."

We kissed again. As whiskers brushed my face, wings sprouted from my back. Why couldn't I have a feline form instead of a dragon one? I wondered if Kit could take on a dragon form of his own. I had a newfound preference for animal reptiles over humans who acted like them.

I lifted my head, but the trees were dark clumps in the night. "How late is it?"

"Past supper. It took a while to break Ninya's spell, and I talked to you for hours before you listened to me."

I thought about everything that had happened, trying to absorb it. I couldn't believe it was still the same day I'd returned...

"The reunion!" I sat upright. "They've started without us!"
"After all this, you still want to go?" Kit asked in amazement.
"It's why I came," I answered. "Besides, we have to tell everyone about Ninya."

I cast a light spell, which worked perfectly, and after retrieving my satchel and tidying my clothes, we arranged pears into a Jumping Circle. We embraced as Kit transported us back to the university.

DRAGON'S BLOOD

MICHELE ACKER

"What'cha got for me, Nells?"

I picked up a hefty slab of bloody meat and plopped it down on the scale. "Prime, grade-A unicorn. An adult mare. Meat's tender and juicy, best to be had anywhere," I said with justifiable pride. Unicorn wasn't an easy animal to hunt and I was the best unicorn hunter within a thousand miles. No one else knew the secret to catching them while preserving the flesh's aphrodisiacal properties.

"So you say, so you say." Grady pursed his lips. He turned his head and spat, the inky black juice landing on the dirty, straw-covered floor. "I'd like to figure that out for myself if you don't mind."

I didn't know when the floor had last been swept and I didn't much care. Grady's butcher shop paid well and that's all that mattered. What he did with the meat after I left was his concern, not mine. "How much is it worth?" I asked. Prices for poached animals, especially magical ones, changed on a day-to-day basis.

Grady finished weighing the meat, gesturing for me to remove each slab and replace it with another. Using the abacas he held and doing some figuring in his head, Grady finally said, "I can give you two hundred for the lot."

"Two hundred? That won't even buy me a good plow horse. I got fields to plow and seeds to plant. Are you saying horse flesh is worth more than unicorn?" I shook my head in disbelief. "Six months ago, you'd have given me five times that."

"Times change and so do tastes. Ever since Lord Randall served dragon steak at his birthday party, everyone's been clamoring for it. Problem is, not many hunters are capable of catching the beasts. Now if you were to bring me dragon meat..."

I shook my head. "I don't hunt dragon."

Grady shrugged and spat again. "Sup to you. But unless you got something else to sell, our business is finished."

I thought for a moment, trying to decide what was more important, pleasing my wife, or keeping my family fed. I sighed. There really was no choice. I headed out to my wagon, reached under the seat and pulled out a package wrapped in linen. When I got back inside, I opened the package and showed Grady a beautiful pelt, white as snow and completely unblemished. I had planned on giving it to my wife, but I knew she'd understand.

Grady fingered the pelt's softness and then held it up to the torchlight to reveal the faint, but unmistakable shimmer of silver. "Beautiful," he breathed. "I'll give you three hundred fifty."

Pitiful, absolutely pitiful. A pelt this fine should have brought a thousand easy. But there was no sense in arguing. Grady's was the only place within a week's ride that bought illegally hunted animals, magical or otherwise. No other shop in South Fork would buy from me or those like me. I had no choice but to accept his meager offer and the bastard knew it.

"What about the horn?"

"Already sold it." The sale of that had been almost as

disappointing as the sale of the meat. Altogether, I barely had enough for the new horse, let alone for the seed I needed to plant. And planting season was approaching quickly. If I didn't have my seed in the ground in the next three months, I might as well forget planting anything this year at all. No planting meant no crops and no crops meant no money.

"That's two hundred for the meat and three fifty for the pelt. Take it or leave it."

"I'll take it."

We shook, sealing the deal. Grady counted out the payment and passed it to me. "Sure you won't consider bringing me a dragon?"

"I don't hunt dragon. I won't."

"Why not?"

I shivered. "They're spooky. It's said they can read people's minds, make them see things. I don't want those... creatures... reading my mind. It ain't right. It just ain't right."

Grady shrugged. "Suit yourself. But if you ever change your mind—"

"I won't."

"If you do. The pay is fifty a pound."

Fifty a pound? And dragons weighed what, half a ton? A ton maybe? Fifty thousand for one kill? I could buy all the seed I needed, plus have enough to try that new tobacco crop I'd heard so much about. If the crop was successful, I could stay home with my family. I'd never have to hunt again. It's not that I didn't enjoy hunting, I did. But it kept me away from home for more than half of every year, leaving my wife and children to fend for themselves, and me to worry about their safety.

Then I thought about all the rumors, the horror stories of those who'd tried to hunt dragon in the past. Tried and failed and in most cases, tried and never returned. What good would it do me to hunt a more valuable animal if it meant I'd never go home at all? "I don't hunt dragon," I said again, but my voice lacked conviction. And if I could hear it, so could Grady.

He did. "And the blood too. The witches in Mir'lok pay hefty for a cup of the stuff. I've heard they use it in their spells or something."

"No dragon."

Grady shrugged and called for his assistant to take care of the unicorn meat.

I grunted and left the shop, the payment stuffed inside my boot. I could just imagine my wife's voice when I got home and showed her the money. "We'll get by, we always do," she'd say. I sighed, climbed in the wagon and headed home.

"We'll get by, we always do," my wife said later that night when I told her the story and showed her the pitiful wad of cash. "We'll just have to cut back, eat a little less, make our clothes last another year. Don't worry, my darling, we'll be fine."

I looked into those loving, forgiving eyes and felt guilty. She never pushed me, always accepting my decisions. Sometimes I hated her for it, wishing she would argue with me once in awhile, yell at me, something. But she never did.

I kissed her gently and then rolled over to sleep, knowing that in a week's time I'd be in the forest at the foot of Razor Mountain, hunting dragon.

By the time the sun dipped below the horizon a month later, I still hadn't found anything that even remotely hinted at the presence of dragons, no prints, no scat, no burnt foliage, no stripped bones or rotting flesh. Nothing. All I'd seen since I started this trip was a small family group of unicorns a week's walk back towards home. If I didn't find anything by tomorrow, I'd head back and try for the mare. It wouldn't bring me as much, but what choice did I have?

I shivered, pulling my jacket tight around my body and looked for a good place to camp. The nights were colder the higher I climbed and there was a hint of rain in the air. Though I'd spent most nights outside, tonight I was hoping to find a cave or some kind of shelter. Sleeping in the rain didn't appeal to me.

A short while later, I happened upon a small cave. Lighting a makeshift torch made from a strip of cloth and a small amount of rendered cooking fat, I used the light to explore the interior. It appeared to be empty. A few bones and scattered bits of desiccated scat indicated some sort of wild animal had sheltered here a long time before, a bear or maybe a griffin, but I could find no signs of recent use. A stream flowed just inside the cave's entrance for a short ways before disappearing underground, forming a small pool of clear water.

Gathering together the makings for a fire, I boiled some of the water and used it to make tea and soften the dried meat I'd brought from home. Afterwards I unrolled my blanket and fell into a deep, dream-filled sleep.

When the sun rose, I was still dreaming about nothing in particular, content, my belly full of bloody raw meat... then something bit my foot. I woke with a start, a knife already in my hand.

A baby dragon, maybe two feet long—tail included—was gnawing on my boot. It reminded me somewhat of a puppy, a puppy with scales and too many teeth.

I stood, my chest tight, eyes searching. Where there was a baby, of any species, there was always a mother. She couldn't be far away. But where? I'd seen no sign of dragon the night before. But now, with daylight shining inside, I spotted a passage in the rear of the cave, hidden by several large boulders. The baby must have come from there.

I turned to my pack, my hands shaking slightly. Now that the time had come, I began to wonder if I'd made the right decision. Rumors and facts scrambled themselves in my brain until my head felt like it might explode. I had no idea what I'd find on the other end of the passage and that scared me more than anything. I was the best unicorn hunter around because I knew how the animals moved, how they defended themselves. I'd studied their actions, their habits. They were no longer a surprise to me. With dragons, all I had were snippets of other people's experiences.

Readying my weapons, I got into the hunter frame of mind. In order to best the creature, I needed to be calm and focused. Calm and focused. Easier said than done. I looped a couple of knives to my belt and picked up the other weapons I'd brought, a half moon axe that could cleave a man's head with as little resistance as a knife cutting tomatoes and an eight-foot spear with a fire-sharpened metal blade.

111

Again I felt that sleepy contentment, the feeling everything was right with the world. There was no need to hunt, was there? Why not just stay here and relax. Sleep... Play...

Play?

The baby started towards me to nibble on my boot again. I pushed her away with my foot. She—I had no idea how I knew she was a she, I just knew—squeaked with surprise and suddenly my good mood vanished. Then I realized. It had come from her. The rumors were true. Dragons could project their thoughts into human brains.

I hesitated and took a deep breath. Calm and focus. Calm and focus.

Quietly and more slowly than strictly necessary, I started down the passageway, weapons ready, searching for my first adult dragon. A musty odor permeated the air, faint at first but growing thicker the farther in I hunted. She was here, I was certain of it. I hoped I could take her by surprise, make the kill fast and easy before she had a chance to turn me into a human torch. Of course I'd have to transport the body back to town, but I'd worry about that later.

Sooner than expected, I rounded the corner into a spacious cavern, the ceiling more than forty feet above me. A couple of other baby dragons played along one wall. I didn't notice much of anything else because she was right there, waiting. How she knew I was coming, I have no idea.

She was enormous. I couldn't help but be impressed. A good twenty feet long from snout to tip of tail, she was covered with glittering scales of black and silver. She was bigger than I'd expected, bigger than I could ever have imagined, and when she reared up on her hind legs, roaring, jets of fire spouting from her open jaw, I saw nothing else. She was my whole world. The last thing I would ever see.

Until that point I thought I was ready to hunt dragon. I'd been hunting other animals since I was six years old. I had the right weapons, the right frame of mind—though calm and focused had long since vanished. I knew what to expect, or thought I did; where the tender spots were, where the scales didn't quite overlap, where the killing blow should land.

But all the preparation in the world didn't prepare me for this. Faced with the reality of a fully grown, fire-breathing dragon, I realized I could no more kill her than I could stop a herd of stampeding elephants. If I'd had the element of surprise, if she'd been sleeping, maybe... but not like this.

Then she attacked me, not with fire, but with magic.

Images slammed into my brain with the force of a hammer blow, shredding my mind, blinding me. I couldn't see, yet, at the same time, I could. Burning forests, spilled blood, smoking flesh. I could smell it, see it, almost touch it, it was so real. I felt sick to my stomach, appalled by the destruction and horrified by the death. Pain and fear drove waves of emotion through me like spikes of hot metal, so vivid and inescapable, I couldn't breathe, couldn't think. My skin itched; it felt like I was falling apart. My heart stopped, and then started again, pounding unnaturally fast. I tried to get away but I couldn't move. Or maybe I forgot how.

I tried to cover my eyes, to block the images somehow, but I couldn't raise my arms. They were glued to my side. The images continued unabated until my eyes wept with sorrow and my mind sobbed with horror. I had to do something to stop this or it would kill me. I couldn't take much more.

Suddenly, the images stopped and I could move again. My legs wobbled. I staggered and almost fell. But I couldn't give into my weakness. I had to get out of here, get away. I couldn't endure another attack. She roared again and I panicked. Dropping my weapons, I ran, just ran until the pain faded to a whisper. When I saw she wasn't following, I stopped to catch my breath. By then I was back in the forest.

113

I'd lost everything. My weapons, my pack, the rest of my food, everything. It was all back in the cave, and though I could see it from here there was no way I was going back. No way would I willingly endure that agony again. I had no choice but to head home.

Before I'd gone more than a few steps, I heard something snuffling in the underbrush. Carefully parting the shrubs, I found the baby dragon looking for something to play with. She'd wandered away from the cave. Looking back to make sure the mother wasn't around, I scooped up the baby and began jogging towards home, putting as much distance between baby and mother as possible.

The baby squeaked in alarm, her emotions those of a frightened child. Using my experience as a father, I soothed her with gentle nonsense words to keep her quiet. For the most part, it seemed to work.

Perhaps I could salvage something out of this disastrous trip after all. There wasn't much flesh on a dragon this size, but I remembered what Grady said about witches and dragon blood and how they'd pay handsomely for even a cup full. This baby, once drained, should produce five times that much. It wasn't as much as I'd get for a full-sized dragon, but it was certainly better than nothing. Besides, I told myself, she had other babies. She wouldn't miss this one. I needed it more than she did.

Day after day for the next two weeks, I trudged closer to home, burdened with a baby dragon that cried piteously every night for her mother. I thought numerous times about killing her now instead of later, but I knew the blood needed to be fresh and the best way to keep it that way was to wait and kill her when I arrived at my destination. So I continued to comfort and feed her, keeping her alive until I made it home.

Even now, so far from the cave, and though I knew she had other babies, I feared the mother finding us. More, I feared those horrific visions. I saw her once, flying far overhead, a dark shadow blocking the moon. The baby went wild with excitement and I had to gag her to keep her quiet. Afterwards, she seemed depressed, as if she realized she'd never see her mother again. I thought about my own children and how I'd feel if I would never see them again. I couldn't help but feel guilty. Even so, I had no intention of letting her go. Providing for my family was more important then the life of a dragon, even a baby dragon.

After two weeks, she began to accept the changes in her life. She missed her mother, but her mother was no longer

114

around. Her place had been taken by this strange two-legged creature. He became both mother and provider. When she was hungry, he provided food. When she was thirsty, he provided water and when she was lonely, he provided companionship. With the narrow attention span of a young child, he'd become everything to her. He'd become her whole world.

Three weeks after I'd stolen the baby, and when I was still more than a week from home, I made camp one evening beside a small, gently flowing stream that provided us with both water and food.

Wading out into the creek, I caught several fish, tickling them out of the water and up onto the bank. The baby, I named her Rena—in the old tongue it meant 'beautiful' and she was in an odd, reptilian sort of way—gobbled up the fish as fast as I could catch them. When she seemed satisfied, I caught a couple extra for myself, gutted them, and then stuck them on a branch to roast over the fire I'd built earlier. When they were done, I ate my fill and tossed the leftovers to Rena who snapped them up with obvious relish. She enjoyed cooked flesh as much as raw.

Full and content, I settled back to sleep, watching Rena do her nightly inspection of the campsite. It was so cute, watching her protect us. If she found anything that didn't belong, a snake, a squirrel or even a spider, she'd raise her tiny wings threateningly, hiss and open her mouth to spray fire. But there was no fire. I wasn't sure if it was a skill she'd develop naturally as she grew older, or if it was something her mother would teach her. Then I remembered. She wouldn't live long enough to learn and I was going to be the one to kill her.

When I first took her, I had to tie her up to keep her from running away, but for the last week, ever since we'd seen her mother fly overhead, I'd let her wander free. I think I was hoping she'd run away. Then I could blame my curious emotional weakness on something other than myself. But she never did. Since that day, she hadn't once tried to escape. Her emotions,

115

less intense than her mothers, told me she felt comfortable with me. I wasn't exactly sure what that meant, but it scared me. My emotions scared me. I knew I had to kill her, but as time went on, the thought of doing it became more and more abhorrent.

I was almost asleep when I felt her settle in beside me, curling up to my body for warmth. She almost purred, her feeling of contentment was so strong. I fell asleep, my arm draped over her protectively.

"Eh, what's this? Lookee here Myngo. This here man's got hisself a pet dragon."

"Really, Erb? A pet dragon you say? Lemme see. I wanna see."

Later I'd have to say it wasn't the voices that woke me that night, it was the sudden spark of anger, like a freshly lit furnace, that shot through my body. Rena's anger. She woke and hissed, opening her jaws to spit fire at the intruders.

They laughed at her. "Aw, look Myngo, the little beastie is trying to burn us."

"Trying to burn us, Erb, trying but not doing too good."

I sat up, assessing the situation, my hand moving slowly to the knife I kept on my belt. Two men confronted us, both dressed in leather skins that were worn, discolored, greasy with food stains and ripe with salty sweat. Though they were dressed alike, there the similarity ended. One man, the one called Erb, was tall, skeletal and balding. There were burn scars on the back of his left hand and along the left side of his face and neck. When he took a step forward, I saw he had a limp. I wondered what sort of accident would scar a man like that.

The other man, Myngo, stood a few steps to Erb's right. He was short and squat with a large, bulbous nose, yellow teeth and huge hands with tiny sausage-like fingers. I wasn't sure which one scared me the most. But I knew I didn't dare take my eyes off either one. Both men held their weapons loosely pointed in my direction, Erb a spear and Myngo a crossbow, a quiver of arrows hanging at his side. Hunters.

I stood slowly, keeping my knife hand hidden behind my back and stepped in front of Rena to protect her. "Who are you and what do you want?"

I braced myself. There was a weasely sort of shiftiness about them I didn't trust. I had a feeling they'd rather steal someone else's food then catch and cook their own. And they'd kill anyone who got in their way.

Erb twirled his spear in some complicated display. I watched the weapon carefully, ready to duck if necessary. It stopped as quickly as it started.

"Me, I'm Erb, and this here's Myngo. Ain't that right Myngo?" Myngo answered from further to the right. "That's right Erb, that's my name. Myngo." He'd managed to circle around me and I hadn't even noticed. He stared at Rena with a look of such hunger, it frightened me. A man with a look like that would do anything to get what he desired. Anything at all.

But to be honest with myself, why should I care if Rena was captured or killed? That's what I planned to do. Kill her, make money off her. She was just some stupid animal after all, an animal whose blood was worth a whole stable full of horses.

I told myself that, but I didn't really believe it. She meant more to me than that, but just what I didn't know. I didn't want to know. Somehow she'd wormed her way into my affections. I knew I had to protect her no matter what.

"We answered your question, now you answer ours," Erb said. "Who might you be? And how do you come to possess a dragon whelp?"

"None of your business," I said. "Now leave. This is my campsite and I'd rather not have company right now."

"Hear that, Myngo? This here fella's being down right unfriendly like." His tone turned venomous. "Where'd you get the dragon?"

"Again, none of your business. What's it to you?"

"Dragons is very valuable creatures and hard to find. Myngo and me have been out looking for six, seven weeks and ain't seen hide nor hair of the beasties. And here you got a miniature one all for yourself. There ain't much flesh on the whelp, but I reckon there's plenty a blood to go around. Wouldn't you agree, Myngo?"

"Yeah, Erb, plenty of blood for everyone."

Myngo had changed position again and now he was behind me. I backed up, trying to see both men, but they were too far apart.

Rena stuck to my side, her feelings a child-like mixture of anger and fear. I knew exactly how she felt. Not only was I outnumbered, I was out-weaponed as well. Two knives against a spear and a crossbow were terrible odds indeed. But Rena was my dragon—I'd found her, I'd taken care of her—and no shifty hunter was going to take her away from me. "I won't share. She's mine. I captured her and I'm keeping her. Now get lost."

Erb shook his head. "There he goes again, being uncharitable like. What do ya think we oughta do about it, Myngo?"

"Let's kill 'em, Erb. Can I do it? Can I kill 'em?"

Erb winked at me. "Always the impetuous one, my Myngo is. Acts first, thinks later. If he thinks at all that is." Still watching me, he said, "Not so fast, Myngo my friend. Let's not be hasty." He smiled, but it only managed to stretch his scared face and make him look even more sinister. "You heard my friend, he wants to kill ya. But even though you been rude to us, I kinda like ya. So I'm gonna give ya an option, a chance to live if ya will. Give us the dragon and we'll let you go. Give us the whelp and we'll let ya walk away, nice and easy like. Now what could be fairer than that?"

"You can't have her, she's mine." Quick as thought, I flung the knife at Erb. I missed. The blade stuck in a tree a few inches to his left. Just for an instant he looked startled as if he hadn't expected me to fight back. Before I had a chance to try again, something hard and unyielding slammed into the back of my head and darkness closed over me.

118

When I woke, Rena was gone. While it was light outside, I had no idea how long I'd been unconscious. It could have been a few hours or a few days, though judging by the emptiness in my stomach, I figured it was probably closer to a day, day and a half. That meant they had at least a twenty-four hour head start on me. But I'd find them. I had to.

It took me three days to track them down. I was an excellent tracker, the best around. I had to be to hunt unicorn. Wiley beasts, unicorns, hard to find and even harder to kill. But in the end, it didn't matter. The two men had left a trail my five-year-old could follow. They probably thought I was dead. I felt like it. The blow had raised a lump the size of an orange on my head and I felt weak from hunger and loss of blood. I spent the first day after I woke just trying to gain my strength back. A couple meals of fish restored some of the energy I'd lost and enabled me to start looking for Rena.

The two men had set up camp inside an abandoned silver mine. The silver had run out a good fifty years earlier, but hunters and various others still used it on occasion for camping or as shelter from bad weather. I knew about the place, but never used it myself. It had a notorious history of cave-ins. People had died during those cave-ins, lots of people. But for some reason that never seemed to stop anyone.

I approached the entrance cautiously and peered inside. Both men sat in front of a fire, their backs to me, gobbling down chunks of cooked flesh. At first I thought they'd killed Rena, but then I saw her in the corner, her snout bound shut with twine and her legs and fledgling wings wrapped tightly to her body like a turkey on a spit.

She radiated hunger and thirst so intensely; it felt like a physical blow. I could tell she hadn't been fed since they'd stolen her. How could they be so cruel? How would they like it if no one fed them in three days? Couldn't they feel her hunger?

I snuck in quietly behind the men, intending to do what, I wasn't sure. I had no weapons. When they stole Rena, they'd taken my knives as well, including the one I'd thrown at Erb.

Once inside, I saw the men's packs stacked haphazardly against the wall. I didn't see the crossbow, but the spear lay in plain site. If I could get to it, I might be able to get both Rena and I out alive.

119

I moved slowly towards the spear. I might have made it too if Rena hadn't spotted me. She began to squeak with delight, attracting the hunter's attention. I couldn't blame her. She was just a baby and didn't understand what was going on. She only knew I was there to rescue her.

Both men looked up. They saw me. I was trapped, no weapons, no way to defend myself.

"Hey look, Myngo, it's dragon boy, come to claim his little playmate."

"Dragon boy. I like that, Erb. Dragon boy." Then he giggled. I shivered. His laugh had a high-pitched childish quality, but no child's voice had ever held such murderous intent. "You shoulda let me kill 'em, Erb."

Erb gave a dramatic sigh. "You're right, Myngo, but sometimes I jus' don't like killin'. It's a failing of mine."

Both men stood, the already drawn crossbow in Myngo's hand. "I changed my mind," Erb said. "Kill him now."

With those words I moved, launching myself across the mine towards Rena. I didn't quite make it. Something punched into my back, lifted and slammed me against the rock wall. Pebbles and bits of ceiling rained down and dust stung my eyes. The pain stopped my breath. It was all I could do to remain conscious. I couldn't see it, but I knew I'd been hit with a crossbow bolt. When I tried to move, I felt the blade scrape against my spine.

Erb crossed in front of me and grabbed Rena, but she would have none of it. Anger overcame her hunger and fear. She twisted forcefully in his arms. He barely hung onto her. He cursed and grabbed her tighter, but she'd managed to free one of her clawed feet and, even though she was a baby, those claws were capable of severe damage. She raked them across Erb's belly. He cursed and flung her violently to the ground, so violently I heard her wing bones snap. Her whimpers tore at my heart. I started to crawl towards her, but it hurt. It hurt so damned bad. I was dying. But I had to protect Rena.

120 Erb stood staring down at Rena, blood leaking from the wound she'd inflicted. There was such a look of raw fear and hatred on his face, it gave me chills. I knew he meant to kill her, never mind the money she'd fetch if she were still alive. She'd hurt him, frightened him, and a man like that would die before letting anyone know a baby, even a baby dragon, could get the better of him. He wanted her to suffer like he'd suffered. I couldn't let that happen.

Slowly, I pulled myself closer, picked up a rock and smashed it down on his foot. I didn't have the strength to do much damage, but it was enough. Erb screamed in rage and kicked me in the face. My jaw exploded with pain, but at least he'd left Rena alone. He kicked me several more times, then stopped just as suddenly.

My mind floated in pain as I thought about my wife and my children, how much I missed them and how much they'd miss me. But I knew they'd be all right. My wife was strong, capable. They'd survive. I worried about them, but at this point there was nothing I could do to help them. They were safe, protected. Rena was not. She was nothing but a baby. Vulnerable. My wife would agree. But even if she didn't, I had no choice. I had to do something. I had to help Rena. They were going to kill us both and I couldn't let that happen. I fought through the pain and continued to move towards her, fighting with every ounce of my remaining strength to get to her before I lost consciousness again. She was my focus, my remaining will to live. I wouldn't give up. I couldn't.

Erb seemed to think the whole situation was some kind of hilarious joke. He laughed at my pathetic attempt to rescue Rena. "Kill them," Erb finally said, bored of the whole situation. "Kill them both. And make sure no one finds the bodies."

I turned my head and saw Myngo aim the crossbow at the unstable ceiling and fire several bolts in rapid succession. When the mine shook and debris started to fall, I understood. He was trying to bury us in a cave-in.

The mine rumbled as even more rock and stone rained down on us. I crawled faster towards Rena, ignoring the pain as best I could. I reached her and pulled her body under mine for protection. It was the only thing I could do.

121

Pebbles became boulders, smashing into my legs and back, crushing my spine. I cried out in pain and horror. I whispered, "I'm sorry," to a wife I would never see again. Then the whole ceiling caved in and I knew nothing more.

When I woke, the pain was gone. At first I thought I'd died. How else could I have sustained such serious injuries and not be dead? Then something bit me on the foot and I knew I was still alive. I sat up and saw Rena gnawing on my boot the same way she'd done all those weeks ago. Or maybe this was still that day and everything else had only been a dream. An awfully vivid dream...

I looked around. I was no longer in the mine; I was back in the cave where I'd met Rena. Nothing had changed. My pack was still there, beside a dead fire. What was going on? How did I get here? Was this all a dream?

I'd just begun to think the last month had never happened when the mother dragon came stomping out of the back cave. Then I knew. The last month wasn't a dream. It had really happened. I looked towards my weapons, which were next to my pack, but I had no real intention of using them. If she was going to kill me, so be it. I deserved to die. Besides, I'd already died once. How bad could a second time be?

The dragon touched me with her snout and took a sniff. Whatever she smelled seemed to satisfy her as she licked me with her scaly tongue. Was she trying to decide whether to eat me or not?

Then the images came, slowly and painlessly, and I began to understand. I saw myself dead. I saw Rena's mother move stone and debris to find us. I saw her find Rena under me, alive but unconscious. I saw her... what... breathe on me? Then my wounds closed as if they'd never existed. I saw her carry us back to the cave. She saved my life. She healed me. Why?

The images changed. I saw myself pulling Rena underneath me before the cave collapsed. I understood. She saved me because I'd sacrificed myself to save her daughter.

122

"But I tried to kill you," I said. "I thought dragons were blood-thirsty animals. The images you showed me before, the blood, the burned bodies... "

More images came, the same ones as before, but this time slower. I gasped. She hadn't shown me what dragons had done to humans; she had shown me what humans had done to dragons—killing, burning, destroying their habitats, slaughtering their young, selling their blood and flesh for profit, raiding their nests. When I attacked, she'd been afraid of me. Of me! I could hardly believe it.

I was ashamed. "I'm sorry," I whispered. "I'm so sorry."

The dragon watched me for a long moment then rose and led me into the back cave, Rena following behind. The other babies were there, but they stayed back, afraid of me as Rena had never been. She picked up a fist-sized stone from her nest and dropped it into my hand. I understood this was her way of saying both thank you and goodbye.

I pocketed the stone and leaned down to give Rena a quick hug, wishing both her and her mother well, knowing they'd understand my feelings if not my words. Walking back to the front cave, I picked up my pack and weapons and headed towards home.

Much later I remembered the stone in my pocket. I pulled it out and looked at it. It was dark red, almost black, with unpolished, rough edges. I smiled. When I got home I'd have to tell my wife I wasn't hunting anymore. We'd have to find some other way to provide for ourselves. I tossed the stone in the air, caught it and put it back in my pocket.

Once she saw the ruby, I had a feeling she wouldn't mind.

No Time for Dragons!

Tina Morgan

Clarine tapped the desktop impatiently as she waited for the web page to load. She had read a rumor on one of her magic-users' chat groups that there was an ancient formula for removing sticky substances from spider hair. She winced at the thought of her pet tarantula, Francesca, with bright blue bubble gum clinging to the hair on her back and legs.

It didn't bear contemplating, best to focus on the task at hand and find that formula before her next workshop. She couldn't take Francesca in her current condition and since the topic was "Improving Communication with your Familiar," she couldn't leave the spider at home.

The page loaded with nail-biting slowness. Clarine peered at the image and groaned. The formula was a tattered and faded picture of a hieratic tablet. From the spider symbols etched in the side of the tablet it appeared the formula would remove sticky substances from arachnids. She hoped it would work on Francesca. Printing out the page, she carried it into the kitchen. Her knowledge of hieratic was moderate since she'd taken several classes in ancient Egyptian spells at the local wizarding co-op, but the carvings in the picture were worn and blurry. She surrendered and donned her reading glasses. There was no one to see her wearing them in her own kitchen. It just wouldn't do for word to get out to the other witches that she couldn't perform a simple vision correction spell.

With the picture in a little better focus, she began to compile her ingredients and set her cauldron on the stove. A knock on her front door made her pause. She wasn't expecting visitors. A cold chill ran down her spine. What if it was Enari? That witch had a talent for finding out everyone's secrets. She would be sure to spread the tale of Francesca's predicament and Clarine's glasses. Slipping the offending glasses back into her skirt pocket, Clarine tiptoed into her dining room and peeked around the corner. The L-shape of her house allowed her to see through the dining room window. She could just make out the back of a man's blue business suit.

A frown creased her forehead. That wasn't Enari. The rival witch was a portly older woman with impossibly bright red hair-not the orange shades of a true redhead, but bright crayon red like a dye job gone bad. Not that anyone would dare question Enari's spell casting abilities. That would earn the busybody's eternal wrath.

Clarine debated whether to return to her work or answer the door. She hadn't started the formula yet; it was safe to leave it for a few moments. After all, it had been some time since she'd had a male visitor. She stepped back into the kitchen and surveyed her reflection in the glass front of the microwave. It wasn't a very good mirror but she could tell her brown hair remained bewitched into an attractive (no grey showing) style. Her eyes were bright and her cheeks were flushed at the thought of a male visitor. Maybe she could entice him to stay for lunch, and maybe a dip in the lake later.

Certain that her appearance was acceptable, she hurried through the dining room and down the hall to the front door. She pulled it open but her merry "Hello" died half spoken. Instead of a man, she stared into a pair of golden eyes set within a dragon's blue scaled face. The scales were two shades brighter than his conservative suit, and the contrast was enough to warrant a call to the fashion police. Instead of standing up like a plume, the purple ridge scales adorning the back of his head and neck were flattened against his skull and he looked like he'd been attacked by a bottle of superglue. He held a book clutched to his chest and she could see just enough of its title to know which religious text it was.

"Greetings citizen," the dragon began in a gentle tone. "Are you familiar with the teachings of the Great Nartal?"

"I don't have time for dragons!" Clarine snapped and slammed the door in his face. With an angry huff she returned to her kitchen. "Dragons wearing suits and preaching pacifistic gospel. Really! They're mad. Whatever possessed them to think they could become vegetarians and eschew magic?"

Slamming the ingredients for her formula down on the counter, she tried to bring her temper under control. Francesca needed her help. She couldn't afford to mess up the mixture. She winced at the sound of persistent knocking on her front door. Surely the dragon wasn't still there? Peering around the corner, she crouched down so she could see the creature's head below the edge of her lace curtains. Sure enough, there he was. Answering the door had been a major mistake; now he would knock until she talked to him. She didn't have time for such silliness. The Church of Enlightened Nature need not send such missionaries to her house. She was a fully accredited witch and she knew magic was real!

Ignoring the knocking, she turned back to her work. Within moments she was humming as she cut up the ingredients. Her spell casting might not be as good as other witches' but she excelled at formulas and potions. It was her favorite part of being a witch as it combined magic and cooking. Within moments she'd forgotten all about the dragon. Until the glass in her kitchen door rattled. He hadn't given up. He'd moved to the side of her house where he could peer through the window and see her working.

Dusting her hands on her apron, she stormed over to the door and yanked it open. "I told you, I do NOT have time for dragons. Now begone before I cast a spell on you and turn you into a toad."

What she supposed was a condescending smile crossed the dragon's lips. The gleaming incisors that hung just past his bottom lip shattered the effect. The dragon hadn't been hatched that could pull off an innocent look. "Citizen, if you would consider the Great Nartal's words 'and so magic had never existed despite the claims by the disillusioned that it had,' I'm sure you would find comfort in his benign and gentle teachings."

"Go away. I have a formula to mix and you're interrupting." Clarine closed the door and tried to remember where she was in her preparations. The dragon continued to knock on the door, his nose pressed to the screen. The sound was beginning to make her head hurt. If he persisted, she'd have to make some chamomile tea to ease the pain.

Just as she remembered that the next ingredient was finely chopped snake liver, the telephone rang. She jumped and cut her finger. Cursing long and low under her breath, she used the corner of her apron to apply pressure to her finger as she walked toward the phone. The dragon knocked again and Clarine cursed louder.

"Hello?" she snapped.

The cheerful voice on the other end of the line made her cringe. "Why hello, Clarine. Malen said you have a dragon knocking on your door. Is it a Church of Enlightened Nature missionary? You didn't let him know you were home, did you? Would you like some help getting rid of him?"

"No Enari, I'm fine, but thank you for the offer. He'll go away soon, I'm sure."

"Really, dear, you're so gullible. These missionaries never leave once you've let them know you're home. Why don't you let me come over and get rid of him for you?"

Clarine gritted her teeth at the condescending tone in Enari's voice. "That won't be necessary. I'm getting ready to fly to the store. He won't follow me through the air; you know they've all eschewed flying as blasphemous."

"Well, if you say so," Enari said skeptically. "But I haven't had the opportunity to turn a dragon into a toad for a long time. It would be fun."

"Thanks for the offer but I don't have time right now. I'm in the middle of a potion and I need to pick up some ingredients before it spoils." A wicked grin crossed Clarine's face and her eyes lit up with mirth. "But I could send the missionary over to your house if your heart's set on turning him into a toad."

"That's quite all right, my dear." Enari paused and Clarine rushed to say good-bye but the busybody cut her off. "Do you need someone to come sit with your potion while you're at the store?"

"No, it's fine. Thanks though. I've really got to run. I'll talk to you later," Clarine said and quickly hung up the phone. The dragon was still knocking.

She looked down at her sliced finger and walked back into the kitchen to clean and bandage it. The dragon saw her and knocked even louder. She grabbed the door and jerked it open. "I'm very busy. You have five minutes. Sit at the table and don't interrupt, just run through your spiel."

The dragon blinked his golden eyes. "Really?"

He hurried into the house as if he were afraid she'd change her mind. Clarine ignored him and returned to the sink to finish cleansing the cut. The dragon hovered over her shoulder.

"You're hurt," he said.

"Sit!" Clarine ordered. "And stop stating the obvious. Besides, this is your fault. If you hadn't knocked on the door, I wouldn't have been startled and cut myself."

"Perhaps I could help?" The dragon opened the small briefcase he'd been carrying and rummaged around inside. He pulled out a tube of antibiotic cream with a pleased expression. "Here, this will help it heal."

Clarine stopped what she was doing to stare at him, her eyes half-lidded and her mouth drawn down into an angry frown. The "Enlightened Nature" church obviously wasn't living up to its name. Use a chemical compound when she had herbal remedies? Not this witch! She picked up a small pot of her favorite poultice and smeared a tiny bit on the cut, then covered the wound with a bandage. It really wasn't fair to accuse him of making her cut her finger though. That was Enari's fault, calling her when she was already in a state about poor Francesca. "You're using up your five minutes making silly suggestions. Sit."

"Yes, yes, of course." The dragon wrapped his long tail around his waist and perched on the edge of one of her kitchen chairs. He looked so ridiculous trying to assume a non-threatening pose that she almost laughed out loud. The urge to laugh quickly faded as he launched into his thoroughly practiced speech about the church and its doctrine. Having a fire-breathing predator spouting pacifistic rhetoric in her kitchen did little for her concentration and she regretted letting him inside. Still, with the dragon in the house, Malen couldn't see him and she would have to gossip to Enari about something else.

The pain in Clarine's head continued to build with each "Praise Nartal!" that came out of the dragon's mouth so she put a pot of water on the stove. Chamomile tea might help, but it would take a few minutes for the water to boil. While she waited, she uncorked a bottle of peppermint oil and dabbed it on her temples. She set the oil on the counter and returned to her work. She didn't notice the dragon's eyes begin to tear and his skin turning a deep greenish blue until a resounding sneeze made her jump and drop her knife. She turned to see him trying to choke back another sneeze while the curtains over her sink burned. Grabbing the fire extinguisher from its hanger in the broom closet, she put out the curtains and turned to glare at her guest.

129

"What in blue blazes was that about? I thought you Church of Enlightened Nature missionaries weren't allowed to use flame."

"I'm so sorry," the dragon muttered between smothered sneezes. "It's the peppermint oil you opened. I'm allergic. I'm so very sorry about the curtains. I'll pay to replace them."

Clarine's jaw dropped and she stood looking at the dragon's red-rimmed eyes for several seconds before it occurred to her to go wash the peppermint oil off her temples. How could she keep Enari from finding out she'd let the dragon in her house if he torched the darned thing? "No harm done, you just surprised me. I'll fix them later. I'm quite good with interior decorating spells."

The dragon stifled another sneeze, then peered at her through watering eyes. "I wish I could convey to you just how much it would change your life for the better if you would consider converting to the church. The use of magic is dangerous and it creates more problems than it solves."

"I thought the church said magic wasn't real." Clarine arched an eyebrow at him before returning to her work. She was pleased to note that his eyes were showing signs of drying up and he'd stopped sniffling now that she'd washed off the oil.

The dragon gave a heavy sigh. "You believe magic is real, that's all that matters at this time."

"Don't patronize me! Mister...what is your name?" She stopped stirring and brandished her wooden spoon like a club. He blinked his eyes at her in the disconcerting way of all dragons with their nictitating eyelids.

"You may call me George," he tried to smile again but she thought it would be best if he kept his mouth shut and didn't reveal so many sharp incisors.

"George? What kind of name is George for a dragon?" she asked. "Shouldn't you be named something like Firebrand?"

The dragon stopped smiling and looked at her with narrowed eyes. "I'm named after Saint George."

She started to make a caustic reply but decided it would be best not to interrupt his spiel again so she could finish the potion. Turning back to her printout, she stared at the last ingredient with dismay. A dragon incisor? How was she supposed to obtain that? Ever since their conversion to the Church of Enlightened Nature, the dragons had stopped allowing their body parts to be used for magic. They were currently trying to pass a bill in congress that would put an end to what they called the "exploitation of dragon products". As if they really cared about the use of a tooth. They shed them like sharks. They had more teeth than they knew what to do with, especially now that they'd all converted to vegetarian diets.

The silence became unnerving and she realized George hadn't launched back into his practiced speech. She must have upset him with her question about his name. She turned to see him draw himself up with great dignity and start for the door. "I can see that you do not wish to be enlightened. I'll bid you good-day."

"Wait!" Clarine called. "Please, I'm sorry. It's just that I'm having a bad day and I've let my temper get the better of me. I'm so sorry. Please sit down and tell me more about your church."

He gave an injured sniff. "You're clearly not interested so it would be best if I move on to the next house."

"Please, George, I'm truly sorry. Stay. Have a cup of tea and a brownie." She turned and grabbed a platter of freshly baked brownies off the countertop. With the plate in her hands, she rushed to the door and blocked his exit. "Brownie? It's a new recipe and I'm concerned about the amount of vanilla. Would you taste one and let me know what you think?"

The dragon looked down his nose at her but lifted a brownie from the plate with two delicate claws. Skeptically, he turned and walked back to the table. Sitting down, he took a small bite while she watched. His golden eyes opened wide with surprise. "This is excellent!"

"Thank you." Clarine blushed as she opened her cabinet to look for a cup for his tea. All of her delicate porcelain cups seemed too tiny for his toothy snout. Glancing over her shoulder, she attempted to estimate the size container she would need to serve him.

"A bowl will work fine."

She nodded and lifted a small bowl out and filled it half full with the chamomile tea she'd been brewing. Pouring herself a cup, she sat down at the table and stared at George, trying to think how to ask him for a tooth.

He choked on a swallow of tea. "Do I have something on my face?"

"No, no, I was just admiring your fine teeth. It must be nice not to have to worry about cavities."

The scales on his cheeks turned a darker blue and he batted his eyelids. "You don't think they're too frightening? I try to put people at ease by smiling, but I'm afraid it only shows more teeth."

131

"I think they're beautiful." Clarine smiled and leaned closer. "Can I see?"

George blushed once more but leaned closer and pulled his lips back to form what she was beginning to recognize as a smile. She stared intently at his teeth in hopes of seeing a loose one. There were two teeth on his upper left jaw that were hanging by the tiniest bit of gum.

She tried to keep her voice blasé. "You have a loose tooth. Does it hurt?"

"Oh no," George replied. He opened his mouth to speak but stopped and glared at her. Clarine shifted in her chair and struggled to maintain her calm demeanor.

"Why the sudden interest in my teeth?" His golden eyes narrowed even farther. "You want a tooth! You're trying to exploit me!"

"George! I'm insulted." Clarine sat up straight and feigned indignation. "I'm a nature lover. I'm interested in all forms of life."

The dragon stood abruptly, causing his bowl of tea to slosh all over Clarine's white tablecloth. She bit back a reprimand. She had to have that tooth.

"You are a witch and witches use dragon body parts for vile and degrading practices."

"Well...I...well!" she stammered as she tried to come up with a valid excuse for her interest. She stood and looked over at the burnt curtains. "Really George, I forgave you for nearly setting my kitchen on fire. I thought we were learning to get along."

"You are atrocious," he said, pausing on each word to give it extra emphasis. "Nartal's teachings are wasted on you." He tried to stand up straight but the scales he'd held flat to the back of his head now flared in fury and brushed the overhead light. He flinched.

Seeing her only chance at a dragon's tooth slipping through her fingers, Clarine stepped toward the door. "I thought Nartal taught patience and tolerance for the unenlightened. Surely you don't wish to leave without explaining how the great Nartal came to his wise and educated philosophies?"

George huffed and started for the door. Desperation set in

132

and Clarine looked frantically for a way to stop the dragon. Her gaze fell on the bottle of peppermint oil sitting on the counter. She stumbled forward as if to grab his arm but bumped into the counter and knocked the bottle to the floor. It shattered into thousands of tiny fragments and splattered peppermint oil across the bottom of his trousers.

He jumped back and roared in anger, "Woman, you're a menace! Are you trying to kill me?"

"I'm so sorry! Let me help you." She grabbed a towel from a drawer and dropped to her knees to dab at his pants, being sure to slop the towel through the oil on the way.

George jerked away. "What are you doing?"

She stood and waved the towel in the air. "Oh, I'm so sorry! I'm such a klutz some days, please forgive me."

George's eyes watered as he tried to smother a sneeze but lost the battle.

"Oh dear," Clarine moaned and muttered more apologies while pressing the oil soaked towel into his claws. In the confusion, he did just as she hoped and wiped his nose with the towel. He began to sneeze violently and his eyes were almost swollen shut.

"Get off me witch!" he yelled and fumbled for the door. Unable to see or stop sneezing, it took him several moments to find the doorknob. Clarine had dropped all pretense of helping him to grab her fire extinguisher and put out the flames that were threatening to engulf her kitchen. As she put out a blaze on her countertop, she found what she had hoped to see. There in the ashes was a perfect incisor.

The dragon shouted insults about her lineage and intelligence but continued to search for the door. Having what she needed, Clarine escorted him outside. He staggered off down the street screaming about witches and their insidious plots to take over the world.

Clarine went back to cleaning her kitchen and putting out the smoldering flames that had once been her toaster. It was a small price to pay for a dragon incisor. She added the tooth to her potion and after giving it a final stir, set the cauldron to one side to cool. As she mopped up the peppermint oil, she

133

found two more dragon teeth. She whistled happily to herself as she carefully sealed them in an airtight jar. For once, a visit from a dragon had turned out for the best.

Later that evening, after she and Francesca returned from the workshop, they sat before the TV watching reruns of "Charmed". A contented sigh escaped Clarine's lips as she gently stroked the spider's silken body. The potion had worked beautifully.

"The workshop was very informative, don't you think?" she asked. The spider tapped her forelegs against Clarine's thigh in a positive response. She rubbed a fingernail along one of the spider's legs. "I'm glad you agree."

Silence filled the air when Clarine muted the commercials. Francesca jumped off her lap to capture a large moth that had flown too close to the lamp sitting on the nearby end table. Clarine watched her kill her meal before asking, "You're going to stop chewing gum in bed, aren't you? I'm not sure I'll be able to get another dragon tooth if you don't."

She couldn't be certain, but she thought she heard a mischievous chuckle escape the spider.

FOR YOUR EYES ONLY

J.M. BUTLER

Ruita leaned her head against the rough camel stall. "I can't help it," she whispered, tears clinging to her lashes. "Matuha, unless we have your father's blessing, I won't marry you. There are some things that shouldn't be done, regardless of how strong the feelings. Right is right."

Matuha sighed, extending his arms with helpless confusion. "But I love you, Ruita. I'm willing to give up everything to marry you! Why won't you say yes?"

"I promised I'd marry you when your father gave us his blessing."

"Father won't give us his blessing unless you can prove you truly love me." Matuha sank onto the splintering bench, adjusting his orange cloak so it avoided the filth-covered straw.

Ruita brushed her fingertips over his dark cheek. It hurt her to know no one believed she loved Matuha. And there was no way she could really show or prove that. Anger at their doubt swirled in her heart, but at the same time, understanding. The words choked from her mouth. "Your father is wise. He's not sure what to think now. And you can't blame him after what Jakunda did to your brother."

Matuha grasped her hand, the hard edge in his voice intensifying as he recalled his brother's death. "But Eltok was blinded by lust. He couldn't see that Jakunda was only after his money."

"Yes and your father doesn't want the same thing to happen to you." Ruita ducked her head. The loss had devastated Matuha's family. Perhaps, she consoled herself, if it had not happened, his father would have been more trusting.

"But I'm not blind!" Matuha pulled her into his arms, burying his face in her thick hair. "I know you love me, Ruita. We were meant to be together since before time began. But it could take years for Father to see that."

Tears choked Ruita's throat. Years. She closed her eyes, inhaling the sweet scent of his cedar and spice cologne. Usually, the smell comforted her, but now it only intensified her loneliness. "If we can still love one another this passionately then," she whispered. "Even after we've waited, our love will endure through all time."

"Waiting is so hard." Matuha leaned his forehead against her brow. His long eyelashes brushed against hers. "But who said loving was easy."

Ruita forced a smile and flicked away a tear. Matuha was such a wonderful man. Sometimes, she wondered if she even deserved him.

136

"The only way we can cut the time short is if we can soothe Father's doubts. Father suspects your love is bred of money. How can we prove it's not?"

Ruita brushed back her thick black cornrows as she rose from his embrace. Love endured for ages, but her chores had to be finished before the end of the afternoon. She picked up the rough pitchfork. "You think, but I need to finish taking care of the camels."

Matuha grabbed the shovel leaning against the stall. Stepping in beside one of the camels, he dug it deep into the mire. The stench intensified with this movement, causing him to grimace.

"Ugh. I think we need to finish this up so we can get out of this place. Who can think clearly here? Hey, Bulbo! Stop that!" He swatted the big camel.

Bulbo looked at him, a reproachful arrogance in his dark brown eyes. But then he shifted his gaze back to Matuha's thick crop of black curls. Matuha moved away from the camel as he tried to take another bite.

"Does Tamm have a hair fetish?" he asked, jumping back.

"Only if your hair's black." Ruita smirked, digging the pitchfork into the pile of fresh straw. She lifted it up and tossed it into the clean straw on her right. Matuha, usually so confident and graceful, lost his typically fluid movements as he struggled into Tamm's stall. "And usually I move the camels out before I try to clean up. You weren't meant to clean camel stalls."

Matuha grimaced as he glanced back at her. "I agree, but this is called an act of love. For better or worse, eh?" He swatted the flies buzzing around his head. "I hope you appreciate it."

A smile tugged at the corners of Ruita's mouth. But inside, she felt sadder. Matuha came from a noble heritage, his father being the head of the city. By lowering himself to helping her in the camel stalls, he demonstrated how much he loved her. But no opportunity ever presented itself for her to show him the same.

These thoughts tormented her as they worked in silence, tending to various duties. After Ruita finished putting fresh straw in the stalls, she hauled water to fill the stone trough. Matuha came up beside her as she heaved a bucket of cold water up. He put his hands on her shoulders. "Don't worry. If the worst comes to the worst, then we'll just wait another three years. If only we could find you a good dowry. Then Father would see that it wasn't my money you were after."

Setting the bucket down, Ruita wrapped her arms around his neck.

"And what dowry do I have? I'm a foreigner, Matuha. I'm

137

lucky to have a job tending camels and horses. I'm barely able to save a few extra coins at the end of each month." She sighed, resting her head on his chest. Tears burned in her eyes. "Even if I worked a hundred years,
I'd never be able to save a dowry large enough!"

Pulling her closer, Matuha remained silent for a moment, chewing his lip in contemplation. "I've got it!" he exclaimed, shaking her shoulders. "We'll get the treasure from Dragon's Canyon!"

"Dragon's Canyon?" Ruita fell back a few steps, her eyes wide with shock. "But that place is cursed!"

"No one's seen the dragon in years." Matuha grabbed one of the saddle bags and threw it on Bulbo's hump. "Go and fill those water skins. I'll saddle the camels and we'll be on our way."

"But—" Ruita held up her hands.

"No time to argue. Come on." Matuha thrust the worn water skins into her hands and pushed her out the stable door. "The sooner we leave, the sooner we'll have your dowry."

Ruita turned, but no words left her mouth. There wasn't anything else to say. She sighed, hugging the water skins close. She had seen him get in these moods many times, and when he did, there was no reasoning with him. The only thing she could do was fill the water skins and be ready to travel.

Walking to the edge of the well, Ruita wondered how Matuha could be so bold. Was he truly that brave or was it just the intoxication of riches? Lowering the skins into the water, Ruita couldn't help but wonder if the dragon really was gone. The cool water reached up her forearms, washing the heat from the sun and hard work away for a few pleasant moments.

138   "Water please," an old voice beside her croaked.

Turning, Ruita saw one of the blind beggars, kneeling beside the well. His ragged brown wrap fell away from his arms, revealing the scars he'd received for getting in people's way. If the guards caught him dipping from the well before dark, he'd be beaten. The skin around his mouth cracked and bled as he spoke. No matter how many times she saw it, it still wounded Ruita's heart.

Kneeling down, Ruita offered him one of the skins, placing the cleaned lip against his mouth.

"Drink and may it soothe your pain."

Ruita found the words slipping from her mouth before she could stop them. Some of the other men and women at the well gave her disparaging glances, their faces taut with disapproval.

Ruita closed her eyes, wishing she could jump in the well. Why had she said that? She could have just given him a drink. There were enough problems with being a foreigner. She didn't need to emphasize it. Sighing, Ruita began filling the other skins. What did it matter? Her red-brown skin proclaimed for everyone to see that she wasn't a native of this land.

The man drank from the water skin for a few long moments, some of the liquid making a darker trail down his ebony jaw. When he had finished, he pressed the container back in her direction.

"Thank you."

Ruita took the skin and refilled it, screwing the plug back in place. She watched as the beggar hobbled off, ducking to the side to avoid bumping into people.

A dowry. The thought of glistening gold coins and sparkling gems excited her heart. Once she had the money to spend, after her marriage to Matuha was finalized, she would use the gold to build a place for the blind to live. They were no more cursed than the average patron of these streets and it wasn't right for them to be left to fend for themselves in this way.

These thoughts startled her. She had never really thought of having money to spend, not even in her daydreams of marrying Matuha. But now, a door opened in her thoughts. Foreigner or not, she could help these people.

"Ruita?" Matuha scooped up the water skins, tilting his head to the side as he tried to meet her gaze. "Ruita, are you all right?"

"I'm fine." Ruita forced a smile.

"Was one of those blind devils bothering you? You shouldn't help them. They could curse you too," Matuha said.

This remained one of the few areas where they disagreed. But Ruita didn't say anything. She knew he wouldn't understand. "How long will it take us to reach Dragon's Canyon?"

"If we leave now, we should be back by late evening." Matuha guided Tamm over and helped Ruita up onto the bright saddle. "Of course, I'll have to marry you after that. Not much gets past the gossips of Kalidat. And you know how good they are at making up stories to match circumstances."

Ruita held her tongue, knowing full well that some of the looser tongued members of the city were nearby. At times, she didn't know why she even wanted to be accepted and for people to know that she really loved Matuha for himself. No matter what she did, it was flawed because she was foreign and they could draw scandal just from the way she braided her hair.

Matuha climbed onto Bulbo's back, shaking the reins. "Let's go!" He shoved his long orange cloak back and smacked the camel across the left flank.

Ruita squelched a startled cry as Tamm ran after Bulbo. People scattered in the street, some frowning and others laughing at their comrades' shocked expressions. The swaying motion made Ruita thankful for the saddle; otherwise, she knew she would have been thrown from the dromedary's back in just a few moments. Matuha showed no signs of any such problem. With each of Bulbo's strides, he reacted, leaning in and out so the two of them moved with the grace of one animal. Ruita was certain some of the laughter was targeted at her and it made her cheeks burn. She couldn't even show Matuha she loved him by appearing dignified and regal.

They soon left the town and the camels' broad hooves dug into the sand, carrying them closer and closer to their destination. With each step, Ruita's thoughts grew darker. She had only lived in Kalidat for four years, yet in that time, she had heard many tales of the Dragon's Canyon. The horror stories rose in her mind like ominous graves, tendrils of fear nibbling at her thoughts. What would they find? She closed her eyes, letting the searing wind blow through her hair. Would the dragon be there? Would they really find wonderful treasures? Or would they discover death's lair?

After a time of moving at their unusually fast pace, the camels slowed to a sauntering walk. Their slow stride reminded Ruita

140

of a large dancer, moving to a slow beat. To her imagination, however, it was only a death-paced drumbeat.

"Maybe we should go back and wait until your father warms to the idea of our marriage," she said, glancing over at Matuha. Sweat trickled down her dusty cheeks.

"Why?" Matuha reached over to pat her hand, though his fingers barely brushed her arm. "Come on, Ruita. This is an adventure. Cover your head so you don't get sun stroke. I know where we're going. I've got guider's blood in my veins. Not one member of my family has ever gotten lost."

"There's always a first." Ruita pulled her scarf up over her hair, adjusting it so it wouldn't tickle her ears. She didn't usually feel this pessimistic. But somehow, nothing lifted her mood.

For the first part of the journey, she and Matuha talked of little things. But as the heat increased, their conversation faded and they stopped a few times for brief water breaks.

"We can only drain two water skins at the most on our way out." Matuha corked one of the skins after he'd taken a sparse drink. "That way we'll still have two on the way back."

Ruita nodded. She held a sip of water in her mouth for a few moments before swallowing. She still wasn't used to the crushing heat of this place. While the ocean's waves lapped along shores not more than three days away, this land remained nothing more than a desert as far as she could see, with the exception of a few oases. The relief of their drink quickly faded after riding awhile longer. Her lips ached and burned from her nervous nibbling and her tongue felt like it filled her whole mouth now.

"Are we almost there?" she murmured, holding her hand up to shade her eyes. 141

"We should be there soon." Matuha looked over at her, his eyebrows drawn with concern. "Are you all right?"

"I'm fine." Ruita readjusted the scarf on her head.

The heat grew more unbearable by the second. Tamm's swaying sides made her legs sweat and itch where the saddle blanket didn't cover the animal's coarse fur. And the smell of hot camel and human wasn't pleasant. How a dragon could survive in this forsaken land, she didn't know. Through this entire trip, she hadn't seen one snake or lizard. No birds sang to stir the silence. All she could see were the unpredictable patterns the wind carved in the sand dunes.

The oven-like air smelled of death the farther they traveled, a rotting stench of thousands of camels' carcasses lying beneath the baking sun. Ruita searched for dead bodies as they rode on, but nothing met her eyes. What was that smell? Looking up, she saw scavenger birds soaring in never-ending circles against a cloudless sky.

"There it is!" Matuha shouted, rising up in his saddle. "Look, Ruita! There it is."

A shudder raced down Ruita's spine as she stared ahead. The heat caused shimmering waves to dance across the horizon, but after a moment, she saw the canyon. Was the dragon dead? Was that what they smelled? She turned to ask Matuha what he thought, but realized he was urging Bulbo to a faster pace down the sloping hill.

"Come on, Ruita! We're almost there. If we hurry, we can get this done and be back before nightfall." Though Ruita felt hesitant, Tamm responded to Matuha's voice, trotting forward like a giant dog.

Matuha came to a stop in front of the canyon's edge. Sliding out of the saddle, he uncorked a water skin and sipped the water.

"We're there, Ruita. Just a few moments and you'll have a dowry fit for a queen. Here. Get something to drink."

Ruita managed a weak smile as she climbed down beside her fiancé.

"Wonderful." Closing her eyes, she took a drink of the water. Though warm and dusty on her tongue, it provided welcome relief to her parched throat. She wanted to pour it over her face and let it sink into her skin, but that would be wasteful. Wedging the leather plug back in place, she hung the skin from the saddle. Soon this adventure would be over and life would be better.

Matuha grabbed some rough homespun bags from Bulbo's saddle and reached for her hand. "Come on. Isn't it beautiful?"

"Yes." Ruita had to admit it was breathtaking, but in a disturbing fashion. The canyon dove away from the land,

142

a stark red gouge in the golden sand. "But are you sure the dragon isn't here?"

Matuha pulled her close and kissed the top of her head. "The dragon's dead. No one's seen him for years. That treasure is just down there for the taking."

"Then why hasn't anyone else thought of this?" Ruita cast a nervous glance over the side of the canyon. The wind howled up at her, like the low growl of a sick dragon.

"Because they're too afraid." Matuha led her to the edge and then down the coarse rocks. "But who knows? Maybe someone did take some of it, but they headed toward Lindoc, although we surely would have heard about it. Anyone that found the dragon's treasure would be sure to become a hero. Surely Kalidat isn't the only land with story tellers."

Ruita managed a weak laugh, although it wasn't particularly funny. She just needed to do something to relieve the tension building within her. The path leading down the valley made it hard to keep her balance. One misguided step could take them both over the side onto the hard red rock bed below. As they walked around a bend, a jagged cave entrance jutted into view.

"Oh, Matuha, look!" Ruita pulled on his hand and pointed toward the opening.

Bleached bones lay on the ground in front of the cavern, some crushed into piles of splinters. For a moment, both remained silent, their ears straining to catch even the faintest sound of danger. But nothing reached their ears, aside from the wind's low growl.

Matuha hesitated, no longer oozing with the confidence he had shown earlier. "It's all right. If there was anything down there, it'd have come out by now. Besides, those bones could have been here for a long time. Maybe jackals brought them down." He rested his hand on the hilt of his sword, giving her half a smile. "Come on."

The chills of fear made it hard for Ruita to follow him down the rest of the way. But she knew she would follow him into the cave, no matter how frightened she was, because her place was by his side. Matuha was probably right. If an animal had been in there, it would have come out with the sounds of their approach.

143

After they reached the valley floor, Matuha laid his hand on her shoulder. "I'm going in. You stay here."

Ruita's mouth fell open. "Why? No. No, Matuha. I'm going in there with you. I can't let you go in alone."

Matuha took a deep breath, as if he wasn't sure how to say this. "Listen, Ruita. I don't know for sure what's in there. I'm just going to go in and make sure it's safe. Then you can come in. Otherwise, I'll be worrying about you."

"But what if you need help? What if you fall and I can't hear you?" Ruita grabbed his hands, squeezing them with all her might. "I can't let you do this! We should have brought someone with us. What if we go back and get one of your servants or one of your friends. You can't go in there alone. Who knows how far it is to the treasure."

"I'll let you know when it's safe for you to come in." Matuha pulled his hand free, his tone growing firmer. "If you go in there with me, you'll distract me. I won't be as alert because I'll be worried about you. If I don't come out or you don't hear anything from me by the time the sun's rays hit that rock over there, then leave."

"No." Ruita shook her head, tears pressing. "The dowry isn't worth it. Let's just go back and bring someone with us."

"Ruita. We've come all this way and if Father hears about what we're doing, he might not give me permission to go. If you love me, do this for me. I'll be back soon."

Falling silent, Ruita ducked her head. Why did he have to say that? She had been so desperate to show him her love, but now he asked her to do something that contradicted the very thing she longed to demonstrate. But what choice was there?

"I'll stay," she whispered.

"Good." Matuha reached into his pocket and removed a miro stone. He gave her a quick kiss, leaving a sweaty imprint on her cheek. "Everything'll be fine. I'll see you in a moment."

Hugging herself, Ruita watched him go. She watched Matuha strode into the cave entrance, saw his confidence wasn't as strong as his swagger suggested. He was worried. She could see it way he walked, in the way he held the stone, and in the way he had kissed her. Inside, she seethed. She knew she had been terrified to follow him into the unknown, but if she had gone with him, at least he wouldn't have felt so alone.

As soon as Matuha entered the darkness, the miro stone glowed with a dim red light. Ruita stepped forward, her heart beating faster. Soon he became only a dark figure in the blackness, outlined in dull red.

"It's looking all right, Ruita," Matuha called back after a few moments of tense silence. "I found it! I found the treasure! And something else—"

A deep-throated roar erupted and Matuha cried out in agony. He fell, his outline disappearing as the miro stone slipped from his hand.

"Matuha!" Ruita screamed. Racing forward, she plunged into the darkness. She didn't know where he was or what was going on, but she had to reach him. Suddenly, she tripped over a body. Scrambling on all fours, she realized it was Matuha. Her hands and knees bled from falling onto the hard stone, but she grabbed him anyway, determined to drag him out to safety. His weight proved too much for her, however, and she collapsed. The miro stone shone just a few feet away, casting a faint glow on her surroundings. Matuha still lay on his back, his eyes shut and his mouth open in a silent scream.

"Matuha," Ruita cried, shaking his head. "Say something!"

Matuha didn't respond. Ruita slapped his cheeks and rubbed his wrists. The dust on his arms burned her hands, her blood staining his skin.

"Wake up, Matuha, wake up! What happened?"

Stinging smoke whooshed over her. Looking up, Ruita fell back in terror, wondering why she hadn't seen the golden-eyed dragon resting just behind her.

"What are you doing?" the dragon growled, its voice rumbling like a lion's roar.

Ruita swallowed hard, her hands and voice trembling. The horrendous stench was far worse in here. The dragon wasn't dead after all and he was very angry.

"I'm sorry, noble dragon. Forgive us for disturbing you. Please don't eat him."

The dragon snorted, disdain huffing from his fist-sized nostrils. "Felz dragons do not need food or drink."

"Then what's wrong with him?" Ruita grasped Matuha's hand, squeezing it tight to give him strength. Matuha moaned, clenching his gorgeous black eyes shut even tighter. "Why is he unconscious?"

"He tried to steal my gold," the dragon responded, drawing one of the stray coins that had fallen back into his pile. "He's blind now."

"Blind?" Ruita felt her heart skip a beat. "But why?"

"I cannot afford to lose anymore gold," the dragon bellowed, his smoky breath wreathing her face. Ruita fell back against Matuha's body, holding her ears.

"Please, noble dragon," Ruita whispered, tears strangling her voice. She rose to her feet and then bowed at the waist as far as she could. "Please, give him back his sight. Please. It will destroy him if he can't see."

"He would have destroyed me. This is his punishment." The dragon settled down on the pile of golden treasures.

"Destroyed you? No, no!" Ruita held up her hands, her desperation giving her courage. "No, all he wanted was to find enough gold to give me a dowry so we could get married. People couldn't see that I loved him. They thought it was because he was rich. So he thought we could find a dowry and make them see otherwise."

"As I said, he would have destroyed me." The dragon's voice grew softer. He didn't say anything for a moment as he began rubbing his face in the mass of coins. "I waited till he tried to take the treasure before I struck. My punishment is just."

146

"I don't understand. Please..." Ruita couldn't hold the tears back. They trickled from her eyes. "Why would that have killed you? We don't know. Honestly, we don't."

The dragon remained silent for a moment. "Many years ago, I fell ill with a strange disease. It blinded me after a month of feverish chills and frantic mirages. The disease continues in my eyes, robbing me of my sight. That's the stench. Day after day, pain is my only companion. I need more gold to staunch the infection, but I can't see to track it down."

"But what does the gold do?"

"When there's enough, I will melt it down and use it to bathe my eyes. Only then will I be healed. After I am healed, then all those I have blinded will regain their sight as well, if they're still alive."

"Matuha brought some gold!" Ruita cried. She dropped to her knees, digging into his pockets. There were a few golden coins and some jewelry. She set them down at the edge of the pile and then pulled some of the decorative rings from his fingers though she left the thin band she had given him on their engagement. "Is that enough?"

The dragon shook his head. "Woman—"

"Wait!" Ruita pulled the golden band Matuha had given her from her finger and then removed his. "Here. That's all we have with us. But we'll go back and bring more."

For the first time, the dragon seemed to relent. Sliding off the pile of treasure, he stood in front of her, setting his enormous clawed-paw on her shoulder.

"You don't have enough. I have not even reached half the quota. I need almost another ton."

The dragon's words kicked Ruita in the stomach. "A ton?" she whispered, feeling faint. "But there isn't that much in all of Kalidat! Isn't there some other way? Please, you don't understand. Matuha is the prince of Kalidat. If he is blind, he'll bring disgrace on his whole family. They'll say he's cursed! His own father may disown him."

Smoky breath engulfed Ruita's face once more as the dragon sighed. His golden eyes shut for a moment, before he opened them again. "There is one other way. But the price is high."   147

"I don't care. If I can pay it, I will!" Ruita laid her slender hand on the dragon's claws, ducking her head. The dragon's heavy paw remained on her shoulder for a moment longer.

"Gold is the usual requirement. But if a person gives me their sight willingly, then my eyes will be healed," the dragon said. He leveled his massive snout with her head. "You would have to give me your sight."

"My sight?" Ruita fell back a step, trying to comprehend

this. "My sight? I would be blind?"

"Yes. And there is no cure for that. You would be blind for the rest of your days." The dragon shrugged, causing some of the coins and gems to clatter to the ground. "It is a huge price to ask of anyone. Take your fiancé and go. You can prove your love by caring for him."

Ruita stared into the darkness past the dragon, not seeing anything. How could she take Matuha home like this? It wasn't her fault but she felt responsible. What would it be like to be blind? Would Matuha still love her? Tears blurred her vision as she remembered how he'd talked about the beggars. Would she join them? Would he disown her? Would he say she was cursed too? But what would he do if he was blind? He would feel so worthless. And if his father disowned him, Ruita knew she couldn't earn enough money tending camels' stalls to take care of both of them. The more she thought about it, the more she realized she had no choice if she really loved him.

"I'll give you my sight," she whispered. She looked up at the dragon, her vision blurring with tears. "But may I please have a few moments? I want to see all I can."

The dragon nodded, curling his tail around his polished scales.

Ruita sank down next to Matuha. She ran her hands over his face, devouring every detail. This is the last time she would ever see him and it hurt too much to understand. She knew she would never again see the way his lips parted in a half-smirk when something amused him or the way his eyes sparkled with delight. She would never see his face light up with joy when he saw her. Darkness would always hide this and so much more. Trapped sobs strangled her as she buried her head in Matuha's chest.

For several moments, she sat there, absorbing as much as she could. But finally, she looked up at the dragon. Taking a deep breath, she held Matuha's hand.

"I'm ready."

The dragon rose and inhaled.

That was the last thing she saw. Ruita felt his thick breath whoosh over her like a consuming curtain stinging her eyes and forcing sleep on her body. Gentle swaying finally woke her while something wet and salty fell on her lips.

"Ruita," Matuha whispered. "Ruita?"

"Matuha?" Ruita opened her eyes. Fear exploded in her mind when only darkness met her. Suddenly she remembered what had happened. She was blind. Blind forever now.

Matuha pressed his lips to her forehead and then her cheeks, his tears falling on her face. A cool breeze brushed over her like a gentle veil. Night must have come. She had been unconscious for a long time.

"It's going to be all right, Sweetheart." Matuha stroked her hair. "Everything's going to be all right. Father can't possibly doubt whether you love me or not now."

Ruita buried her face in his shoulder, almost afraid to ask.

"You still love me? We're still getting married? You want to marry me?"

"Of course I do!" Matuha's voice trembled. "Ruita, nothing's changed."

"Your father won't let us get married," Ruita whispered. The words would have stabbed her through the heart any other occasion, but this time, they weren't nearly as painful. Matuha still loved her, even though she was blind. He hadn't changed his mind!

"Yes, he will." Matuha continued to stroke her hair, his voice growing stronger. "He won't doubt it."

"Why?" Ruita managed a weak smile. "Anyone could make up a story like this to try to explain away a disaster."

Matuha leaned down, brushing his lips over hers. "The dragon sent as much gold as Tamm could carry. He said if people still told stories, he'd come to Kalidat and set it straight." He laughed, but the sound was weak. His heart beat against Ruita's ear like a vibrating drum. "I'm so sorry, Ruita. If only I'd known. Please forgive me."

"I forgive you." Ruita touched his face, running her fingers over his cheeks. She knew what he looked like now. His black eyes would be filled with compassion and his jaw would be trembling. She felt the muscles shaking when she touched his chin. If only she could see him again. "Things are going to be

149

very different now that I can't see."

Matuha pulled her hand away from his face, squeezing it tight.

"You're blind now, but I can guarantee that no one else can fail to see you really do love me. And whether you can see or not, we still have many adventures to take."

SHATTERED DREAMS

KEVIN TISSERAND

"We're almost there Becca. Now close your eyes."

"I don't know James, what if I trip? There are loose rocks all over the place."

"Don't you trust me?"

"Sure I trust you, but..."

"Then close your eyes."

"Oh, all right." Becca closed her eyes and held out her hand for James to lead her the last few steps to the crest of the hill.

James took her hand and led her forward. "Left a bit, now straight, straight, good, lift your right foot a bit higher now, perfect, just a few more steps, now stop." He moved behind her so as not to obstruct her view. "Okay, open your eyes."

She found herself looking out over a magnificent vista.

"Oh James, it's beautiful!" The wooded hillside dropped away below them, revealing a sparkling stream running down to join the glistening waters of Unicorn Lake. An eagle soared majestically overhead while songbirds hidden in the trees filled the air with music. She could just make out a pair of water nymphs frolicking near the shore of Pixie Island in the middle of the lake. "Oh look! That must be Peter and Nathan in their fishing boat." Then she pointed to a tiny village nestled on the lake's eastern shore. "Is that really Grant's Landing? It looks so tiny from up here. Yes! There's my house! Mother must be inside preparing Father's lunch about now."

She stood there looking out over the spectacular view for several minutes while James put down their picnic lunch along with his bow and quiver, then waited behind her, glad he had chosen this location. Finally she turned to him.

"James, it's wonderful. How did you ever find this place?"

"Just one of the benefits of being a hunter. I've been all over these hills tracking deer, foxes, and dragonettes."

Becca frowned at the mention of dragonettes. "I worry about you, you know. Isn't it dangerous wandering around the woods alone? What if a flock of dragonettes decided to attack you?"

"Don't worry. They only flock a few days a year at the end of summer, just before they migrate south. Most of the time they're alone or in pairs, and they're pretty small and timid."

"What about that troll?"

"That only happened once, and it was three years ago. Other than that one time there hasn't been a troll around here for decades. Come on Becca, it's safe, and you know it. Otherwise I'd never have been able to talk you into coming up here."

She smiled and relented, moving in for a quick cuddle. As she hugged him she looked out at the spectacular view once again. "Okay, you're right. Thanks for bringing me here."

"Glad to."

After a moment they parted and James indicated the bundle of food. "Shall we eat?"

"Yes!" Becca declared. "I'm famished after the long hike up here." She bent down and started untying the twine that held it together.

152

James stood back, waiting for her to discover the string of Promise Beads he'd tucked in with the food. Becca was the best thing that had ever happened to him, and he was ready to pledge his love to her forever. This moment, in this place, was one both of them would remember for the rest of their lives. Everything was perfect. He felt his heart beating faster as he watched her unfolding the blanket. Any second now she would see the Beads.

Then he noticed the silence. The songbirds were quiet. The eagle was nowhere to be seen. There was one small rustle in the underbrush, then nothing. Something was wrong. He reached for his bow and arrows.

It appeared suddenly, descending from out of the sun. Immense green wings created a gust that swirled dust and dirt into his eyes and threatened to knock him over. Becca screamed. A huge scaly head appeared in front of James, dark red eyes the colour of blood glaring at him.

"Run, Becca, run!" he screamed. He tried to fire an arrow into one of those hate-filled eyes. The shaft sped toward the dragon, but missed its target by mere inches, glancing harmlessly off the impenetrable scales. He didn't get a chance for a second shot.

A whiplike tail lashed at him, snapping his bow in two. Giant claws gripped his torso, making it nearly impossible to breathe. As he gasped for air and struggled to free himself, he looked around for Becca. He couldn't see her, and prayed that she at least had escaped.

His last thought was wonderment that a dragon was here. The nearest dragon sighting in the past fifty years had been over a hundred miles away. Then everything went dark.

As James slowly regained consciousness the first thing he was aware of was the darkness. Had he been blinded? No, he could make out a few shapes, it was simply very dark. The second thing he became aware of was how much he hurt. As he raised himself to a sitting position he felt severe pain in his chest. Bruised ribs, he thought. The rest of him was covered in small hurts, but there appeared to be nothing that wouldn't heal in time.

Peering through the gloom he realized he was in a small enclosed space, perhaps eight to ten feet across and roughly circular. The only light was coming from a few small cracks in one wall. He staggered to his feet and approached the light. The wall was stone. In fact, he now realized that he was in a small cave, with the entrance blocked by a large boulder. He gave it a tentative shove, but was not surprised when it didn't move.

As his eyes became accustomed to the darkness, he saw that he was not alone. Three large shapes, roughly man-sized, lay in heaps on the floor. Could one of them be Becca? As much as he wanted to see her right then, he hoped not, for it would be far better if she had escaped.

He approached the first shape. It smelled strongly of burned flesh and James felt a wave of nausea before realizing that it was the carcass of a deer. The second shape turned out to be a pile of branches, freshly torn from a fir tree. The third shape was Becca.

Becca! He found her throat and felt for the rhythm of life. She was alive! He lifted her head into his lap and stroked her hair.

"Becca, wake up." He could feel her breathing, but she did not awaken immediately. "Please Becca, wake up. We have to figure out how to get out of here."

After a few minutes she began to stir. When James' hand passed over a large bump on her head she winced, reflexively pushing his hand away. She moaned and squirmed a little.

154 "Becca, I'm here."

"Oh James, what happened?" She sat up. "Where are we?"

"In a cave, blocked in by a boulder, but other than that I have no idea."

"That was a dragon, wasn't it? Dragonettes don't get that big, do they?"

"No they don't; not even close. As hard as it is to believe, that was definitely a dragon."

"But then," she gulped, "why are we still alive? Why did it put us in here?"

He hesitated. "I don't know."

He wasn't fooling her. "But you have an idea," she said.

"There's a burnt deer carcass in here. I guess in a way we're lucky to even be alive. I think we're being kept in a sort of... pantry."

She stood up quickly, then leaned on the wall as a wave of dizziness washed over her. "We have to get out of here."

"I know." He'd been trying to think of a way to escape. "Besides us, the only things in here are the deer and a pile of branches. How do you feel? Can you help me push on the boulder?"

"Is there a choice?"

The two of them heaved on the boulder as hard as they could, but it was simply too big. It wouldn't budge.

"What about the branches?" asked Becca. "Can we make a lever?"

"They're too thin, too green," he replied. "They'll just bend."

"But there's got to be something we can do," she said.

"If we can't get out," he said, "probably the best we can do is be prepared when the dragon returns." He thoughtfully patted his hunting knife which was fortunately still in its sheath at his side. "I'll need the leather thong from your hair."

James went through the branches and chose the straightest, sturdiest one he could find. While far from an ideal spear shaft, it should at least extend his reach a bit, hopefully enough to blind the dragon. The eye was one of the few weak spots in a dragon's scaly armour. After stripping off the smaller twigs, he lashed his knife to the stick with Becca's hair thong.

"Now what?" she asked.

"Now we wait." he said. He wished there were more they could do, and they both wracked their brains for ideas, but nothing they thought of could get them past that boulder. They huddled together in one corner, wishing for their chance at freedom, but dreading the return of the dragon.

They didn't have to wait very long. Less than half an hour had passed before they heard scuffling noises from outside. Then the boulder moved away.

They were blinded by the sudden brightness, but they leapt to their feet, watching for any chance to escape. As their eyes

155

adjusted, a huge claw entered the cave and prodded them. They had no choice but to emerge or be skewered.

Outside the cave was a small clearing. The low cliff wall behind them stretched both left and right, with the nearest trees being about fifty feet away in either direction. The emerald green behemoth stood before them, watching intently, but not moving to stop them as they began edging along the cliff face. It towered over them, its head at least twenty feet above theirs. The late afternoon sunlight glinted off its metallic scales. If it weren't so deadly, they would have found it beautiful.

"What's it doing?" Becca whispered.

"I don't know. Stay close." It was pointless advice, as she was already glued to his side.

They got within ten feet of the trees before the dragon moved. It was fast. One second it was standing still, peacefully watching them, the next instant a tremendous claw slammed down in front of them, narrowly missing James and completely blocking their path. The hunter in James noted that there had been no warning. No tensing of muscles, no quickening of breath, nothing. If this dragon wanted them dead, the attack could come at any time.

They backed slowly along the cliff face, past the cave entrance, and tried the other direction. Again they were stopped as they neared the trees.

"James, we have to get out of here." He could feel her trembling. "We have to get out of here now."

"I know, Becca, I know. Believe me, I want to leave as much as you do. But at least it doesn't seem to mean us harm, at least not yet."

"It's playing with us, James. Like a cat plays with a mouse, before..." She couldn't finish, but she didn't need to. And with a sudden realization James knew she was right.

"Stay here," he whispered, "and be ready to run." James started edging away from her, back toward the cave. With luck, he thought, at least she'd be able to escape.

As they separated, the dragon seemed to become agitated. His dreadful gaze swept back and forth between the two of them. When they were about thirty feet apart, James feinted as though to run. The dragon quickly blocked his route with a claw and lowered its massive head to growl threateningly at James. With this movement, Becca had a chance for freedom. "Go Becca! Now!" he yelled, and with all his might he thrust his makeshift spear at the dragon's eye. He missed as the beast jerked aside and let out a deafening roar. James was close enough to see saliva dripping from dagger-like teeth. He lunged again, this time aiming for the mouth. The larger target brought success! The knife's blade sank into the unprotected tongue.

The dragon screamed in a mixture of rage, pain, and hatred. It snapped its powerful jaws, severing the spear's shaft, then whipped its head back and forth until the weapon came free and flew harmlessly away.

Then the dragon's huge claw caught James before he made it even half way to the trees. He was certain this was the end, and prayed only that Becca had made it to safety. He felt himself being flung back into the cave, where he hit the back wall with bone-crushing force. His left arm shattered in mind-numbing pain. He lay in a heap, momentarily unable to move as he heard the enormous boulder sliding back across the entrance.

He heard the dragon crashing off into the forest and whispered to himself, "Run, Becca, run."

As he lay there concluding that his ruined arm would never heal properly, and then chiding himself for worrying about that when he would clearly be dead before long, he noticed that he could still see fairly well. It wasn't as dark as it should have been.

He turned to face the cave entrance and saw that the boulder wasn't completely blocking the opening. In its haste, the dragon had failed to push the boulder all the way across. The gap was small, less than a foot wide, but it might be just enough.

James staggered to his feet, pain lancing through his injured arm. He realized it was bleeding as well as being badly broken, but at least the blood loss was minimal. He moved to the opening and tried to squeeze through. It was a very tight fit, and at one point he became stuck, but by exhaling completely he was finally able to struggle out.

There was no question in his mind as to which way to go.

He didn't know if there was any hope left for either of them, but if Becca was still alive he had to see if she needed help. He tried not to think about how much help he could be with just one good arm. Pausing only to retrieve the broken spear and untie his hunting knife from the useless shaft, he followed the obvious trail of destruction where the dragon had plunged through the forest after Becca.

It didn't take him long to catch up to them. He heard the dragon roar in rage somewhere ahead. When he got close enough to see anything, the dragon was standing on a rocky outcropping looking down over the far edge. Then he heard Becca scream. As James watched helplessly, the dragon belched forth a huge ball of flame. Becca screamed again and the dragon roared in response, its tail twitching back and forth in frustration.

Then, with a final deafening screech, the dragon launched itself skyward and turned to fly back in the direction of the cave. James crouched behind a tree until he was sure the dragon had gone, then he moved forward to where the beast had been a moment before. Looking down over the edge, he saw a drop of about forty feet. At the bottom was a narrow ravine, filled with thickly tangled thorny vines. The top layer was scorched and smoking, and below that he saw Becca, thoroughly entangled and bleeding from numerous small cuts and abrasions.

"Becca, I'm here."

She looked up. "Oh James, you're alive! I thought..."

"I know, me too. Hold on, I'm coming down."

"Are you all right?"

"My arm's broken." What an understatement, he thought. "What about you?"

"I'm stuck in here," she said. "I can't move. And I twisted my ankle."

James made his way carefully down into the ravine. It was difficult with only one good arm, but eventually he was able to cut her free with his hunting knife.

"What now?" asked Becca. "Do you have any idea where we are?"

"Yeah, once we got out of that cave and I had a chance to

look around I recognized the area. We're straight across the lake from home." He lifted her arm around his shoulders. "Here, lean on me."

"Ouch!" She settled her weight on her good foot. "There, that's better."

She was still grimacing, but there was no way he was going to leave her there. "Can you walk?"

"I have to," she said through gritted teeth. "Our families, everyone in the village, they must be warned."

"Yes. Life will be completely different with a dragon in the area. We may all have to leave."

They walked on in silence, each dealing with their own physical pain and drawing strength from the other. It was slow going with Becca's bad ankle, but they made steady progress by staying near the lakeshore where the terrain was easier. Still, the sky was growing dim by the time they were half way home and they knew it would be foolish to continue in the dark with her injury. Fortunately James' arm was no longer bleeding, and he was able to find shelter for them in a depression between some large rocks. They were both hungry, but resigned themselves to having no food until the next day.

"In the morning I'm going to climb back up and get our picnic lunch," said James.

"Don't be ridiculous. You know it's not safe up there, and we can get food at home just as quickly."

"There was more than just food in that bundle."

"What do you mean? What else?"

James sighed. "This isn't how I planned on doing this, but there's a string of Promise Beads in that bundle. Becca, I want you to marry me."

159

She looked at him, stunned, then threw her arms around him. "Oh James, I love you!"

"Ooh! Watch the arm!"

"Sorry," she said, and let go of him.

Their gazes locked, and all James could see reflected in her eyes was love that would last forever. Still, he had to hear it. "Does this mean you accept?"

"Of course, if you still want a wife who can hardly walk."

"I do, if you'll have a husband with only one good arm."

They both knew it wouldn't be the life they'd dreamed of, but they'd be together and somehow that made it bearable.

"Aw, Mom, you promised."

"I did no such thing."

"Yes you did. You said I could get one as soon as we finished moving to our new place."

"I said I'd think about it."

"But all the other kids have them."

"No, they don't. But I haven't said no either, have I?"

"Does that mean yes?"

"It means maybe. Having a pet is a big responsibility. Are you sure you're ready for it?"

"Sure I'm sure! I'll feed it, and play with it, and take real good care of it."

"And what exactly will you feed it?"

"Uh..." So maybe she had a point. But he was willing to learn. "Okay, I'm not exactly sure. But I promise to do all the work if you teach me what to do."

"Oh, I suppose it's all right then."

"Hooray!"

"But listen carefully. Humans can make nice pets, but they can also be dangerous. You have to look after them properly."

"Okay." He forced himself to calm down. He wanted this so bad it was worth paying attention. "What do I do?"

160

"The first thing you need to know is that they can be dangerous in large groups. You need to find one or two alone. They tend to wander off from their herds from time to time, so if you're patient you'll get your opportunity."

"Okay, got it."

"Humans are much happier if they're kept in pairs, so you should get two. Try to get a male and a female if you can."

"How do you tell them apart?"

"It can be pretty difficult, especially since they usually wear artificial skin over their real skin. If you can catch them without it, just look for the floppy bits sticking out from the front. Males have one, females have two. Otherwise, if you find two together, but separate from their herd, chances are it's a male and female. If not, that's fine too, as they'll probably still be happy since they were together when you found them."

"Okay Mom, anything else?"

"Food. They don't eat the same things we do. First of all, they like their meat cooked."

"Cooked? What's that mean?"

"It's kind of like burning it, but just a little."

"Eewww, that's gross! And then they eat it?"

"Yes. Can you handle that?"

"Sure, it's easy enough. Just kind of disgusting, that's all."

"And they eat plants too."

"Okay," he said. He knew most of the animals he devoured ate plants themselves. Not something he'd do, but at least it made sense. "That's easy enough, the forest is full of plants. Can I go and catch some humans now?"

"All right, just remember they're your responsibility. I don't want to end up looking after them for you. If I find you've been neglecting them, I'm going to let them go. Is that clear?"

"Got it Mom."

"You can keep them in that little cave down the hill. Just make sure you keep the entrance blocked or they'll get away."

"Okay Mom. Bye."

You're back. Did you find some humans?"

"Yeah."

"You don't sound very excited about it. Did they get away?"

"No."

"What's the matter?"

"Well, I caught them no problem. Two of them, alone, just like you said. But they tried to get away at first so I gave them a little squeeze. Then they just stopped moving. I thought maybe I killed them, but they were still breathing so I don't think so. I put them in the little cave with some food, but they're still not moving. Somehow I thought they'd be more fun. You know, do stuff. I thought I could play with them."

"You know, you have to be careful with humans. They're pretty fragile, but if they're still breathing they'll probably be fine. They tend to go unconscious easily. Just give them some time and check on them every now and then. Eventually they'll wake up."

"Okay Mom."

"That's it! I give up! Forget the whole stupid pet human idea!"

"Oh dear, I take it things didn't go very well."

"No, they didn't! Lame little creatures."

"Do you want to talk about it?"

"I went to check on them again. They were awake, so I figured I'd let them out of the cave and play with them a bit. It was okay at first. They just walked around, and I kept them in the clearing near the cave. Then they got all nasty and tried to escape. One of them poked me right in the mouth with something really sharp. My tongue still hurts! Then the other one ran off. I tried to get it back, but it got stuck in a ditch full of tangled vines. It was too narrow for me to get in, so I had to leave it there. Then, when I got back to the cave, I found the other one had escaped too. So now they're both gone!"

"I'm sorry. Why don't you try again? There are bound to be more of them around."

"No, forget it. They're no fun after all. Nothing but a big pain in the tail."

A Darkness of Spirit

Eric Diehl

A'qil sa'n Alar strode to the central court of his walled fortress and raised the horn to his lips. It was an ornate instrument; looping coils of polished brass flaring sensually into a gleaming bell. The sounding began as a deep bass rumble, rattling the windowpanes in their frames, and when A'qil pressed a valve the note rose to a piercing bay. He sounded it six times, and between each soaring trumpet the echo reverberated throughout the mountains. The armies that floundered nearly broken before the walls of House Alar blanched with new fear—they'd heard the stories, they knew what would follow.

The sounding of the Great Horn was a grim augury, a call to the slaughter.

Dal had just finished a long climb to crest a high ridgeline when the keening wail reached her ears and white fury flashed in her heart. But just as fast as the anger emerged, she snatched it back, thrusting it into the far corner of her soul where she kept it sequestered and repressed. Dal edged down to steepen her dive, hastening her descent to the Shii'e'tu caverns—home to her collective. Her thoughts ran with the shadows.

The two-legged one, A'qil—he calls the Drakaa forth once more. I must forestall Zax and his coterie lest they further darken the spirit.

Old Riven waited as she approached, speaking before she came into sight.

"Dal, it is too late. Zax and a dozen others are already away."

Dal growled low in her throat and huffed a thin cloud. "So soon? They've taken the underground passage?"

"Yes. As before, they will meet the two-leggeds in the caverns below their stronghold, and there they will allow themselves to be rigged for this monstrous desecration." Even as he tried to repress his emotion, Riven's tone quaked. Dal remained silent as she glided in, and then, spotting him on the rough terrain near the cavern's entrance, she landed. This was even worse than she had expected.

"You say a *dozen* others have joined with Zax?" She settled back on her haunches and gazed down upon Riven—in his ancient years he'd begun to shrink away from his prime.

"Yes. Four others have gone over to his ethic, including Kestar."

Dal hissed softly. "*Kestar*, even?" She could scarcely believe it; Kestar had been so adamant in his opposition to Zax's beliefs.

Riven loosed a rumbling growl. The crown of armor between his widely spaced eyes glistened dully and he bared his front row of teeth. "It is so. I argued with them, but the reverts have lost their identities—they're now little but reflections of Zax. They loftily claim their actions are the true way of the Drakaa—a way falsely repressed—and that to vent their desire in this manner is only natural. They claim that this sates their bloodlust... for a time. They insist that it involves joining in a savagery already underway, and that it is thereby an atrocity not of their making."

Riven snorted and a cloud of grey smoke puffed from his

nostrils. "I assured them theirs was a foolish and dangerous argument. Zax countered, rather darkly, that the alternative would be a pent need—ultimately erupting into violence among our own."

Dal hissed again. That was new. Never before had the betrayers hinted of violence in the collective. It was true, then, what she suspected. The spirit grew ever darker, claiming more reverts to the ways of old.

"I must follow them, then—intercede before they act."

Riven shook his massive head. "If they scoff openly at Riven, Elder of the Elders, I cannot believe that they'd heed any other, not even you. And even were you to hasten now, you'd not catch them in the caverns. They've too much of a lead. They've got the blood frenzy, Dal; I remember it from my youth. You'd do well to stay away; it would be dangerous to cross them now. Their vision has narrowed and a curtain's drawn, shutting out all light of reason."

But she had to try. Dal left Riven still protesting while she pumped her wings steadily, climbing through thin air toward the pass between the Guardian Brothers. She was a minute speck in a blue sky as she flew between the towering triplets of alps, and once through she canted her wings to begin a fluttering descent, her heavy breathing gradually returning to normal. The temperatures were frigid up so high. Her breath fogged in white clouds and a sheen of ice clad the stony landscape. She angled out from the peaks to gaze down upon the fortress of the two-leggeds far below. The striped black-on-orange pupils of her almond-shaped eyes narrowed as her vision focused and she studied the mayhem.

165

The chalky soil beyond the fortress walls lay dark and soaked with blood. Broken bodies lay still across the broad mesa-top and a trail of wounded straggled behind the army limping away. Dal strove to peer through the thick smoke; so much of the scene was shrouded by black plumes that roiled upward, drifting apart into a broad, grimy haze.

She hissed softly. There was the feeling of raw evil here.

Dal drifted on the updrafts, floating above a scene of carnage silent from this height. Suddenly the gates of the fortress were flung open and thirteen Great Drakaa moved out in a wedge pattern. She focused grimly on the leader.

Yes… it is Zax. And there is Kestar, immediately behind.

She shook her head in frustration. Zax had carried little sway before the reversions had begun, but Kestar—normally so equable - he'd rivaled Riven and herself in influence on the collective. And now in wonder she looked down upon Kestar rearing on hind legs and raking extended talons, roaring and snarling unintelligibly on a bloodied field of death. Her blood warmed at the faint sound. She spat dark bile and a growl rumbled low in her throat. Her mind extended to the spear of Drakaa bearing down on the fleeing two-leggeds. Riven had been correct, the curtain was drawn. She picked up no structured thought, just raging frenzy pulsing hot and livid.

She watched Zax plunge without hesitation through the straggling clusters of wounded, the V-shaped ridge of his tail sweeping a wide path and decimating those he hadn't trampled. The two-leggeds did not attempt to stand before his thirst, simply dropping their weapons and turning to flee. She listened to their faint screams, not of the mind, and she watched with growing fascination.

Zax is headed for the able warriors. He desires the whole blood of those not already fallen…

Kestar dropped behind and fell upon the wounded, snatching them up in his jaws and shaking his head. Separated body pieces and bright gushes of blood spread across the ground. He tilted his head back and Dal watched his neck pulse and bulge as he swallowed. She could not avert her eyes. She was possessed. Her second heart kicked in, doubling her pulse and flooding her mind with coursing heat. She flew a circling pattern high above the carnage, her structured thought dissolving into a haze of wanton, unremitting desire.

166

Zax reached the mass of the able-bodied two-leggeds. Surprisingly enough, some turned to form a thin line facing him. They thrust and jabbed their tiny lances and swords at the Drakaa and he thrust his neck forward in return, two streams of viscous fluid jetting from glands beneath his extended tongue. The line of two-leggeds, doused with venom, howled and fell to the ground. The writhing bodies erupted in blue flame when Zax surged through the broken line.

Dal's eyes shifted to the two-leggeds riding atop the raging Drakaa. Perched in elaborate saddles, they were suited in lustrous black battle armor, with polished red helms styled like the head of a Montar. The lust was on the two-leggeds also. They brandished their lances and loosed flights of arrows into the ragged mass. The mounted warriors howled in animalistic glee and Dal felt a deep hunger building within her thoughts.

Another of the fleeing two-leggeds, larger than the others, stood his ground with a huge battleaxe. Zax's head snapped down like a striking serpent, his jaws closing over the two-legged's torso and snatching him off the ground. Dal's senses were so sharp now, she heard the steel breastplate crumple like an eggshell, transforming the piercing scream into a choking gurgle. She abruptly reared back and sprayed a dark mist of poison into the air.

She blinked, dazed. She'd never known it before, the exquisite taste of black death. She shuddered. The glands beneath her tongue swelled and her muscles hardened with the strength of a doubled heart rate. Her breath came fast and heavy and suddenly she canted her wings to plunge down toward the carnage glistening blood red.

Her eyes, greedy now, sought out a target on a portion of the battlefield not yet broached by the spreading wedge. All thought was gone. There was now only bright glowing vision, rapturous taste and scent. She flexed her talons, extending them long, and saliva trailed from both corners of her gaping muzzle. Her jaw muscles flexed, opening and closing, and a red haze crossed over her vision. 167

"Dal! Break away! Do it now! I cannot hold the collective together without you!"

Dal blinked, confused.

What is this? Who speaks my mind?

"Veer away, Dal! You must!" Riven's voice echoed in her mind.

She forced her focus away from the carnage. Was there something important she should remember? Something to be wary of?

And then she did remember... some of it.

I must...turn away. Not join in the slaughter. But where to go? Not to the collective...not like this. How can I break the frenzy? How can I break it...without taking of it?

Dal forced herself to bank away, angling back toward the forest climbing the steep slopes. She could not return to her collective, not without first breaking this dementia and the deep instinct awakened within her understood only true violence could stop it. She shook her head and roared in black anger, swerving into the flat anvil of stone she flew alongside and slamming herself against its unyielding surface. There was the briefest flash of white and color and then nothing.

A full cycle of the moon passed before Dal could again attempt flight. A cold cycle spent alone and in pain. She drew on deep body stores to survive. Riven's mind ventured to her, cautiously at first, and when satisfied she'd broken the reversion he withdrew. He told her she needed time alone to heal.

Even once physically recovered she stayed away, working to fully cleanse her mind of the malignance that had come so near to claiming her. By then Riven came to her regularly, a welcome touching. She trusted Riven to be strong enough to see her for only Riven—once, long ago—and now Dal, had proven resilient enough to break the bloodfrenzy without the taking of blood, without the tainting of Spirit.

Time did pass, now more than a full circle, and Dal rejoined the collective whole. But the darkness continued to build unabated and she sensed a black wave cresting, ready to break its fury over everything she knew. She watched the others closely and continued to fear for them. Group thought was finished, sentiment shuttered in and open sharing long since faded away. The collective members now conversed secretly, selectively, a fateful omen.

How had it come to pass that the two-leggeds assumed overbearing control of the Spirit, as though the callous savagery living in their hearts had usurped the devout stewardship

long pledged by the Drakaa? How could that be, when the
two-leggeds were such a young race and their intellect not yet
developed? The two-leggeds didn't yet recognize the Spirit's
existence, much less understand what it was, what it meant...

A'qil sa'n Alar stood at a high window in the southwest
donjon, looking past the compound walls to the mesa and
the yawning Flat of Gal'tar beyond. Word had just arrived -
House Tyrgon had assembled the largest military force ever
seen on Kast'ar, in large part by assimilating the armies of
other Houses vanquished in recent years. That armada now
moved across the Flat, approaching Alar, intent on a stellar
prize never before taken.

A'qil smiled thinly. So be it then. His lust for dominance
fed his ruthless tactic and he'd surely need both in the weeks
ahead. But once Tyrgon was finished there'd be no others
worthy of challenge.

He chuckled softly. In a way the absence of worthy opposition
might prove a disappointment. His barbaric nature seemed in
particularly fine form of late.

"I overhear thoughts from small groups." Riven mindspoke
in a black tone. "They see the armies again gathering on the
battlefield, easily the largest ever assembled. They are excited,
giddy even, at the prospect of what is to come." Riven hissed
his disgust. "Worse yet, those I overhear are not of the original
group of reverts. These are new, young males mostly, but even
females join now."

Dal nodded grimly.

"I've suspected as much, the malignancy gathers itself. I will
call the collective; perhaps together we can throw this off."
She began to turn away but she stopped to study the odd glow
in Riven's eye. She cocked her head at him and he nodded
before speaking aloud.

"I feel its influence, Dal. I feel it strongly. The shadows tug at me, insistent, and they *tempt* me. It becomes ever more difficult to resist. I fear for the others; I fear even for myself now."

Dal flew through the deep caverns, the steady *wh-whump* of her wings the only sound as she sped through the darkness toward the home of the two-leggeds. As Riven had predicted, the meeting of the collective had gone badly. When she'd finally coerced group thought she'd been shocked at the resultant cacophony. Jumbled fervor and hysteria, often no distinct speech at all, stretched by raw, charred, emotion. Zax had easily carried the assembly. It seemed the collective had come to view Dal more as an obstacle than a leader. Even from those who'd not yet admit to it, she could feel the darkness of spirit on them.

Now nearly all the collective eagerly awaited the sounding of the Great Horn, lusting for the call to carnal savagery.

Dark Spirit coursed through the lower caverns. After a long passage, Dal climbed to a higher level, entering the primal dungeons below the stead of the two-leggeds. Here, incoherent moans and screeching tore at her soul. Through the deep shadows she caught fleeting glimpses of captives chained to ankle posts or hanging limp from manacles. She picked out the gloating chortle of some debased practitioner inflicting his ministrations and she pushed on to land farther away, under an iron-barred grate through which daylight filtered in from above.

She could sense the two-leggeds, not so far away now, and she sent her mind out to the one. She sent her voice to A'qil, to the cruel one, and she waited, determinedly holding on to measured thought.

Soon he arrived, alone.

A'qil approached with two greatswords slung over his back. He carried a huge crossbow fitted with twin bolts, harpoons almost, and he held it pointed loosely toward Dal.

"Why do you come now, Drakaa?" His voice echoed through the cold silence. "The war is not yet won. I've not yet sounded the slayer's horn." He peered stonily at her. "My victory must leave no doubt among the Great Houses—Alar will *never* fall. Only after I've sounded the horn, only then comes your time to feed upon the broken enemy." He pushed shaggy hair away from his eyes, his blunt fingers leaving smudges of dirt or blood. "That is our agreement."

Dal hissed softly, struggling to push down the white anger that flashed to the surface, and her second heart gave a single beat before she forced herself calm. A'qil's eyes widened and he stepped back.

"You and I have no such agreement, two-legged. Your vile pact is with others of my pod."

With feet planted wide, A'qil raised the heavy crossbow, training it on Dal's chest.

"These are armor-piercing bolts, Drakaa, dosed with d'arkfire. If you've come to kill me, you'll fail."

Dal shook her head and she spoke carefully. "I do not come to kill you, A'qil two-legged; that is not my purpose. I've come to change the way you think, the actions you take, before all hope is lost."

A'qil dropped the point of the crossbow a few inches, chuckling mirthlessly. "You, a craven beast, would presume to change the way of A'qil sa'n Alar, the greatest warrior of the greatest race?"

Dal caught her breath as the fury flashed blood-red, a pulse pounding behind her bright eyes.

To kill him now... it would be so easy. I taste the venom sweet...

Her eyes widened as she recognized her own intent, and again she pressed the burbling rage down. She spoke slowly. "You do not understand, two-legged. You know nothing of the Spirit, even though you take of it and return to it. You do not see its darkening as the spiral accelerates your savagery and you don't recognize this as a self-feeding prophesy. Every brutality accumulates and drives further atrocities." She sought the words that might convey her vision.

"We teeter on the sheer brink of insanity: a mindless, unbounded chasm awaits our plunge. Ours is a race much older than yours, more attuned to the Spirit, and for that reason I

171

fear we'll be the first to fall to the darkness. But you'll follow soon enough, as you can surely intuit from your mounting abominations. Think, A'qil two-legged! Your breed was not always this way."

A'qil squinted at Dal with a calculating expression. "So —you come to me, the great warlord A'qil sa'n Alar, seeking your own salvation? Why should I care if the Drakaa survive? I need no Drakaa to win my wars; their passing would mark no loss for me."

Dal ground her teeth, tasting the anger sweet.

How can I hope to get through to this simple fool, when I can no longer communicate even with my own?

"We all require untainted spirit. It's integral to our lives. If it continues to cloud over, then all will ultimately perish. But our races can work together to begin a restoration of balance, beginning with the cessation of rampant warfare."

A'qil snorted and raised his crossbow, waving it in the direction she'd entered. "I don't believe your words or your intent, Drakaa beast; I would have you leave now. Return with your ravening pack only when I sound the Great Horn."

Dal fought her quickening pulse, and then she accepted it.

I must risk descending...

Her coiled haunches launched her with a quickness not expected. Dal sprang forward, thrusting her head low as A'qil loosed both bolts from his crossbow. The prongs shot past and before he could unsheathe his swords she was in his face, her rows of teeth bared and glistening red in the flickering torchlight. A'qil stood frozen as Dal crouched rigid over him, her tail thrashing, so very close to simply finishing him. But in moments the red haze lessened and she held herself abeyant. She snorted and blinked her eyes as her pulse came down, and she spoke to his mind.

"I... do not mean to kill you, two-legged. If I did, I would be forever lost. What I must do now," she forced her cramping jaws closed, "is show you how we might both live."

"How... do you mean?" A'qil's voice quavered.

"You do not believe my words. Will you accept the unmasked truth of my thoughts? I will enter your mind, and open mine to you." She reached toward him. "I must have contact."

A'qil took a step back. "How do I know you won't simply kill me?"

"If that was my desire, then why do you still live?"

A'qil spoke carefully. "If your race loses itself to this... this *spirit*, as you call it, you'll come for us, won't you?"

Dal nodded grimly. "Yes. It would be the first stage of descent. Your race is plentiful and easy. But ultimately we'd turn on each other. Already I see signs of it."

A'qil remained silent, trembling but making no further attempt to move away. She took his head between her talons and four thin trickles of blood trailed from where she held him.

"First I will release, just a little, the thin control that I hold over myself. You will see what will come should the darkening continue."

She entered his mind and he gasped as she opened herself. She went back, back to the time she'd so nearly broke, and she replayed the vivid memories. Her second heart picked up and filled with savage warmth and glee, a cloying scent rising from her hide. A thin black slaver, oddly foaming, dripped from her clenched maw. She wanted so badly to open her jaws, to snap forward, crunching down, but she held fast to the last strand of control. She watched in her memories as Zax and Kestar ripped chunks of flesh from the two-leggeds and her mind surged jubilantly toward the violence.

And then with great effort she thrust the memories back— able to do so only because she'd once before come so close to the edge. She sagged back on her haunches with her eyes closed, struggling to force calm on her racing hearts.

Suddenly she staggered backward, a flash erupting across her senses as A'qil reversed the exchange. He thrust himself forcefully into her mind. On top of her raging emotions the raw influx of fury stunned her. Her eyes blinked open to see A'qil's leering, triumphant grin as he unleashed a savage intent paramount to her own.

He lunged forward, pulling a greatsword from its scabbard while stooping to sweep a handful of gravel toward her eyes. Dal hissed and flashed a forepaw out to catch A'qil around

173

the chest, pinning one arm useless. Her jaws snapped shut, grinding the thrown gravel and breaking teeth. She fumed a dark cloud that covered A'qil in oily, noxious smoke. With his free sword arm A'qil hacked at her and she yanked him off the ground. He screamed and dropped the sword as her grip tightened and a rib broke with an audible pop. She drew him in close to her muzzle, all slimy with dripping black slaver, and she bared her teeth, tasting the sweet venom. Her tongue snaked out to taste his sweat, and she reveled in the sour fear she found there.

And then she paused, shaking her massive head in confusion. *Los...I'm lost?*

She struggled to grasp the thoughts that flitted through her raging mind, but she could hold none of them. She felt the collective playing at the fringes of her jumbled psyche—no words, no coherency, just blind frenzy—urging her, goading her on. She felt the others gathering in ecstasy.

Gathering...

Senses exquisitely acute, she tasted the pulverized stone mixed with her blood and broken teeth and the narrow slits of her pupils focused on her prey. She could smell the stench of pure panic.

She roared suddenly, angry with herself. This was wrong for it to end this way. Why? And what of the others?

The others... gathering... can I somehow...take it from them?

Dal struggled to concentrate, to put her thoughts together. She understood her mind was fast slipping away. If she could hold to just one thought for a time. She ground her teeth together, tasting the stone.

174   *Stone, use the stone...take it...take the gathering to stone!*

She turned her eyes back to the small creature she'd momentarily forgotten. It struggled in her grip. She reached for its head with her free manus. It kicked its puny feet and snapped its teeth in a ridiculously futile defense. Her talons pierced its scalp and set firmly on bone while her eyes focused on his. He screamed when she drew hard on his mind, as she entered and pulled his darkness to her. In short moments the creature's spastic flailing went limp. Dal threw her head back and roared, hurling a great swath of fiery rage to burn senseless against the stone ceiling of the cavern. She flung the limp body across the stone floor and turned her eyes to the iron grate overhead, leaping toward it.

She slammed against the grate, taking the bars in her talons and wrenching them loose, raining clumps of broken stone to the floor. She clawed at the opening, tearing chunks of rock free until she could push through. The distant clamor of battle went unheard. She opened her wings and bounded into the blue sky.

She repeated to herself, over and over, lest she forget.

Gathering, to the stone...gathering...to the stone.

She could feel the collective with her now, wild with unrestrained exultation, clamoring for more. She felt their fury swell but hers was greater and she drew on them. Her twin hearts beat faster than ever before as she climbed and her rage darkened.

Up and up she climbed, feeling more power than she'd dreamed possible. The voices spoke to her, shouted at her, but she could understand no words. Only the feelings—the bright, intense, bloodfrenzy.

Gathering... stone...

When she could climb no more without her hearts bursting, she ducked her head and pitched over, beginning the dive. She scanned the rockscape below and bared her teeth in baleful exaltation. There, she found it, her prey. She pumped her wings until her speed was too great and then she folded them in, feathering just enough to guide her plunge.

Stone...

She narrowed her lids as the wind tore at her. The voices 175 howled now, incoherent, and she picked out a few though she couldn't remember many. One she recognized, ancient and different from the others. She was surprised she could understand it. It told her to stop, begged her to not do this thing. Irritated, she placed it to the rear of her conscious where it couldn't distract her purpose.

And there, on the rear fringe, she recognized another voice, louder than all the rest, exhorting her on, goading and gloating. A name came to her.

Zax.

She snatched that consciousness up and thrust it to the front of her mind, shoving from behind as she plunged toward the jagged mountainside. She forced its vision through her eyes and it quailed. The entire collective felt his fear and stepped back.

She could no longer remember why; she simply knew it had to be. The fury drove her, the excitement of the bloodlust and the realization that the others now feared her. She reveled in it and just before impact reversed herself, wings breaking backward she extended her talons and roared a gout of flame toward the sky.

The stony spire impaled her underbelly, plunging up through her chest and hearts. She slammed to a halt with the gory pinnacle rammed through the ridge of armor along her spine. Her blood spattered and mixed with the venom of her ruptured glands and blue flame sprang up and quickly burst into a blazing inferno. The intense heat shattered the cold stone, melting it, and the landscape was consumed.

On the battlefield, warriors paused in their struggles to gawk in astonishment at the huge torch erupting on the distant mountainside, too bright to look at for long, loosing a roiling black cloud of oily smoke to the heavens.

A'qil again stood at the high window of his donjon, his chest splinted and bound, watching the massive army retreating from his walls. He cocked his head to listen, shaved scalp puckered with stitchwork. In the distance, raucous bedlam resounded from the mountains among the Drakaa. He'd never before heard the like of it.

He sighed, absently fingering his knife. He looked down and drew the edge across an open palm. So sharp it was—the tissue took a moment to recognize the cut, but then a bright flow of blood welled. He stared at it moodily. He felt none of the old excitement. He put his hand to his lips, tasting blood.

Still nothing. He spat bloodied phlegm on the polished horn lying at his feet and he looked back at the retreating army.

It's not cowardice, what I do...

He looked hard at his battered reflection in the pane of glass.

Is it?

He shook his head.

I let them go, perhaps to one day regroup and come again even stronger. I could finish them now, they have nothing left. Even without the cursed Drakaa I could finish them...

A'qil sighed and he rubbed a rough hand across his bristly chin. He rang the bell to summon an attendant. It was decided. He'd send emissaries to all the Great Houses.

He could scarcely believe it. He—A'qil sa'n Alar, never defeated and most feared of all the warlords—intended to speak of peace.

DRAGON FRUIT

KIM RICHARDS

Lord Anton moved among the circle of virgins gathered beneath the flickering torchlight of the amassed villagers. Gravel crunched beneath his boots as he stepped across the village's marketplace. No other sound dared disturb the solemn atmosphere.

To each girl, he held out a silver bucket filled with ivory tabs. One by one they reached in and chose their markers, holding them closed tightly within their fists until the time of revealing. He dared not meet the questioning gaze of any of the maiden candidates. He had once and it nearly killed him to do what was required of the Dragon Lord.

The choice was not his, though the duty rested squarely upon his shoulders. No, it's much easier to simply not see the desperate pleading in their young and beautiful eyes.

Anton looked, instead, at the faces in the crowd. Many of the girls were at the age where they should be standing in this circle, drawing their lot. More than a few wore pitiful, vacant expressions common among girls who had their virginity raped from them most recently.

So, this is what we've become: men who deem incest and violation lesser evils than the choosing. It disgusted him and he let his opinion be known by the way his hard gaze cowed each father guilty of it. They withered before him and still he longed to plunge his sword into each of them. It took a massive gathering of will to force his attention back to the task at hand.

After each girl secured her fate, Lord Anton stepped out of the circle, letting the bucket fall to the ground with a clatter. He had no need to see each individual marker's symbol. Their reactions would say it all.

As one, the maidens stepped forward, stretching their arms out before them and stopping once their fists touched. Then at the same moment, all revealed the marker nestled in their palm. Anton watched as shoulders dipped and chins lifted in relief, except for one. The chosen one.

That one trembled and stumbled. The maiden to her left caught her and whispered in her ear. Then the chosen one stood and squared her shoulders. Her strength both pleased and saddened Anton. Many times he'd seen the chosen one panic or fall to her knees in despair. This one shed no tears, not yet anyway. She stood tall with all the bearing of a queen, her golden hair glistening in the torchlight.

Anton stepped forward, shouldering between two unchosen maidens dancing and clapping at their good fortune. He wanted to yell at them but instead faced the one who would be sacrificed.

179

"What is your name child?" he asked the golden chosen one, forcing himself to meet her gaze. *What beautiful green eyes!* It broke his heart.

"Arum," she said.

She started to say more but Lord Anton turned away, wanting to distance himself from the weeping and joyous laughter of those not chosen. He saw no celebration in all of this. He took her hand and, ignoring all others, led her down the streets of town towards his small keep. Tonight she would be treated as a queen, for at dawn she would meet her fate...and her king.

The yellows and pinks of the early sunrise brought no beauty to the heart of Lord Anton, nor any of those daring enough to bear witness to the sacrifice of Arum. They dutifully escorted her up the winding path towards the sacrificial clearing of the dragon's mountain, carrying banners and swinging brass braziers of burning incense suspended on chains.

The whole of them sang the song of ascent, though none knew what the odd, sad, syllables they uttered meant. They all learned it at a very young age and knew the language to be one of ancient Dragon. Anton sighed and wished he'd taken the opportunity to learn the meaning in his youth. He'd been arrogant and self-righteous back then, unable to see the rarity and value in what he'd been offered. Hindsight is a terrible thing.

Arum made no effort to dishonor them, instead helping them chain her to the marble post by placing her wrists within the silver shackles. She held her chin high in an almost defiant way.

Anton counted his lands fortunate. He'd heard tales of dragons who devoured the maiden sacrifices before the horrified onlookers, leaving blood stains on the ground and their souls. This dragon preferred to take his offering away with him and for that Anton felt grateful.

Within moments of securing Arum to her post, a great wind picked up, swirling her skirts and quickly unbraiding her long golden hair as it tore the crown of roses from her head. People ran for cover.

All of them except for Anton, who stood grim-faced at the clearing's edge. The whipping, dusty wind scourged him and flayed his exposed skin, but not hard enough for him to consider it a penance for what he must let happen. No, that would require blood, which he knew would not come.

The whomp and whoosh of the dragon's great wings grew deafening. Still Anton stood his ground, forcing himself to

180

witness as the enormous scaled body blocked out the sky, its silvery scales shimmering like those of a river trout in the morning sun.

In one swift motion, claws like polished steel wrapped themselves around Arum, ripping her marble post from the ground. Then as quickly as it came, the dragon departed. The winds died quickly and dust settled. The entire clearing ached in its silence and the hot sun.

That's when Anton noticed something moving within the hole left by the marble post. He drew his sword as he hurried forward.

He paused at the lip of the hole and knelt, laying his sword on the ground by his knee. There in the soft upturned earth lay a baby, wrapped in a thick blanket. It looked up into Lord Anton's face and smiled. He recognized something in its soft, pale complexion, raven hair and eyes of the palest dove gray. He saw himself.

The boy child grew and Anton named him Nynin, which meant 'winged protector' in the old language. He taught him to hunt and to read, to pray and to sing, to count and to be fair. Anton kept him near always, instilling in him the art of warfare and the diplomacy of peace—all of the things necessary to someday become the Dragon Lord and rule well.

During that time a neighboring Lordship's holding fell at the hand of the Green Army, a new threat from the north. Wutherwood's demise came with sudden intensity, which surprised Anton, especially the lack of refugees. He sent word offering support but his letters returned unopened in the hands of abused messengers who told of threats towards any coming near. Since the invading army abruptly turned west, Lord Anton fortified his own borders and remained wary.

Anton had no heirs and the boy, no family to speak of. They had only one another. Nynin grew into the spitting image of

Anton, exacting enough that none questioned any absence of relation between them, though there'd been rumors of magic in the earliest days.

Lord Anton kept nothing from his young protégé, particularly with regard to the decadal choosing. He knew one day Nynin would have to preside over the proceeding and wanted to impress upon him the importance and seriousness of the event.

The boy confounded him with a perpetual bombardment of questions.

"Why do you allow it to happen?" Nynin asked.

"It's not a question of allowing it, my son. It is one of duty and fulfilling our end of an ancient bargain struck between mankind and dragonkin."

"What kind of bargain requires people to be sacrificed?"

"The kind which allows both dragon and man to co-exist," Anton explained. "The details of the bargain were lost long ago so I do not know them. I do know the dragons gave up much more than mankind. They gave up freedom when they moved underground. For a creature of the skies, this is an enormous concession."

"But our people *die!*" Nynin was appalled. "Do they suffer the sting of death as well?"

Anton knew there were things Nynin would not, could not, understand fully until he became Dragon Lord himself. For now he was forced to explain as best he could. "Yes, of a sort. It is an equal trade of lives. Dragons lay their eggs once every ten years." Seeing Nynin's expression of confusion, Anton continued, "One egg every ten years. Our sacrifice is timed to coincide with that event. We sacrifice a maiden, they destroy an egg. It's simply a life for a life."

"Won't they eventually die out?"

"That is a possibility. However dragonkin live for centuries at a time. It is not something we will see in either of our lifetimes." Anton drew in a deep breath and let it out heavily. "They are resourceful creatures. I'm certain they will find a way around it."

It pleased Anton thoroughly when, in his teen years, Nynin showed displeasure at some of the villagers' attitudes towards their daughters. Perhaps he would be the one to change their outlook on it all.

Anton watched his son and thought back to the day the title of Dragon Lord had been bestowed upon himself. He'd inherited a land where girl babies were given in marriage upon their births to prevent the choosing. He thought perhaps allowing marriage only after participation in the choosing would be the solution. He was terribly wrong.

Now, life for women had worsened: more illegitimate children than ever, less security in the home, and fewer hands to do the work. It hung heavy upon Anton's shoulders.

Soon after, Nynin turned to Anton at dinner and asked, "Who is my mother?"

And so he was told the story of his abandonment by their dragon. After that, Nynin grew thoughtful. Quiet as he was, his eyes took in much around him. Anton was pleased.

The attack came swift and precise, cutting through the Dragon Lord's holdings the way a hunting knife slices open a downed stag. Anton lost half his men before the warning horns sounded. Refugees, those of his own people left living, crowded the rooms and halls of his keep. Servants and soldiers alike worked night and day to ease the hurt and dying.

In the boldness of daylight, he sent sixteen year old Nynin to the next holding for assistance. He watched, his lips pressed tightly in a straight line, as his 'son' rode away, letter in hand and saddlebags filled with gold taken from the floor safe. He prayed for the young man's safe and successful return.

Two weeks Anton waited, fought off the persistent attacks, and waited. In the middle of the third week, Nynin came to him at midnight. The youth stepped quietly through the bedroom doors, looking haggard and beaten. From the regret in his gray eyes, Anton knew there would be no help forthcoming. He beckoned his son sit and served him food and drink while he rested. Then the two of them sat in an awkward silence beneath the flicker of candle light and a stray moonbeam from among the window tapestries.

After some time, Nynin drew in a deep, shuddering breath and began. "First I went north to Brakenstone Castle. There's nothing left but ashes and rubble."

"I'm sorry," Anton could think of nothing better to say.

"Further north, I found worse at Fenwich Keep. There were people stuck on..." Nynin let out a sob. He gave Anton the full force of his pain when their gray eyes met. "They were still alive, Father. Screaming...crying out. I slit their throats. I could do nothing else for them."

Anton patted his son's arm. "You gave them peace." He hoped his pitiful words sounded reassuring.

"Then they saw me. A patrol of the Green Army. I fled across the flatlands, into the holdings east. They chased me as far as that old manor, the one whose lord fell when I was six." Nynin paused to take a sip of his wine and wipe his brow.

"Wutherwood," Anton remembered of whom he spoke.

Nynin continued, "I crossed the river's edge and ran headlong into an army encampment. When...when I told them where I'm from, they took me into the manor house. They chained me to the dining room table and woke the Lord of the keep.

"He is part of this, Father. He gives them food, weapons, gold."

Confused, Anton said, "If that is true, then why are you here? Why were you not...not..." He choked on his words.

Words Nynin finished for him in a hard tone, "Why am I not dead? Revenge. Pure and simple. I never told him I was your son. He sent me back to ensure you knew who wanted The Dragon Lord dead."

"Revenge?" Anton shook his head in disbelief. "What did we, I, ever do to them? I sent offers of help. They refused. I don't understand."

"He says you murdered his daughter."

Anton reeled. This was insane! "What daughter? I never met any daughter of his."

"Her name was Arum." Nynin leaned in close to his father and stared deep into his eyes, "Did you? Did you kill her?"

Remembering, his voice barely a whisper, Anton relented, "I did." His entire body trembled at the realization. "She was a chosen one. I took her to the clearing myself. That same day, the dragon left you."

Nynin threw down his goblet. As the red wine stained the carpet like so much blood, he turned on his father, his face twisted in anger. "I cannot believe you would put that stupid ceremony above the welfare of those people." His voice rose in tone and in volume, "She came to us asking for assistance during a siege and you put her into the circle and made her choose a marker. How could you do that?"

"I didn't know," Anton said softly. He hadn't known.

The faces of those fathers came to him, the ones willing to do whatever it took to save their daughters from the choosing. They hadn't told him who she was, passed her off as one of their own. Worse, he hadn't asked. He'd thought himself better than they and now he knew better.

The Dragon Lord, shamed and sick to his stomach fell to his knees. Nynin left him as he prayed for forgiveness.

The midday sun found father and son fighting side by side on the walls surrounding their keep. The attack began with the sunrise and, so far, neither side had made any headway. Both men avoided speaking to one another, preferring to immerse themselves in the battle at hand.

Then, with a sudden surge, the Green Army burst through the walls and the side gate almost simultaneously. All hell broke loose as the formerly well organized defenses turned to chaos.

Arrows flew and blood ran as the air filled with curses and the stench of sweat and urine. Tired muscles guided weapons as shields met with clanging steel. Men fell. None did the Green Army spare; women and children sprawled in the red mud at the swing of a blade. It was a horrible, terrible massacre in which few managed to survive.

Nynin finished off a trio of mace wielding opponents and turned to see a long blade part the ribcage of his father and reach the soft tissue inside. Not missing a beat, Anton slashed sideways with his shorter weapon, neatly slicing the throat of his assailant.

Nynin rushed to his father's side, taking care to be certain the attacker was dead.

Hesitating a moment, the young man looked about for oncoming soldiers. It seemed they'd entered the manor house itself and busied themselves within. He hurried, knowing the reprieve would be brief.

He grabbed the long blade and looked to his father for consent. Anton nodded and gritted his teeth. Nynin quickly removed the steel from the Dragon Lord. Anton let out a terrible roar as the discarded blade landed in the mud.

Noble blood flowed, stubbornly resisting Nynin's attempts to stuff the wide cut with his cloak but eventually man won over wound and the bleeding lessened. He lifted his father enough to maneuver behind and wrap his arms about the older man's torso, clasping his hands over the wound to keep it tightly bound. Then he dragged Anton through the broken side gate.

Nynin found a horse, covered in its rider's blood, fidgeting nervously. The dead soldier lay on the ground at its feet with the reins tightly wound around one hand. Grateful for this bit of luck, Nynin managed to get his father into the saddle. Anton grew weaker by the minute, but held on long enough for his son to cut free the reins and swing up behind him.

Shouts told both men they'd been spotted. Nynin kicked his heels and turned the horse towards the dragon's mountain. Crossbow bolts flew by as they fled into the dense woods. From their steed's faltering gait, Nynin knew the stallion was nearly spent. Still, he urged it forward until they reached the mouth of the dragon's lair.

Anton fell more than climbed off the horse. Nynin set it free with a hard slap on its rump to send it galloping off through the trees. Then he assisted his father into the cave, going as far into the darkness as he dared.

"Nynin..." The older man placed a trembling hand on his son's shoulder.

"I don't fear the dragon. Let it take us," Nynin said defiantly. "It's a far better end than at the hands of those bastards." He waved his hand 'out there' towards the clearing.

Anton nodded and allowed himself to relax. His son had chosen a good place within the cave for them to hide, just behind a tumble down pile of rough stones and roots. They wouldn't be seen from the cave mouth. There among the warm scent of earth and something else, something faintly acrid, they both fell prey to exhaustion and slept.

Nynin woke with a start and immediately reached for his weapon, but a steel-toed boot quickly pinned him at the wrist. He surveyed the warrior standing over him bit by bit, amazed at the elegance in the curvature of the leg armor. *What kind of metal is that? It looks almost like silver, yet soft around the edges. A trick of the torchlight perhaps.*

His gaze traveled upward to the most amazing set of scale mail he'd ever seen. Each scale rounded and precisely placed. It shimmered with the warrior's movement and made no clinking sounds. Nynin longed to touch it. Instead he looked into the face of his captor. A distinctly effeminate face with dove gray eyes. His eyes. And Anton's.

"Are you elven?" he asked.

The warrior's lips parted in a smile, and a side to side movement of the helmed head indicated his guess was incorrect. Again, the intricacy of the helm intrigued him. The head of a dragon. Not just any dragon but *their* dragon, recognizable once the visor was pulled low, both intimidating and gorgeous in its design.

Movement to his right brought focus to Nynin's mind as he realized there were other similarly armored warriors around him. Six of them, carrying lozenge shaped shields, devoid of ornamentation. A seventh held the oiled torch above their heads. All of them delicate of feature and gray of eye.

Nynin looked about but saw no sign of his father. "Anton?" he called out.

187

The boot released its hold on him and the warrior, reaching out an open hand, said in a soft voice, "Come. This way."

Nynin stood and allowed himself to be escorted. To be surrounded by these dragon warriors seemed safe somehow. He felt no need to locate his weapon or seek a means of escape.

They led him down the winding tunnel, which never at any point narrowed. He found that fitting and decided he was about to meet with the dragon himself.

Eventually the tunnel walls changed. Nynin peered at them, slowing his walk as much as the dragon warriors would tolerate. Thin pillars of white marble striated the sides, giving the opening a more square appearance.

The instant he saw them, Nynin knew where the pillars came from. The sheer number of them boggled him. *There's a sacrificed maiden for each one of these; and there's got to be thousands!*

The pillared hall ended, opening into a cavern large enough to hold all of Lord Anton's holdings, plus those of Brakenstone Castle and Fenwich Keep. The center of it lay bare, except for a myriad of carpets touching side to side and covering miles, reaching the lip of the cavern opening.

As the dragon warriors led him across it, Nynin saw building after building, entire cities in fact, stretching along the cavern walls into the distance. Everything was carved of the same white marble. He paused before a field covered in high piles of broken egg shards, each larger than his entire body. His escort nudged him forward.

He watched battalions of the dragon warriors drill on the edges of the open area, their armor shimmering like the scales of a river trout in the morning sun. The entire kingdom, for that is what this seemed to him, was bathed in warm light shining through a silvery, rippling ceiling. Nynin gaped and wondered how many countless men, like himself, had fished that lake not knowing its true purpose.

Already he loved this place, knowing his father would too. He hastened his steps at the thought of Lord Anton.

The dragon warriors escorted Nynin into a large temple-like structure, though he saw no images to indicate any deity of worship. Once inside, they paused to set their shields against

188

the wall. The warriors then removed their helms, letting long raven tresses, some plaited, some tied with leather thongs, fall down their backs. Nynin realized these were indeed not elves of any kind, they were women.

The first, who'd helped him to his feet earlier, took Nynin by the hand. Her firm grip sure and commanding. She stepped forward, pulling him with her.

"In here. Anton lies this way." As they walked she said, "They await your arrival."

"They?" Nynin wondered.

Inside, just beyond a set of large double doors, the dragon warrior paused. She bowed her head, placed her hand on the small of his back and gave a quick shove which sent Nynin on into the heavily incensed room. He glanced back to see her take a guardsman's stance at the side of the door.

"Welcome," the male voice seemed familiar, drawing Nynin's attention forward.

The words came not from his father, for Anton lay in state on a large rectangular platform. Dressed in robes of white linen, his hands lay at his sides and his eyes remained closed in death. The Dragon Lord Coronet circled his pale brow.

The sight of him brought a deep pain into Nynin's heart.

"You sacrificed him!" Nynin cried out.

"We honor him," the male voice corrected.

Nynin looked up into the face of the man who spoke and recognized it. He gaped, recognizing the same features he saw every time he looked at Anton, and also those he found in the mirror each morning. Though this one's age seemed... indeterminate. Thirty perhaps? It stunned him.

189

On either side of this enigma stood six women of varying ages, all garbed in fine robes of red gossamer. The youngest woman, pregnant and near her birthing time, Nynin recognized as the last Chosen One. Who could forget that fiery red head, just a handful of years older than himself? From the sly smile she gave, he knew she recognized him as well.

The next older woman, perhaps in her early thirties, stepped forward. Her deep blue eyes and golden hair captivated his heart. He couldn't shake the thought he'd seen her portrait somewhere.

She took his hand in hers. "Your brother's wounds were mortal. It was his time and his destiny. Do not be sad for him."

"Brother?" Nynin looked from the woman to Anton, then to the man, who nodded his confirmation. He remembered the story Anton told him about his founding. "Then you are my..."

"Father. Yes." After a short pause he continued, "Don't fret, it will all become clear once you have time to sort through your thoughts and feelings."

"I don't want to take time for any of that," Nynin blurted out in exasperation. "Explain it to me... NOW."

His demands seemed to amuse his real father because a sparkle came into the older man's eye and his thin lips parted in a toothy grin. He stepped past Nynin and strode through the double doors. Nynin had no choice but to follow him.

At the temple entrance, they stopped. The man turned to Nynin, then with a sweeping gesture of his arm indicating the whole of the underground kingdom, he said, "All of these are my shieldmaidens, my children. They are all dragon fruits, if you will."

Though he knew in his heart the truth of it, Nynin balked, "You can't tell me you are the dragon."

"Indeed I am." In response to the youth's skeptical scowl, he sighed heavily, "Must I resort to shape shifting to prove my point? You know it to be true. Look about. Do you see any large, scaly beast out there?"

Nynin shook his head. He had to accept the surreality of it. There could be no other explanation.

"Are they all women?" he asked.

190   Dragon nodded.

"Why?"

With a shrug, Dragon replied, "That is simply the way of things, the cycle of life. I have no control over which babe will turn male. It just happens every century or so."

"Why not keep the males, then...if they're so rare."

"They are destined to be the Dragon Lords."

"You are the Dragon Lord, now that Anton is gone." Both men turned to face the woman who spoke. She stood behind them in red gossamer. The one from the portrait—Nynin suddenly remembered where he'd seen her. The oil and canvas image hung in a dining hall where he'd recently been chained to the table. At Wutherwood.

"You're Arum."

She nodded.

"Your father...he exacts revenge on your behalf."

Arum moved to stand next to Dragon, allowing him to wrap an arm about her waist. "My father is a fool. He thinks me dead and has no idea of the honor your people bestowed upon me."

"You are a hard woman," Nynin's voice shook with disgust. "Don't you care about all the people dying up there."

"No. I don't. They are no longer a part of me, just as I am no longer a part of them."

"Aren't you going to ask?" Dragon's voice belied mirth.

"Ask what?"

"Why this dragon doesn't devour the maidens?" He laughed at Nynin's look of disgust, "I would've asked it."

"Then I'll ask," said Arum, her voice light hearted and sweet. "Why haven't you devoured us?"

Laughing, Dragon leaned over and kissed her forehead. "It's because I love you."

Nynin could take this no longer. "Why don't you do something?" he demanded. "Men are being slaughtered on your lands."

Dragon's expression turned dark and serious. "I care nothing for the affairs of mankind. Let the evil and the greedy slaughter one another. The world will be the better for it."

Dragon indicated the entire cavern with a sweeping arc of his arm, "These are my lands, given to me by the bargain. I keep my end of it. I do not meddle in the affairs of men."

"Then why have a Dragon Lord at all?"

"To organize the choosing and to oversee the egg-death. To assure that the bargain remains intact and fulfilled. Nothing more."

Nynin stood on the temple steps, looking out over the dragon realm for hours. Then an idea came to him. He returned inside to where the red ladies busily rubbed Anton's body

191

with scented oils. They paused in their ministrations to watch him as he leaned in close to his brother's corpse, talking in a low voice. He reached out and gingerly removed the coronet, placing it upon his own head.

He stood tall, then walked briskly to the shieldmaiden at the guard post. "Take me to my father."

They found Dragon at the edge of the carpet field, watching shieldmaiden troops go through their drills. One of the older red ladies stood at his arm. She smiled at Nynin's approach, turning Dragon's attention in his direction.

"If I am the Dragon Lord...," Nynin began.

"You are," Dragon interrupted.

"If I am the Dragon Lord," Nynin started again, "I would use these warriors to take back what is ours and bring peace again."

At Dragon's signal, several of the shieldmaidens marched over. "So be it," he told Nynin. "Our dragon army is under your command."

"Thank you," Nynin walked towards the warrior commanders. He paused, half turned and said, "There will be no more Choosing, you understand?"

Dragon just smiled.

After Nynin and the others had gone, Dragon turned to his red lady, "I like this one. He is strong willed. Just like his mother."

She hugged him tight and then looked into his face, "Are you really going to let him do away with The Choosing?"

He kissed her forehead and patted her hand. "Oh, he will learn."

A DRAGON'S DAWN

DANA SISSON

As far as she knew, she was the last of her kind. She hadn't seen another in… eons. And she was tired. Very tired. She watched the darkness settle over the land and damned herself once more. It would be so easy to let go… No, actually, it wouldn't be easy. If it had been easy, she would have been able to see to her own ending ages ago.

And now she was hunted. No matter what she longed for, she knew she would fight to survive again. The Peloponnesians hadn't been able to destroy her, the Romans were like children fighting in the dark and the Spartans hadn't begun to come close. Neither had the French, the Spaniards or the Goths. It made her wonder, briefly, if she could be killed, if she could die, even though the others of her kind must have been driven into extinction.

Candles burned throughout the room, emitting a soft glow

and softer fragrances. Lilacs spilled from a short, wide vase and added their scent to that of the candles, as soft and sweet as first love. She moved to the sofa and settled down, picking up the glass of wine she had poured earlier and taking a sip. The wine was chilled and tart, settling on her tongue like young apples and sunshine, leaving a taste of blackberries and shadows as she swallowed.

She had had a family—once, twice, and then a third time —only to watch them age, marry, bear their own young, and die. She had long since lost track of the descendents, not because she wasn't interested but because she couldn't stand the thought of losing them again and again. Better to lose them once and live with the memories, both bitter and sweet.

Logs lay on the hearth and she waved a hand, sparking a flame that leapt into the darkness of the recess. Fragrant smoke hovered for a moment and then drifted away as the fire cheerfully consumed the wood. On nights like this one, she sought what comfort she could, when memories and thoughts circled within her mind, chasing each other uselessly. She lay her head on the tall back of the sofa and watched the flames dance, the wisps of smoke twisting their way up the chimney, fighting the depression that threatened to burn her to ash as well.

She grew lonely, she knew that, and most times could handle the feeling with ease. Something stirred on this night though, something unsettling like a chill wind at a funeral, and goose flesh chased itself up her arms. She took another sip of wine, set the glass down and rose again, wondering at the restlessness driving her pacing feet—pacing like a wild animal penned too close. She grinned at the thought. She *was* a wild animal penned too close and had been for far too long. Her form was trapped in this time and space. She wanted to throw her weight against the bars, find what unsettled and destroy them, and that was not like her, either. At least, not since her human families were alive.

She stalked into her bedroom and flicked on the light. Warm glow bathed the room as she stripped to her skin. The robe she pulled on, heavy and old, comforted against the chill that didn't belong to the night but came from her soul. She slipped into the bathroom and stared into the mirror, the light from the bedroom enough for her to see into the eyes that belonging to the stranger she was, masking the glow of the fires within her body. Perhaps it was just that she had spent too long in this form, a strange one to her. She had married into human kind more than once and felt human emotions more than she cared to bear any longer. She picked up the wine and took another sip, watching the image in the mirror match move for move, before shutting her eyes against the lie, turning away from what she saw and moving into the darkness of the bedroom. A wave of her hand turned off the lights behind her. For so long, she had lived without her magic, without her true form, always searching, always hunting, always protecting. Perhaps because she had once given birth to human offspring she could feel for mankind now. She didn't have a name for the emotion, however. Pity, or perhaps compassion. Sorrow, certainly, always there. But mostly, she felt tired.

She lay upon the bed and stared up into a night that didn't know darkness. The remnants of the wine on her tongue lingered both bitter and sweet. She knew it was past time to return to her true form, to sleep through the ages and perhaps wake in some sweeter time. Perhaps her kind was not truly gone, just hidden away. Perhaps the one that hunted her now would lose her. She closed her eyes on the thought and dreamed, deeply, of long sleeps and fragile dreams, hot winds and hotter caves, of fire and ice and thunder. And maybe, just maybe, when she awoke there would be others and her loneliness would end.

195

He flinched awake, the dream startling him from sleep, and sighed as the weight of waking settled on him. He didn't know what he dreamed, didn't often remember. But sometimes, yes, sometimes he dreamed of fire and overwhelming heat. He felt no fear in these dreams, the heat a welcome comfort though the flames licked at his skin. He turned over in the bed and his mind drifted back over the last few days. He trailed something, a prey that moved from place to place. He couldn't identify what it was, or why he followed it, but he knew with absolute certainty it was vital he find it.

He rolled to his back and stared up at the ceiling. His skin itched, a fierce burning that made him long to claw at his skin, to find a pile of sand and wallow in it until his flesh was abraded. He had long ago learned to control the urge. When he had been a child, the itching had forced him from one doctor's office to another, longs welts from his own nails scoring his arms, his legs, his chest and as far on his back as he could reach. The trips to the doctors' offices usually heralded another move into yet another new foster home. As an abandoned child caught up in the system, he hadn't been given any say in where he was deposited.

Those days were over, long over. He sat up in bed and caught a glimpse of himself in the dresser mirror. He was nearly sixty-two and didn't look a day older than a man of thirty. He still wondered about that, learning not so long ago it was not a good idea to let friends and neighbors realize this about him. At the age of forty, he had taken to moving around the country, landing long enough in one spot to earn his keep, save a little money and move on to the next town. America had become a transient society. Very few people stayed in the same neighborhoods, in the same apartment, any longer. Jobs were hard to come by and more often than not, when your company told you to move, you did, packing up the house and family. On the other hand, if you lost your job, you moved to where you could find work. Since most corporations also seemed to be becoming nomadic, chances were also good you would only have a few years before the company took advantage of better deals in other states or countries and it was easier to hire a new staff at a lower wage than to move the previous employees.

This made it easy for him. He had another decade or so before the IRS might start wondering why he still paid taxes but that gave him time to figure out how he was going to get around that problem. Some novels made it sound so easy. Maybe it was. Maybe he should go ahead and purchase a house, a place secluded from others, travel for a while before leaving his property to himself as his own heir. He shook his head, got out of bed, and stretched. The prospect was daunting and to tell the truth, despite his age, he still felt like a puppy, young and foolish and confused.

And on top of all of that, now he felt he was...hunting... something. The feeling had descended upon him recently, a sensation almost as strong as the itching, burning within his heart and gut. He padded into the bathroom as he contemplated these things. He turned on the hot water in the shower and stepped under the steaming spray. He didn't touch the cold water, didn't need it. The temperature of the hot water should have made him feel parboiled, but the water never seemed quite hot enough.

He dressed quickly and headed out of the apartment. That something, something he was looking for—he needed to find it soon. He had no idea where the sense of urgency came from but it burned within him like the itching of his skin burned on his frame. He would find whatever it was—today, tomorrow, perhaps next week—but very soon now. He must.

The sensation of the hunt was indescribable. It was scent, feeling, itch and urge all wrapped up together. It was the throb in the bridge of his nose, the scent of flame burning clean and the anxiety chasing itself around in his belly. When he paced the busy streets, it was an itch along his spine, a pair of eyes following his every move. At times, he felt his head swinging from side to side, his nostrils flaring to catch the scent of what he sought. His prey was close.

197

She woke to sunlight streaming through the windows and a scent both strange and familiar at the same time. It was still distant but drawing nearer, moving beneath her skin like an itch. She rose from the bed and walked to the balcony. She didn't know what had possessed her to purchase this place in the heart of the city so many years ago. Maybe it was the activity. Perhaps she had thought that with all the people, all the motion, she wouldn't feel so very alone any longer. But the city had grown and now it was too much. Looking down upon the masses only made her feel trapped and left a longing for the wide-open skies and barren mountains of her adolescence.

It was past time to go. She had no more to give and wanted only the solitude of the deepest sleep. There were no others, long ago hunted or driven to extinction. She kept no hope for a sweeter future. Tired of this skin, tired of this body, she wanted her size and strength back. She wanted her wings, her scales, her sleep, and her dreaming mountain of gold. She wanted the fire of the earth and the darkness of the deepest caves.

In the matter of a short hour on the computer, she erased all traces of her existence as she had so many times before. It was simpler now in the internet age, but for so many centuries it had been even easier, simply a matter of disappearing when she associated with humans. The world had been much larger then. She sat back and thought for a long moment, trying to remember when she had last assumed her true form. Before flight. Before humans had become as comfortable in the skies as her own kind had been so many centuries ago.

She shook her head and shut down the computer. It would be difficult, finding a place where she could hide herself. Satellites and global positioning systems would make it difficult unless she was very careful. The last thing she wanted was to find a place and then make herself a target for the weapons at the command of so many nations, spending eternity as a stuffed prize in a museum somewhere. She grinned at the irony of being killed by those which had once been food for her kind, displayed as a myth come to life and mounted for their viewing pleasure.

She rose from her seat. It really wouldn't take much to prepare for her departure. She wandered into the bedroom and idly wondered where she had last left her hoard while the daylight beyond the windows called to her. The park was just across the street. She had time to take a walk, clear her head and think of nothing. She wouldn't think of the hunt or being hunted. She wouldn't consider finding a new place or her hoard. She would just walk and let her mind drift while her feet went where they wished. It had been too long since she had taken that sort of time for herself.

Something had changed but he wasn't certain what. Some pressure had been released but still more continued to grow. Work had passed much as it did any other day. He returned to his apartment and perused the contents of the refrigerator. There were times when it seemed like he couldn't get enough to eat. He scratched compulsively at the back of his neck then reached forward and pulled out the package of steaks he had purchased the day before. He barely seared them when he cooked, preferring his meat very rare. The only thing that kept him from eating them raw were the social strictures he had been raised with, that and the memory of a royal beating he had received once when he was about six and helping himself to the burger for that night's dinner.

He felt jittery but couldn't understand why. He cut through the plastic on the steaks and turned on the stove, setting the cast iron frying pan over the burner before rummaging through the refrigerator and cabinets for something to add to the steaks. He gave up the search after only a few moments. Though he was hungry enough to eat a cow, nothing appealed to him beyond the meat. He plopped both steaks into the skillet and inhaled deeply, smoke rising from the pan as they sizzled from the heat. His stomach growled as he flipped both steaks and the next thing he knew, he gripped a slab of meat in each hand and all but stuffed them into his mouth whole. Startled, he dropped one and then the other onto a plate and stared at his hands. He was hungry, yes, but not so hungry he would eat like an animal.

He carried the plate and utensils to the breakfast bar, made himself sit down and eat like a human being. After managing to plow through what was left in very little time he carried the plate to the sink and rinsed it off while his stomach rumbled in response, complaining the meal had not been enough. He scowled as he stacked the dinnerware to dry. He had just eaten two pounds of meat and felt he could still finish the cow itself, hooves and all. Washing his hands and drying them with a paper towel, he shook his head in disbelief.

He looked toward the windows of his modest apartment. It

was a beautiful day outside. It had been sunny without being too hot or humid, though he never had any complaints about the heat. Humidity was a different story, though. Perhaps it was time to seek a place where the heat was dry and constant. Maybe out west somewhere, like Nevada or Texas. He snorted at his own thoughts. Dry as a desert—why not opt for the Sahara or the Gobi while he was at it? Thoughts of either of those desolate places were enough to make him melt with longing. He glanced toward the window again. The park was just a few blocks away and it was too nice outside to sit inside and dwell upon what was bothering him. Especially when he wasn't certain about what troubled his thoughts.

The park was full of visitors. This late in the day, everyone in the city seemed to be here. It was still light enough that the darker element of society had yet to emerge with their drugs and shadowy deals. Vendors did a brisk business in sodas, pretzels and hotdogs and the atmosphere felt light-hearted and festive. It wasn't often such days blessed the city during the long days of summer. The sun would be up for at least another hour, the weather was fine and the air reverberated with the sounds of conversation, music and laughter of children. She strolled along the paths, enjoying the dappling of the sun through the trees, imagining herself someplace where the green extended for miles and not just a few square blocks. But, without another of her kind, she couldn't escape and slip through to a time with no satellites, no GPS, no missiles.

She wandered down to the lake and walked slowly around the perimeter. Adults stood on the banks feeding water fowl while children played with boats along the edges, normal activities among real families. She squelched the yearning for a family of her own, not a human family as in the past, but a real family, a clan of her own kind. Humans' lives were too short and she couldn't tolerate the ache accompanied by watching her children age and die.

She sighed as she stopped at the lake's edge. Life was cruel, resigning her to be the last of her kind. There was no chance of a family for her, not now. No golden eggs to sit amongst her hoard and dream over during long years of gestation. She smiled bitterly over the fact she had put off mating with one of her own kind for so many centuries. Yet, she was dragonkind, strong and eternal. How many humans felt the same during their lives while they chased their careers? How many human women discovered the family they had delayed would no longer be an option? How many of them wept bitter tears over the fact? How many were secretly relieved?

She had watched humans over the millennia, saw the changes in their societies and the transformation of the strictures and the morals. Among dragonkind, the female was the larger and stronger. More fierce than males, the mothers provided for the protection of the future generations. It also had led to the destruction of the females more quickly than their mates, the males remaining better at hiding. As the humans had matured in their societies, some had specialized in hunting dragonkind, learned of the types of places females preferred to lay their eggs and hide their cache. She wondered idly if any others had thought to hide among the predators to survive as she had.

There had been one male that tempted her—a sleek and golden specimen with a deep chest, strong wings and a fabulous twining neck. His scales had been edged with scarlet if she recalled correctly. She wondered what became of him —wondered if he had buried himself with his hoard to sleep away the centuries. Had he changed to a human form as well or had he been hunted and destroyed?

She grimaced and pushed away those thoughts. They served no purpose beyond deepening her melancholy. She stared at the people gathered around her in the park and wondered what they would do if she changed right here, right now. Would they scream in terror if she leaped into the sky breathing fire? She imagined the Air Force would have jets in the air in nothing flat, even if they didn't know what it was they were flying against. For a moment, she wondered how she would fare against fighter pilots. Granted, it had been ages since she had flown but in the air a dragon was grace personified. Riding the thermals, curling into loops and long dives with her wings folded tight against her body before snapping them open to soar upward again—she could almost taste the pure air riding down her throat in the upper reaches of the sky.

Her daydream shattered and she stiffened. The hunter was close. She felt it as plainly as she felt the sun on her face. Her gaze flew around the crowd, searching among the bikers and runners, probing the families at play. She felt him.

The walk had felt random at first, at least until he entered the park. Now it felt guided. The thing that he had sought, the thing that had no name, it was within reach and it pulled at him. So close he wanted to brush his fingers against it, the frustration of not naming the source nearly drove him mad. Like a phantom itch that moved from one spot to another, he felt he had found the itch but couldn't scratch it.

As the last of the day's light blazed and the sun lazed its way toward the horizon, he had walked and dreamed of flying. He often dreamt of flying up high where the air was thinner and cleaner than any found near the ground and had looked forward to the business trips that required traveling by plane. These flights had always a disappointment, however, another thing he didn't understand. The cumbersome take-offs and awkward landings, they both sandwiched the flights which felt long and boring.

Even when he was younger and had splurged for the expense of flying lessons, something... elemental... had remained missing from the excursions and he stopped flying altogether once he earned his license.

He chided himself as he strolled along, enjoying the way the sun fell through the leaves of the surrounding trees. The lake glimmered a short distance away and he turned towards it, his senses continuing a search he didn't understand. His pace quickened with the thought that whatever he sought was finally within his reach. The itch on his neck screamed for attention and chills raced up and down his body. His gaze leaped ahead and his feet begged to keep pace as he walked toward the lake. There, over there. Her. That woman.

She felt the hunter draw nearer and her breath hissed in through her teeth. Not a hunter, no, but some *thing* on the hunt. Dragonkind. She could taste it, feel it's eyes touching her. She looked around and finally saw him, striding toward her with purposeful steps. The expression on his face was intense yet his eyes were clouded by confusion. He was young; not even a century old yet, she could taste that about him. She watched him draw nearer, sensing his aura shift with excitement. He stopped a bare step from her, chest heaving in and out as though he had been running. She smelled the fire within him and inhaled sharply.

He watched her stare at him and his heart pounded against his ribs. He could smell her, taste her before he was anywhere close to her. She tasted ancient and he frowned at the thought. The woman didn't appear to be any older than her mid-to-late twenties but she studied him with an intensity that was unnerving and arousing at the same time. He stopped just short of running into her and gazed into her eyes.

"I thought I was the last of us." Her voice spoke a promise of fire and smoke, subtle and sexy. He blinked at her words.
"Us?"
She cocked her head to one side, gave him a frown and a nod.
"Yes, us. Dragonkind."
"Uh... Dragon... ? Did you say Dragon?"
It was her turn to blink in surprise. Even as she searched

for words, she saw his pupils elongate, his brow ridges arch and scales move beneath his skin. She glanced around quickly. There were still too many people in the park and the sun had not yet finished setting, though the shadows were lengthening with each passing minute.

"Come with me..." She glanced back at him and grabbed his wrist, starting them toward the entrance of the park at a smart pace. The shifting was taking place faster and she saw the confusion and fear in his expression. "Control yourself... Hold your human shape, for pity's sake..."

He followed along meekly, a fever raging through his skin to her touch. "I don't... I don't understand... What's going on? What's happening to me?"

She steered the way out of the park and across the avenue, into her building and across the lobby, the two of them nearly running now. The elevator rang its arrival and she shoved him into the car, punching the number for her floor with enough force to crack her fingernail. He was panting now, his features flushing bright red. He was truly young, a babe really. She slapped him lightly on the face until he finally looked up and met her eyes.

"Who's your dam?"

"What?"

"Your dam, your sire? Who are they?"

He shook his head. "No... no one... abandoned when I was small..." He gasped and nearly folded in on himself. "What's happening? What's going on?"

She hissed and forced his eyes to meet hers, both of her hands framing his face. "You're shifting. You need to stop it. There's no room in here. Stop the shifting..."

He shook his head wildly, panic written clearly on his features. "I... I... can't! I *can't!*"

She felt her own eyes change, felt her voice deepen. "You can, you will. Stop the shift..."

His eyes locked onto hers and his panting deepened when he concentrated on her eyes. He inhaled deeply and let it out slowly, fire and ash riding on his breath.

The elevator stopped and she herded him across the hall into her penthouse. She dragged him through the living room and into the bathroom, not stopping until he was in the shower stall and cold water drummed down on his head. She ignored his sputtering protests.

"You stop the change. You need to get cool. There is *no* room here for us in our natural form… "

He gasped another protest even while he felt the roiling heat and horrible itching subside. His teeth chattered under the spray. "W-w-what are you t-t-talking about? Ch-change?"

She turned off the water and yanked him out of the shower. He stumbled against the sink and she tossed him a towel. He buried his face in the soft folds and scrubbed his dripping hair. She stepped forward and rested a palm against his forehead.

"You're cool enough to last for a little while. Take off your clothes, dry off, and then come into the kitchen."

She turned without another word and stalked from the bathroom.

He trailed into the kitchen a few minutes behind her, one towel wrapped around his waist and another draped across his shoulders. She stopped rummaging through the refrigerator and watched him for a moment before turning back to the shelves. She pulled out a bottle of chardonnay and filled two goblets, passing one across the breakfast bar to him. He took it and gulped down half, his expression one of confusion when he eventually looked back up at her.

"I don't understand what's going on here," he said, shaking his head. "What's happening to me?"

She sighed and gestured toward one of the bar stools. "Take a seat. I think we have a lot to talk about."

He blinked at her—fear, confusion, and hope taking turns on his face. "We're dragons? Real live fire-breathing, flying dragons?" He let loose a weak laugh and downed the remains of his wine before carefully setting the glass on the counter and clearing his throat. He stood up, hitched the towel more securely around his hips and shook his head again.

"I think it's time I left. My shift starts at four… "

"You're close to changing." Her voice was quiet. "So close you won't be able to control when or where it happens." She closed her eyes for a moment and frowned. "I don't know how it was that you were raised as a human, how you were locked into your human form before you should have been able to change at all." She looked at him, the frown still in place but the fires still burning within the depths of her eyes. "When the change comes upon you again, it will be too late. Do you wish to risk those humans that you know, maybe even care about? Because when you change, they will be nothing more than food to you. Nothing more than something to satisfy the hunger burning in your stomach. Do you really want to risk that?"

The itching began again between his shoulder blades and he felt the heat of anger well up within him.

"You're telling me things that I *can't* believe!" He shouted the words at her and she smiled.

"Seeing is believing. Isn't that what they say? You're a youngling, a cub, compared to me. When you reach my years, you can control the change. You can even control the extent of the change." She paused. "Watch."

She centered herself in the large space that was her living room and breathed deeply, closing her eyes. When they opened again, the pupils were elongated and the shape of her eyes had grown to nearly twice their original size. She removed her blouse and bra and he watched, fascinated, as her skin appeared to shimmer. Scales formed, small and perfect across a rib cage that expanded. Wings stretched out suddenly from her back with a wet pop, damp and furled tightly until they
206 stretched to a length the height of her body.

He gaped, jaw working against a shout or words, he wasn't certain which. And he felt, with her changing, something within himself that burst into life like a stoked fire. He leaned back against the stool and watched as all of the changes reversed in her, receding until she once again looked as human as any other person in the city. She calmly bent down and retrieved her blouse, shrugging into it before crossing back to the bar and taking another sip of her wine.

"What am I going to do?" The question was plaintive, quiet.

She looked at him with a small smile.

"*We*. We are going to leave here. Leave this place and find our true forms once again. Myself, for the freedom I had deemed lost long ago, and you to learn what you have never known. The taste of cool air in your throat. The joy of the darkest of caves and your hoard. The dreaming and the sleep. The savagery of the hunt… "

He shook his head at her. "But how? I don't know how… "

"A pair of our kind can travel through time and space." She shrugged. "Perhaps that is what most of our kind have done. I have long since believed I was the last of us. That I had lost my chance to be among others of my own kind. Lost my chance to mate and dream over my eggs and my hoard." She paused. "I have spent too many years as a human. I want to fly into the heavens and wallow in heated sand. I want to stretch my wings and feel the blood of a living thing pour down my throat to quench the fires in my belly as I eat." She smiled wryly. "I have lost the taste for humans, but they're too small for anything more than a snack anyway." Her eyes took on a far away look. "But there are other places, other times, when the hunting is good and the air is pure." She looked at him and couldn't know that the loneliness, the longing in her eyes was what made him decide. He reached forward and took her hand.

They flew high to where the air was so thin it was as nothing. It poured like the finest of wines down their throats as their wings stretched and folded. She slewed sideways on a wingtip, her scarlet and gold scales flashing in the sun when she plummeted toward the earth, her long graceful neck arching to the side as she goaded him to follow. He roared his laughter and plunged after her, spotting the mammoths only a moment after she did. His scales were still maturing, still deepening into gold with etchings of scarlet along the edges.

Together they fell towards the herd and quickly killed two of the beasts, heaving themselves and their meals into the air again. At first changing, he had not believed how large they were as dragons, but the wooly beasts made a fine meal. Soon she would go into the sleep, her eggs newly laid upon her hoard. And they would be there, together, when their young hatched in twenty or so years, as they had become accustomed to reckoning time. Already they had found a deep cave, nestled within the heart of the mountains to the south, a cave filled with the heat of the earth. He would guard her as she rested. And when their young hatched, perhaps this time things would be different. There would be tales of future worlds and assurances that humans tasted nasty anyway.

Inside the Cavern

RICHARD BRAY

Even in the soul-sucking darkness of the cavern's depths, Aina could distinguish each detail of the small chamber. From the striations of gold ore embedded in the walls to the faint wheeze in Carrson's breathing, it all had become familiar and comforting over the last three seasons.

The realization of passing time made her breath catch and the twisting pain in the pit of her stomach squeezed even tighter.

The small figure to her left, curled tight in his woolen blankets, sighed gently as though sensing her presence. In the bed beside him, his brother had tossed the blankets aside haphazardly, preferring the feel of cool, damp air against his scaly flesh.

Aina felt the growing rumble in the distance through the cavern walls, felt the gentle vibrations in the rocks that months in darkness told her was not natural.

They were close now, and as the rumbling drew closer it seemed to Aina that the humans sped up, like hunting dogs that sensed their prey tiring. The thought made Aina's hands tremble.

"What's wrong, Mama? Is Papa home?"

Carrson, still bundled tight beneath his blankets, had awoken and now stared up at her, his eyes shining like stars in the cavern's depths. Aina smiled, hoping her son wouldn't realize how she forced the gesture.

"Not yet." She paused briefly. "I was just checking on you and your brother."

Carrson's face fell, and some of the gleam faded from his eyes. Aina tried not to notice.

"I'm hungry." This time it was Daegel who spoke. "Is it time to eat?"

"Not yet," Aina answered. She sat down on the bed beside Carrson, smoothing out the blankets that covered his slight frame. They were both too thin, she knew, but what food they had needed to be rationed, and without their father here the duty had fallen to her.

Carrgel didn't bring fresh meat anymore, and Aina was terrified to leave her sons behind. The humans had killed Carrgel while he was in the passageways, hunting the rats and vermin that now comprised meals for the dragons beneath the earth. The boys didn't know it yet, but Aina had heard the explosion of rock, Carrgel's distant screams of fury. She had crawled through the passageways the next day, past the dead ends and the roads leading nowhere, until she came to the spot where he had fallen.

210   The rocks there had only recently solidified where Carrgel's fire turned stone to molten liquid. The surface shone a dull red, not because of the lingering heat of Carrgel's rage but because of the sticky pools of blood that remained on the cave floor. Aina could see the trail where humanity's machines dragged Carrgel's body from the scene.

She spent hours alone in the cavern, inhaling the thick scent of recent battle. At times she avoided the blood and made a conscious effort to even look at it. Other times she dipped her hands into the puddles, desperate to make one last connection with the dragon that had been her life-mate for more than fifty generations of the humans who killed him.

She wanted to scream, to release the fury that descended upon her, to hunt the humans responsible and engulf them in flames until the heat of her fury melted their cursed machines and left their bones smoldering in her wake.

Of course, she didn't. To be perfectly honest, she wasn't certain whether it was fear or thoughts of her children that kept her from following Carrgel's blood trail. She knew her flames couldn't melt the human machines. Their gunfire and explosives would rend her flesh in a way her claws and teeth could never hope to duplicate on them.

That was why the dragons no longer flew in the skies above the surface of the earth. That was why the dragons hid beneath the ground, more worm than wyrm. There were places to hide beneath the earth.

Neither Carrson nor Daegel knew their father was dead.

By the time Aina returned home, she had wiped the tears from her eyes and the blood from her hands. As long as her sons remembered him, Carrgel wasn't really dead. Somewhere, he was flying in the open sky again, holding back the human machines. That was what the dragonlings believed. She looked down at them as they stared curiously back at her, their eyes shining in the cavern's darkness.

"I was just thinking about your father," she admitted. Carrson and Daegel leaned forward in their beds, anxious for the story they knew was coming.

"Did I ever tell you two how your father and I met?" It was a stupid question, and the three of them knew it. If Aina asked, either of the boys could have told her the story word for word. Nonetheless, both shook their heads negative.

"Then I'll tell you." In the distance, the rumbling continued. It was closer than it had ever been before, but if the dragonlings noticed, they betrayed no sign.

"Your father and I met in the days when dragons still lived on the surface, when we often shape-shifted into humans. Now, of course, computers and such have made it impossible to live on the surface without detection, but in those days humans didn't even know we existed."

211

Aina allowed herself to grin as she thought back to those years. They were peaceful times, and the daily routine was one of choice rather than necessity. Most of the machines in those days were simple contraptions, rarely more complex than a simple lever or wheel.

"Although many dragons mingled amongst the humans, living in their cities and integrating themselves into their society, my family and I lived in a community comprised solely of dragons.

"My father felt it would be easier to keep our secret that way, and it allowed for us to revert back to our dragon shape without fear of discovery. I think that was truly why my father chose to live there. We raised cows and sheep in the pastures surrounding our village, but we didn't dare try to keep more intelligent creatures such as dogs and horses."

"Because they could tell you were dragons!" Daegel exclaimed proudly.

"That's right." Aina smiled even as Carrson glared at his younger brother for interrupting. "The animals knew. I think they smelled the predator in us."

Aina paused. That rumbling was even louder now, and its constant drumming made it hard for her to concentrate. She was beginning to feel rushed, and it was a story that deserved all the time it took to tell. She wondered how much predator was left within her anymore.

"I had just awoken one morning when word spread that men were coming. King's men. We often had humans come to our village looking for a bite to eat and a bed to sleep in. If they left relatively soon and weren't too inquisitive, we let them go on their way. Some, however, wanted to stay. Obviously, we couldn't have that. If we'd wanted to live with humans then we would have just settled in one of their cities rather than going to all the trouble of establishing our own community. It was a simple enough task making them leave, but unfortunately, it drew some unwanted attention to our little hamlet.

"Complaints of our sometimes brusque methods reached the king, and he had dispatched a company of soldiers to investigate. None of us were entirely certain of what to do."

Carrson and Daegel leaned forward on their seats, their eyes gleaming in the cavern's darkness. Behind them, Aina picked out the gold ore in the cavern's wall. Carrgel had chosen this particular cavern for just that reason. He always had enjoyed the old human stories of dragons hoarding their gold.

"The twenty-man regiment rode straight to the center of the village, a field usually reserved for celebrations and festivals. As they passed by the thatched-roof huts, they were silent, staring at us with the same wariness and suspicion we accorded them.

"Their captain, a pepper-haired man on a mahogany charger, was the first to break the silence.

"'Who's in charge here?' he asked no one in particular.

"I remember how tense his voice sounded, and I knew the rest of the dragons recognized it. The captain knew this wasn't a typical village, but he wasn't sure what he had stumbled into. If he had, he never would have stepped foot within miles of our homes."

Aina stopped. Carrson had stopped paying attention to the story, and his head was now cocked to one side, listening to a sound he didn't understand. Daegel still hadn't noticed.

"The eldest in our village, Pedar, stepped forward from his home." Aina spoke these words loudly, and Carrson returned his attention to his mother's story. "In his human form, he was grey and bearded, with a slow step and a back bent with his years. In his dragon form, however, he could have crushed their entire regiment with a single swat.

"The men's horses seemed to sense this, and as he approached, many of them tried to back away and a few grew quite frightened. This served to make their captain more ill of ease. Given the situation, his response was admirable.

"'My name is Captain Lamont Atwood, sir,' he said, dismounting so he could approach Pedar. '"Might I enquire your name?"'

"Pedar gave him his name in a worn, brittle voice that sounded both wise and weary. The two men stood just a few feet away from each other, each measuring the other.

"Captain Atwood was the first to speak. 'I'm sorry to disturb your hamlet here, my good sir Pedar, but I'm afraid our king has received complaints regarding this village and he has sent me to determine the truth of such claims.'

213

"'What claims might those be?' Pedar asked.

"'That the people of this village practice witchcraft, driving away any and all who do not share in such practice.' Captain Atwood spoke the words calmly, and his heartbeat was only a shade quicker than normal. His men had spread themselves out so they would not be bunched together in the event of an attack, but they were not so spread out as to be too near any of us."

Aina was nearing her favorite part of the story. She began to speak faster.

"'No one here practices witchcraft, Captain,' Pedar said. 'I can assure you of that.'

"The captain's eyebrows rose. 'How can you be so certain?' he asked.

"'It's a small community, Captain.' Pedar's voice was soothing, and it calmed both us and the soldiers. 'I know everyone here and how they spend their days. I can assure you again, Captain, no one here practices witchcraft.'

"'Why have you pressured newcomers to leave your village?' the soldier asked. 'The king has received several complaints.'

"Pedar shrugged his shoulders. 'We're a small, close-knit community that has known each other for a long time. Perhaps to outsiders it appears that we are shunning them, but...'

"The captain cut Pedar off. 'These don't sound like instances of shunning at all,' he said. 'One man's home was burned to the ground, one woman found a deer carcass in her child's bedroom and another claims to have seen the people of this village light flames with a brush of their hand.'

"Pedar barely contained his anger in that moment. As an elder, it had been years since someone last interrupted him. But perhaps worse was the captain's report of humans seeing one of his dragons displaying non-human abilities. He'd known the burned home and deer would be reported, though he hadn't expected them to be taken seriously. Sightings of villagers lighting flames with a touch, however, were the result of mistakes on the part of his people.

"Captain Atwood, however, did not notice Pedar's anger. He was too busy ordering his men to search the buildings.

"'We'll try to make this as quick as possible,' the captain

214

said when he turned back to Pedar. 'I'm sure it will take just a few moments.'

"It indeed took just a few moments. The soldiers, of course, discovered the charred remains of a small hut on the outskirts of the village, but Pedar explained that away as an accidental fire. The soldiers didn't find any sign of magic or witchcraft."

Carrson had once again stopped paying attention. As Aina spoke, the rumbling had grown into a steady hum that even Daegel could now hear.

"What is that?" The littlest dragonling turned from side to side, trying to determine the direction the sound's source.

"Nothing to worry about," Aina lied. Yet, even as she spoke, she worried about the sound and wondered if there was enough time to complete her story.

Carrson gave her an inquisitive look, as though he doubted the honesty of her words. She ignored him.

"Though Captain Atwood's men found nothing, they weren't convinced. The king himself had ordered Atwood to visit our village, and he didn't want to return without feeling that he had accomplished something. I believe he expected to find some evidence of witchcraft in his search of our homes, but dragons don't need books or potions.

"The captain conferred with his officers before turning back to Pedar.

"'I'm glad we didn't find anything,' he said, 'but I'm still concerned. I'm going to leave my best man here, to live amongst your people for a few weeks. If he returns to us safely and in good health, and has been treated kindly by your people, we will consider this matter closed. If he does not return to us, by accident or otherwise'—and here the captain's voice grew deep and dangerous—'the consequences would be dire.'

"The man who stepped forward was taller and more bronze of skin than the rest of his regiment. He was heavily muscled with a thick beard that hid most of his facial features, but could not hide the green sparkle of his eyes. If he was nervous, he showed no signs. Even his heartbeat was steady."

"Daddy!" Daegel squealed delightedly in excitement. Carrson glared at his brother once more for interrupting.

215

"Indeed," Aina agreed. "Your father had chosen to live amongst the humans, and he had been in their company for many years before he visited our hamlet. When the other men left, however, he stayed behind."

The human machines were closer than ever now. Aina had mere minutes remaining. The thought caused her throat to constrict in sorrow and fear, but she pushed those emotions aside. There was time, if she hurried.

"Pedar alone had been able to read through Carrgel's disguise, so when the humans left, there was quite an uproar when he revealed himself in dragon form. It was a trick we'd never even thought to try, disguising ourselves so that even other dragons wouldn't recognize us. We'd never had the need.

"During the weeks Carrgel spent in our village, we fell in love. His life was very different from mine, and his stories of the humans were oftentimes humorous and always educational. I don't know if I'd ever thought much about the humans before that, but ever after they were always close to my mind.

"One day, I asked Carrgel why he chose to live with them."

Both Carrson and Daegel were paying close attention now. They'd never heard this part of the story before, and they knew that what they were about to hear was important.

"'Because I'm not willing to give up on them,' he told me. 'They're foolish and destructive and yet they also unabashedly love at times. I feel as though we should help them, guide them to a better path than the one they follow now.'

"'But why?' I asked. "'Who cares whether their wars and their violence consume them? If we keep ourselves separate from their concerns, we'll continue as we always have. We're stronger than they'll ever be.'

"'I don't know how long that will be true,' he said and seemed sad as the words left his mouth.

"Unfortunately, the rest of the dragons thought the same way I did, and wouldn't listen to him. I wish we had."

Carson and Daegel were staring up at her with quizzical expressions on their faces. The walls were now shaking, and she had to raise her voice above the din.

"We let them develop on their own, assured of our eternal

216

superiority, and that is what has brought us to this point. Now the humans are stronger, and they hunt us with their machines, looking to drive us to extinction."

Dust was falling from the cave ceiling, making it difficult to breathe, and the gold ore in the wall had melted beneath the heat of the oncoming machines.

"Eventually, these humans will make the same mistake. They will forget about us, believing us all dead, and they will search these tunnels no more. Even if they know a handful of us still survive, they won't consider it worth their time or resources to continue. We won't be important enough."

Her sons were beginning to look frightened. Good, she thought. The fear will make them run faster.

"Remember what I've told you. We thought the humans weak once, and they've brought us to our knees. If you're smart and you hide well, one day you will grow strong. You can take back the life your father and I wanted for you."

It didn't take any prodding to get the dragonlings down the tunnel, though they stopped when they realized she wasn't joining them. Daegel was too young to understand, but Carrson knew: if she fled with them, the machines would get them all.

"Go," she said. "You must go and grow strong."

Daegel was crying as he left the cavern. Carrson led the way with a determined gleam in his green eyes, looking so much like Carrgel that Aina had to blink the image away before she began to weep.

When the machines finally exploded through the cavern wall, they were met with dragon fire and tears.

Our titles are available at major book stores
and local independent resellers who support
Science Fiction and Fantasy readers like you.

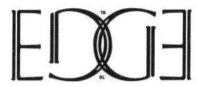

EDGE Science Fiction
and Fantasy Publishing

Tesseract Books

Dragon Moon Press

www.edgewebsite.com
www.dragonmoonpress.com

Our titles are available at major book stores and local independent resellers who support Science Fiction and Fantasy readers like you.

Alien Deception by Tony Ruggiero -(tp) - ISBN-13: 978-1-896944-34-0
Alien Revelation by Tony Ruggiero (tp) - ISBN-13: 978-1-896944-34-8
Alphanauts by J. Brian Clarke (tp) - ISBN-13: 978-1-894063-14-2
Apparition Trail, The by Lisa Smedman (tp) - ISBN-13: 978-1-894063-22-7
As Fate Decrees by Denysé Bridger (tp) - ISBN-13: 978-1-894063-41-8

Billibub Baddings and The Case of the Singing Sword by Tee Morris (tp)
- ISBN-13: 978-1-896944-18-0
Black Chalice, The by Marie Jakober (hb) - ISBN-13: 978-1-894063-00-5
Blue Apes by Phyllis Gotlieb (pb) - ISBN-13: 978-1-895836-13-4
Blue Apes by Phyllis Gotlieb (hb) - ISBN-13: 978-1-895836-14-1

Chalice of Life, The by Anne Webb (tp) - ISBN-13: 978-1-896944-33-3
Chasing The Bard by Philippa Ballantine (tp) - ISBN-13: 978-1-896944-08-1
Children of Atwar, The by Heather Spears (pb) - ISBN-13: 978-0-88878-335-6
Clan of the Dung-Sniffers by Lee Danielle Hubbard (pb) - ISBN-13: 978-1-895836-05-0
Claus Effect, The by David Nickle & Karl Schroeder (pb) - ISBN-13: 978-1-895836-34-9
Claus Effect, The by David Nickle & Karl Schroeder (hb) - ISBN-13: 978-1-895836-35-6
Complete Guide to Writing Fantasy, The - Volume 1: Alchemy with Words
- edited by Darin Park and Tom Dullemond (tp)
- ISBN-13: 978-1-896944-09-8
Complete Guide to Writing Fantasy, The - Volume 2: Opus Magus
- edited by Tee Morris and Valerie Griswold-Ford (tp)
- ISBN-13: 978-1-896944-15-9
Complete Guide to Writing Fantasy, The - Volume 3: The Author's Grimoire
- edited by Valerie Griswold-Ford & Lai Zhao (tp)
- ISBN-13: 978-1-896944-38-8
Complete Guide to Writing Science Fiction, The - Volume 1: First Contact
- edited by Dave A. Law & Darin Park (tp)
- ISBN-13: 978-1-896944-39-5
Courtesan Prince, The by Lynda Williams (tp) - ISBN-13: 978-1-894063-28-9

Dark Earth Dreams by Candas Dorsey & Roger Deegan (comes with a CD)
- ISBN-13: 978-1-895836-05-9
Darkling Band, The by Jason Henderson (tp) - ISBN-13: 978-1-896944-36-4
Darkness of the God by Amber Hayward (tp) - ISBN-13: 978-1-894063-44-9
Darwin's Paradox by Nina Munteanu (tp) - ISBN-13: 978-1-896944-68-5
Daughter of Dragons by Kathleen Nelson - (tp) - ISBN-13: 978-1-896944-00-5
Distant Signals by Andrew Weiner (tp) - ISBN-13: 978-0-88878-284-7
Dominion by J. Y. T. Kennedy (tp) - ISBN-13: 978-1-896944-28-9
Dragon Reborn, The by Kathleen H. Nelson - (tp) - ISBN-13: 978-1-896944-05-0
Dragon's Fire, Wizard's Flame by Michael R. Mennenga (tp)
- ISBN-13: 978-1-896944-13-5
Dreams of an Unseen Planet by Teresa Plowright (tp) - ISBN-13: 978-0-88878-282-3
Dreams of the Sea by Élisabeth Vonarburg (tp) - ISBN-13: 978-1-895836-96-7
Dreams of the Sea by Élisabeth Vonarburg (hb) - ISBN-13: 978-1-895836-98-1

Eclipse by K. A. Bedford (tp) - ISBN-13: 978-1-894063-30-2
Even The Stones by Marie Jakober (tp) - ISBN-13: 978-1-894063-18-0

Fires of the Kindred by Robin Skelton (tp) - ISBN-13: 978-0-88878-271-7
Firestorm of Dragons edited by Michele Acker & Kirk Dougal (tp)
   - ISBN-13: 978-1-896944-80-7
Forbidden Cargo by Rebecca Rowe (tp) - ISBN-13: 978-1-894063-16-6

Game of Perfection, A by Élisabeth Vonarburg (tp)
   - ISBN-13: 978-1-894063-32-6
Green Music by Ursula Pflug (tp) - ISBN-13: 978-1-895836-75-2
Green Music by Ursula Pflug (hb) - ISBN-13: 978-1-895836-77-6
Gryphon Highlord, The by Connie Ward (tp) - ISBN-13: 978-1-896944-38-8

Healer, The by Amber Hayward (tp) - ISBN-13: 978-1-895836-89-9
Healer, The by Amber Hayward (hb) - ISBN-13: 978-1-895836-91-2
Hounds of Ash and other Tales of Fool Wolf, The by Greg Keyes (pb)
   - ISBN-13: 978-1-895836-09-8
Human Thing, The by Kathleen H. Nelson - (hb) - ISBN-13: 978-1-896944-03-6
Hydrogen Steel by K. A. Bedford (tp) - ISBN-13: 978-1-894063-20-3

i-ROBOT Poetry by Jason Christie (tp) - ISBN-13: 978-1-894063-24-1

Jackal Bird by Michael Barley (pb) - ISBN-13: 978-1-895836-07-3
Jackal Bird by Michael Barley (hb) - ISBN-13: 978-1-895836-11-0
JEMMA7729 by Phoebe Wray (tp) - ISBN-13: 978-1-894063-40-1

Keaen by Till Noever (tp) - ISBN-13: 978-1-894063-08-1
Keeper's Child by Leslie Davis (tp) - ISBN-13: 978-1-894063-01-2

Lachli by M. H. Bonham (tp) - ISBN-13: 978-1-896944-69-2
Land/Space edited by Candas Jane Dorsey and Judy McCrosky (tp)
   - ISBN-13: 978-1-895836-90-5
Land/Space edited by Candas Jane Dorsey and Judy McCrosky (hb)
   - ISBN-13: 978-1-895836-92-9
Legacy of Morevi by Tee Morris (tp) - ISBN-13: 978-1-896944-29-6
Legends of the Serai by J.C. Hall - (tp) - ISBN-13: 978-1-896944-04-3
Longevity Thesis by Jennifer Tahn (tp) - ISBN-13: 978-1-896944-37-1
Lyskarion: The Song of the Wind by J.A. Cullum (tp)
   - ISBN-13: 978-1-894063-02-9

Machine Sex and other stories by Candas Jane Dorsey (tp)
   - ISBN-13: 978-0-88878-278-6
Maërlande Chronicles, The by Élisabeth Vonarburg (pb)
   - ISBN-13: 978-0-88878-294-6
Magister's Mask, The by Deby Fredericks (tp) - ISBN-13: 978-1-896944-16-6
Moonfall by Heather Spears (pb) - ISBN-13: 978-0-88878-306-6
Morevi: The Chronicles of Rafe and Askana by Lisa Lee & Tee Morris
   - (tp) - ISBN-13: 978-1-896944-07-4

Not Your Father's Horseman by Valorie Griswold-Ford (tp)
   - ISBN-13: 978-1-896944-27-2

On Spec: The First Five Years edited by On Spec (pb)
  - ISBN-13: 978-1-895836-08-0
On Spec: The First Five Years edited by On Spec (hb)
  - ISBN-13: 978-1-895836-12-7
Operation: Immortal Servitude by Tony Ruggerio (tp)
  - ISBN-13: 978-1-896944-56-2
Operation: Save the Innocent by Tony Ruggerio (tp)
  - ISBN-13: 978-1-896944-60-9
Orbital Burn by K. A. Bedford (tp) - ISBN-13: 978-1-894063-10-4
Orbital Burn by K. A. Bedford (hb) - ISBN-13: 978-1-894063-12-8

Pallahaxi Tide by Michael Coney (pb) - ISBN-13: 978-0-88878-293-9
Passion Play by Sean Stewart (pb) - ISBN-13: 978-0-88878-314-1
Plague Saint by Rita Donovan, The (tp) - ISBN-13: 978-1-895836-28-8
Plague Saint by Rita Donovan, The (hb) - ISBN-13: 978-1-895836-29-5

Reluctant Voyagers by Élisabeth Vonarburg (pb) - ISBN-13: 978-1-895836-09-7
Reluctant Voyagers by Élisabeth Vonarburg (hb) - ISBN-13: 978-1-895836-15-8
Resisting Adonis by Timothy J. Anderson (tp) - ISBN-13: 978-1-895836-84-4
Resisting Adonis by Timothy J. Anderson (hb) - ISBN-13: 978-1-895836-83-7
Righteous Anger by Lynda Williams (tp) - ISBN-13: 897-1-894063-38-8

Shadebinder's Oath by Jeanette Cottrell - (tp) - ISBN-13: 978-1-896944-31-9
Silent City, The by Élisabeth Vonarburg (tp) - ISBN-13: 978-1-894063-07-4
Slow Engines of Time, The by Élisabeth Vonarburg (tp) - ISBN-13: 978-1-895836-30-1
Slow Engines of Time, The by Élisabeth Vonarburg (hb) - ISBN-13: 978-1-895836-31-8
Small Magics by Erik Buchanan (tp) - ISBN-13: 978-1-896944-38-8
Sojourn by Jana Oliver - (pb) - ISBN-13: 978-1-896944-30-2
Stealing Magic by Tanya Huff (tp) - ISBN-13: 978-1-894063-34-0
Strange Attractors by Tom Henighan (pb) - ISBN-13: 978-0-88878-312-7
Sword Masters by Selina Rosen (tp) - ISBN-13: 978-1-896944-65-4

Taming, The by Heather Spears (pb) - ISBN-13: 978-1-895836-23-3
Taming, The by Heather Spears (hb) - ISBN-13: 978-1-895836-24-0
Teacher's Guide to Dragon's Fire, Wizard's Flame by Unwin & Mennenga - (pb)
  - ISBN-13: 978-1-896944-19-7
Ten Monkeys, Ten Minutes by Peter Watts (tp) - ISBN-13: 978-1-895836-74-5
Ten Monkeys, Ten Minutes by Peter Watts (hb) - ISBN-13: 978-1-895836-76-9
Tesseracts 1 edited by Judith Merril (pb) - ISBN-13: 978-0-88878-279-3
Tesseracts 2 edited by Phyllis Gotlieb & Douglas Barbour (pb)
  - ISBN-13: 978-0-88878-270-0
Tesseracts 3 edited by Candas Jane Dorsey & Gerry Truscott (pb)
  - ISBN-13: 978-0-88878-290-8
Tesseracts 4 edited by Lorna Toolis & Michael Skeet (pb)
  - ISBN-13: 978-0-88878-322-6
Tesseracts 5 edited by Robert Runté & Yves Maynard (pb)
  - ISBN-13: 978-1-895836-25-7
Tesseracts 5 edited by Robert Runté & Yves Maynard (hb)
  - ISBN-13: 978-1-895836-26-4
Tesseracts 6 edited by Robert J. Sawyer & Carolyn Clink (pb)
  - ISBN-13: 978-1-895836-32-5
Tesseracts 6 edited by Robert J. Sawyer & Carolyn Clink (hb)
  - ISBN-13: 978-1-895836-33-2

Tesseracts 7 edited by Paula Johanson & Jean-Louis Trudel (tp)
 - ISBN-13: 978-1-895836-58-5
Tesseracts 7 edited by Paula Johanson & Jean-Louis Trudel (hb)
 - ISBN-13: 978-1-895836-59-2
Tesseracts 8 edited by John Clute & Candas Jane Dorsey (tp)
 - ISBN-13: 978-1-895836-61-5
Tesseracts 8 edited by John Clute & Candas Jane Dorsey (hb)
 - ISBN-13: 978-1-895836-62-2
Tesseracts Nine edited by Nalo Hopkinson and Geoff Ryman (tp)
 - ISBN-13: 978-1-894063-26-5
Tesseracts Ten edited by Robert Charles Wilson and Edo van Belkom (tp)
 - ISBN-13: 978-1-894063-36-4
Tesseracts Eleven edited by Cory Doctorow and Holly Phillips (tp)
 - ISBN-13: 978-1-894063-03-6
Tesseracts Q edited by Élisabeth Vonarburg & Jane Brierley (pb)
 - ISBN-13: 978-1-895836-21-9
Tesseracts Q edited by Élisabeth Vonarburg & Jane Brierley (hb)
 - ISBN-13: 978-1-895836-22-6
Throne Price by Lynda Williams and Alison Sinclair (tp)
 - ISBN-13: 978-1-894063-06-7
Too Many Princes by Deby Fredricks (tp) - ISBN-13: 978-1-896944-36-4
Twilight of the Fifth Sun by David Sakmyster - (tp)
 - ISBN-13: 978-1-896944-01-02

Virtual Evil by Jana Oliver (tp) - ISBN-13: 978-1-896944-76-0